Shakespeare's Table

Howard Gimple

Marry, sir, they have committed false report, moreover they have spoken untruths, secondarily they are slanders, sixth and lastly they have belied a lady, thirdly they have verified unjust things, and to conclude, they are lying knaves.

—*Much Ado About Nothing*

Chapter 1

Jordan dropped the keys to the main library door, startled by a screeching gull darting across the pink streaked early morning sky.

"Clumsy oaf!" she chided herself.

Following the bird's flight into an ominous gray cloud, it's sleek outline and hooked beak gave it the aura of a broom-surfing witch. How perfect for the day before Halloween, she thought. Then she saw something that made her gasp, then chuckle.

She grabbed her phone and dialed 3-3-3, which connected her to the campus constabulary. After four rings, a nasally female voice on the other end said, "University Police, Sergeant Colwell speaking."

Jordan heard her chomping between syllables. "This is Jordan Day. I'm Head of Archives and Special Collections at the DeVere library."

"Yeah, I know who you are."

That surprised her. She always tried to keep a low profile. She had once read in a magazine, she couldn't remember if it was Tigress or BizMs, that attractive women aren't taken seriously by senior executives, which is why she hid her long, flaxen hair in a severe bun, wore little or no makeup and dressed in man-tailored suits and high-neck tops. Of course, there was nothing she could do about her long, lean ballerina body, high cheekbones and flawless skin.

"I just thought you should know that we have our first disembodied head of Halloween."

"Where are you calling from?"

"I'm standing right outside the main library entrance."

"Where is the alleged head?"

"It's attached to a spiked finial outside one of the second floor windows. Actually the one right outside my office."

"Who is it this year? Kanye? Trump?"

"It's Spenser Berg."

"Professor Berg, huh?" came the disinterested reply. "That's a new one. What happened, they ran out of rock stars, movie stars and politicians? You'd think those crazy art students would have better things to do."

"I would suggest you have it taken down before too many people see it. It's extremely realistic."

"Yeah." There was a pause. Jordan heard a muffled slurp. "Don't want to freak them out before breakfast. I'll get somebody over there."

Standing in front of the Melville University DeVere Library, she always felt as if she was transported into the middle of a gothic novel. Modeled after the Bodleian Library at Oxford, its spires rose up ominously, like a medieval castle, with turrets and towers and black wrought-iron spikes protruding over ornate oriel windows.

Jordan stared up at the ersatz head. It was Dr. Berg in every detail. The great dome of a bald head that came to a slight point at the top. The dark, bushy eyebrows and narrow almond-shaped eyes that were set a little too far apart. The broad, prominent nose and thick, fleshy lips hung over the double chin. And, of course, the large purplish mole that dominated the middle of his forehead like an all-seeing third eye. She was astounded at how real it looked, down to the jagged, blood soaked neck. Could it possibly be? Could the actual head of Melville University's most decorated faculty member actually be impaled on that spike?

A wave of anxiety washed over her as she felt her heart pounding. She paced unsteadily for a few minutes, then her mother's voice reverberated inside her brain. Grow up! Stop being so melodramatic. This isn't a Gothic romance and you're not a damsel in distress. You're a 29-

year-old university professional with two masters degrees and Melville's youngest department head. Act like it!

Still, she couldn't shake the feeling. Finally collapsing on a nearby bench, she sat, legs asplay, struggling to regain her composure.

It wasn't long before two stalwarts of the University Police arrived. Looking like overaged cadets ready to go on parade in their pressed gray uniforms and shiny black oxfords. One was tall and lanky with a pock-marked face, brown crew cut and a crooked half-smile. The tag on his breast pocket proclaimed that his name was Wheeler. The other was older, heavier, with a shaved head and skin the color and texture of a dried tobacco leaf. His tag read Suarez.

Usually only one officer was required to answer a distress call, but when they heard who had called it in, they argued for several minutes until they finally agreed that they both would respond.

Jordan stood as they approached, her legs still quivering.

"Miss Day, we came as soon as we heard that you called. I'm Brad Wheeler and this is Alfredo Suarez. Our dispatcher was a little unclear about what the problem is."

"Are you feeling alright?" Suarez said. "You look a little pale."

Jordan said nothing. She pointed up at the skewered head.

They both looked up.

Wheeler smiled, "Oh, don't worry Miss Day. It's just a student prank. They do it every Halloween."

"I know. I thought so too. But this is different. Look closely. Does that look like papier mâché to you?"

Wheeler stared at Spenser Berg's disembodied head for several seconds. A starling circled then landed on it and started pecking away at the eyeballs. He dislodged one and flew away with it.

"Jesus. That goddamn bird just ate Berg's eye."

Suarez said, "You mean you're actually thinking that it might be Berg's head up there? That's crazy."

"I know. But I'm not sure. Do birds eat marbles, or whatever else those kids use?"

Suarez shrugged. "How the hell should I know."

Wheeler straightened up. "I can't believe I'm saying this, but until we know for sure that it's not really Berg's head up there we have to treat this as a possible homicide."

Suarez rolled his eyes but kept his mouth shut.

Wheeler took the notebook off his duty belt, turned to Jordan, cleared his throat and said in as authoritative a voice as he could muster, "All right Ms. Day, let's start from the beginning, Did you notice anything out of the ordinary when you came in this morning?"

She pointed up at the bodiless head. "You mean besides that?"

Wheeler smiled contritely. "Yes. Something else. Something suspicious, someone who didn't belong here who might have stuck that, uh, thing on that spike. Anyone with a ladder? Workmen? Window cleaners?"

Jordan considered for a few seconds. "No. No one."

"What about from inside the library?" Suarez asked.

Wheeler shook his head. "I don't think so. That spike is about four feet long." He pointed up. "No way anyone could do it from the inside, unless he was a tightrope walker or a gymnast."

"Well, the head got there some way," Suarez retorted. "It didn't just fly up by itself."

"Actually, the finials are removable for cleaning," Jordan said. "Birds perch on them and make quite a mess."

Wheeler turned to face Jordan. "You mean anyone could just open the window, unscrew the spike, stick the head on it and screw it back on?"

"I'm afraid so."

"Who has access to that window?"

"Anyone who was in the Special Collections reading room could have opened it."

"Was anyone in there yesterday who didn't belong?"

Jordan glared at him. "It's a library, everyone belongs. People are coming and going all the time. Students, faculty, visiting scholars. I didn't notice anyone walking around with a severed head, if that's what you mean."

"I'm sorry, Ms. Day. I didn't mean to upset you," Wheeler said.

"Wait a minute," Suarez said. "Berg was alive last night at the Shakespeare thing in Porter Hall. He made a big scene. Everyone was talking about it back at the station."

Wheeler turned to Jordan. "What time does the library close?"

"The library stays open until midnight. But we lock the Special Collections office when we leave at seven."

"Could anyone have broken in?"

"That's highly unlikely. We have extremely rare and valuable manuscripts. Except for the bank in the student union basement, it's the most secure location on campus."

"Who has a key?"

"I do, of course. And Josh, my assistant. The keys to all the library rooms are in the dean's office." She paused in furrowed concentration. "No one else that I can think of. Perhaps the maintenance people."

"Are the dean's keys secure?"

"I have no idea."

"So it looks like we're back to outside access. What do you think, Fredo?"

"I think we better call this one in."

Wheeler steadied himself, grabbed his phone and hit the push-to-talk button.

"Hello, Chief."

"Yeah."

"It's Wheeler. I'm over at the library."

"So."

"I know this sounds a little freaky, but it looks like there's a head on a spike in front of the library."

"What kind of head? Stuffed? Animal? Plastic?"

"We think there's a chance it might be a human head, sir."

"Who's we?"

"I'm here with Suarez, sir."

After a few seconds of silence. "It's too early for this bullshit. I don't care that it's Halloween. This better not be your idea of a trick or treat joke, Wheeler, or it'll be your head on a spike. Get me?"

"Loud and clear, sir."

"Can you tell who it is?"

"It looks like Professor Berg."

"Spenser Berg? Christ!"

Wheeler looked up and stared intently at the head for a few seconds. "It sure as hell looks like him. If it's not the real thing, it's the best fake I've ever seen."

A guttural grunt came from the other end of the phone.

"Sir, how would you like us to proceed?"

"First thing you gotta do is find out if it's real. Remember the penis in the punchbowl incident a few years ago?"

Wheeler smiled but tried to keep his voice somber. "That was from a cadaver, if my memory serves me."

"I know where it was from," the chief shouted into the phone. "I also remember the mess we had when word of it spread around campus."

"Don't worry sir, we'll keep this under wraps."

"Who's seen it so far?"

"Just the librarian who called it in, Miss Day."

"All right. Until we find out different, treat the area like a crime scene. Have Suarez seal off the entrance. If anyone asks, say it's a possible gas leak. I don't want anyone anywhere near the thing until we know for certain what's going on."

"Anything else, sir?"

"Have you tried to call Berg?"

"He doesn't own a phone. Or a computer. How should we proceed?"

"Secure the area." The chief heaved a loud sigh and hung up.

"Did you take a crime scene kit?" Wheeler asked Suarez.

"Negative. I thought we were investigating a student prank, not a murder."

Jordan said, "Can I go up to my office or is that also a crime location?"

Wheeler glanced over at Suarez, who shrugged, then back at Jordan.

"Sure. Right now, we're not even sure there was a crime."

"What about my assistant, he gets in around eight?"

"What's his name?"

"Josh Campanella."

Wheeler wrote the name in his notebook. "Give him a call to let him know what's going on. We don't want him to panic when he gets here."

"Thank you," Jordan said. She took a few steps toward the front doors, turned and said, "Do you think that could actually be Professor Berg's head up there?"

Wheeler shrugged. "If it is, all hell's gonna break loose."

Chapter 2
12 Hours Earlier

"Christopher Marlowe, in a drunken rage, pummeled his young rival, howling curses and insults with every strike. Held fast by Marlowe's hooligan cronies, Will struggled mightily, finally managing to break free, loosen the rope around his neck and rip the foul-smelling horse blanket off his head. Grabbing a knife off one of the tables, he swung wildly at his captors. Either by sheer luck, uncanny skill or divine providence the blade hit home, plunging deep into Marlowe's eye. Bleeding profusely and in excruciating pain, England's preeminent poet and playwright died a death as gruesome as any his characters suffered onstage."

Harry Gabriel looked up. Melville University's Richard Rogers theater was filled beyond its 300-person capacity. He scanned the audience, gratified to see every seat filled and about fifty more rapt listeners standing around the periphery of the hall.

He continued reading.

"Having killed London's reigning literary superstar and a great favorite of the queen, the best Will Shakespeare could hope for was a quick death by hanging as opposed to the agonizing torture of being drawn and quartered.

"But the young bard wasn't killed. Christopher Marlowe's untimely demise meant that the Crown needed a new playwright-propagandist to manipulate the minds of England's unruly masses. Someone they could control, unlike Marlowe, who was the loosest of loose cannons. Who better than an ambitious young poet from out in the sticks, a bumpkin with no money, no connections and a hangman's noose dangling over his head."

Gabriel put his book down on the lectern and smiled smugly at the crowd.

"Everything I just read is based on the facts as we know them. We know Marlowe was stabbed under mysterious circumstances in a dodgy public house in Deptford, one of the seedier London neighborhoods. We know he despised Shakespeare and was envious and fearful of his burgeoning success. We know he associated with thugs, spies and assassins who would think nothing of slitting a man's throat for the price of a tankard of ale. And we know Shakespeare was in London at the time of Marlowe's death.

"So, could Shakespeare have killed Marlowe? It's possible. Pure conjecture...yes. Just like all of the biographies of Shakespeare ever written. The only difference between my work and all the other so-called Shakespeare biographies is that I'm honest enough to label my book as fiction while the others masquerade as fact."

He flashed an impish grin. "And, of course, my books are best-sellers, while the only people who buy their boring tomes are students who are forced to by their professors." The students in the audience chuckled. The faculty sat stone-faced.

"Now, I'll be happy to answer any questions."

He was about to call on a winsome young woman in the third row when the rear doors flew open. All eyes turned to the back of the auditorium as Spenser Berg strode in. "I have a question," he thundered,

Marching up the center aisle, the imposing six-foot four-inch, 300-pound septuagenarian scholar pointed an accusatory finger at the stunned Gabriel.

"How dare you have the temerity, the audacity, the unmitigated gall to come to this school, MY SCHOOL, and pontificate about something you are less qualified to talk about than the person who will sweep out this auditorium after you, thankfully, leave it?"

Now at the front of the auditorium, he turned to face the audience.

"Harry Gabriel is a brainless dolt, a charlatan and a poser," Berg's voice resounded through the hall. "Just like that uneducated clod from Stratford, who had difficulty writing his own name, much less the most profound works the English language has ever produced."

Gabriel seethed. Muscles taut, he held onto the lectern with a death grip. He glared with hateful eyes down at his former mentor. He wasn't going to let the old man rattle him as he had done years before. This was his night. His crowd.

Breathing deeply, he exhaled slowly and turned toward the transfixed audience. His angry scowl melted into a sardonic smile.

"Thank you, Dr. Berg, for equating me with the greatest writer who ever lived. I'll share doltage with William Shakespeare anytime."

He took an exaggerated bow to some scattered applause.

"The only thing you two share is that you are abject frauds," Berg shouted back. "I shall soon expose you both."

Gabriel gestured grandly at his accuser.

"Ladies and gentlemen, behold the Lear of academe. Once a literary titan, America's foremost man of letters, now a blathering shell, lost and blindly flailing in a storm of his own making. The difference is that King Lear had the good judgment to die in the final act while the superannuated Professor Berg refuses to leave the stage." He pointed to the door. "I'd be more than happy to assist with your final exit."

"Don't threaten me, you guttersnipe! I shall be alive long enough to reveal the greatest literary discovery of all time and expose you as the incompetent mountebank you are."

Berg turned to the audience. "I have incontrovertible proof that the man known as William Shakespeare did not write a single word of any of the plays or poems attributed to him."

Gabriel shook his head slowly, condescendingly. "Dr. Berg has been spewing about his great Shakespearian revelation for the better part of a decade. But all we've gotten from him is self-aggrandizing bluster." He gestured at Berg. "If you have proof that someone other than Shakespeare is the true author of the works, reveal it now and show everyone that you aren't a delusional old fool."

Berg sneered. "I will not share my moment of triumph with an unlettered guttersnipe. That would demean the entire experience, just as you defile this place by your presence."

He turned to the audience. "Tomorrow night on this stage I shall present my discovery. Then I will prove to the world that the man who called himself Shakespeare was nothing but a third-rate hack. And that you..." He gestured malevolently at Harry, "Are a thief and a plagiarist."

Berg strode purposefully to the side door, then turned back and glared at Gabriel.

"When I am through, your unearned reputation will be in tatters and your so-called career in ruins. Enjoy this moment of glory, it will be your last!"

Berg stormed out and slammed the door behind him.

Chapter 3

"Do you want me to get the president on the line for you?" Suman Champati's mellifluous voice called from her desk outside Chief Gregg MacArthur's office.

Though he had no reason, MacArthur couldn't help feeling that Suman was a spy for President DellaRosa. Her husband, Kadhir, had recently been hired as chair of Mechanical Engineering. Part of the compensation package was that his wife be given a job. The only position available at the time was the Chief's administrative assistant, even though she was vastly overqualified, with a PhD in Global History from Bangalore University.

"I don't think that's necessary, Suman."

"Whatever you think is best, Chief," she said pleasantly. "It's just that I remember the president mentioning that if anything came up that could possibly disrupt Saturday's event, you should contact her immediately. And, if you don't mind my saying so, I'm sure the appearance of severed heads displayed on campus could be a source of distraction."

He was about to tell her to stop eavesdropping on his conversations but thought better of it and grumbled, "All right, get her on the phone."

Less than a minute later, his phone chimed three times, signaling that there was someone on the line. He picked it up and a groggy, irritated female voice on the other end muttered, "It's 7:30 am, Chief, what's wrong?"

"Hello, President DellaRosa, you asked me to call you as soon as anything..."

"All right, get on with it."

"One of the librarians saw what she thought was Spenser Berg's severed head on a spike outside a window of the library."

"Why are you bothering me with this? This happens every year around Halloween. Just have them take it down."

"My men think it might be the real thing."

"Then your men are idiots. I saw Spenser last night. Trust me, his head was firmly attached to his shoulders."

"I'm sure you're right, ma'am. But just to be on the safe side, I'd like to make sure he's all right."

"You know Spenser's the ultimate Luddite. He has no phone, no TV, no computer. He writes with a quill pen. He sees himself as the last of the true Elizabethans. If you feel you must verify that he's still alive, you'll have to go to his house and see for yourself."

"I'll get one of my men right on it."

"Not one of your men. You!" she said emphatically. "Spenser doesn't trust strangers. He will never open his door to anyone he doesn't know. Do you understand?"

"Perfectly, ma'am."

Fifteen minutes later, MacArthur walked up the wooden front steps of Spenser Berg's house. Only four miles from campus, the one-story cottage was at the end of a long, meandering road.

The door was slightly ajar.

"Dr. Berg!" MacArthur shouted. "Dr. Berg are you in there?"

Silence.

MacArthur pushed the door all the way open and walked into a very large room. It was furnished like a nineteenth century gentlemen's club, with a large stone fireplace, book-lined walls and a well-worn crushed velvet carpet, upon which stood several antique inlaid walnut parlor tables surrounded by leather club chairs. A large burled oak billiard table, where the renowned literary icon would trounce many of his unsuspecting guests, dominated the center of the room. A brass chandelier was centered above it. Though it was a bright morning, the house was dark, the windows covered by heavy chenille drapes.

A noxious stench immediately gripped his face like five fetid fingers. MacArthur, who had been to the scene of several fatal fires during his fifteen years on the New York City Police Force, recognized the smell immediately. Burnt flesh. Grabbing a small flashlight from his belt, he waded resolutely into the haze enshrouded room. His eyes focused on a charred, bloody hulk lying across the top of the billiard table. He thought it might be the remnants of a whole barbecued lamb or pig. The he realized it was a headless human torso, it's hands and feet bound, a bloody, gaping wound where the genitals should be. Nothing in his experience prepared him for this. The sight of the charred, mutilated corpse combined with the repugnant smell of seared flesh turned his stomach. He retched, as bile coated his throat.

Suddenly, the room was bathed in light. "Hiya Mac, whatcha got?" A booming, cheerful voice shattered the stillness.

MacArthur jerked up, spun around, coughed, lost his balance and did an awkward jig to prevent himself from falling.

"Jesus, Lizzie, couldn't you at least knock or something? I almost wet my pants."

He struggled to regain his composure. And his dignity.

Lizzie Peltz stood in the doorway, hands on hips, with a wide grin. Her eyes darted around the room, her crime reporter instincts resurfacing after twenty years of dormancy. Though a shade under six feet tall and weighing over two hundred pounds, she moved with the grace of an athlete, which she was in her younger days as captain of the Melville University women's lacrosse team.

Oblivious to the stink, she sauntered to the table, dropped her oversized red canvass tote bag on the floor, leaned over and gazed down at the barbecued torso. "Is that what I think it is?"

"How can you stand to be so close to that thing?" MacArthur demanded as he walked over to her. "Doesn't that odor make you sick?"

"Got a cold." She pointed to her nose. "Can't smell a thing." Then at the body. "It's human, right? You think it's Berg?"

"Who else could it be?"

She grinned. "No brains, no balls, smells like crap, could be any one of a hundred men I know."

"That's not funny. A man was butchered here. It's no time to make jokes."

"Sorry Mac," she said, feigning contrition. "Hey, what's this?" She bent over next to the table and resurfaced holding an empty whisky bottle. She examined the label carefully, then said pensively, "I wonder who belongs to this. Berg only drank English ale, Old Speckled Hen."

"Hey, put that back. Berg was probably murdered right here. Until we know for sure, this is now a crime scene."

"So are you gonna process it or what? Once the press find out about Berg's murder, they're gonna be all over this place like maggots on moldy meatloaf."

"I'll have to speak to the president before I do anything. Who knows how she'll want to handle this."

Lizzie held up the bottle. "You know what this is?"

"Yeah. It's an empty whiskey bottle. So what?"

"This is a bottle of 18-year-old Talisker single malt scotch. It goes for close to 200 bucks a pop. Find out whose this is and you'll find your killer."

"I don't think so. We got a lot of drinkers on campus."

"They don't drink this. You can cross every student off your list. Too pricey for them. And most of the faculty drink beer or wine, if they drink anything at all. I'm not sure too many would know the difference between single malt scotch and hopscotch."

"So right now our only lead is an empty bottle of expensive hooch that no one on campus drinks. Not a lot to go on." MacArthur headed for the door.

Lizzie followed him out and closed the door behind her. "There happens to be someone on campus right now who is known for drinking pricey single malt whisky."

"Who?"

A Cheshire Cat grin meandered across her face. "The same person who almost came to blows with Spenser Berg last night in Rogers Hall."

"Harry Gabriel?" MacArthur turned and glared at Lizzie. "And how do you know he likes that, what did you call it, Talonscar?"

"It's Talisker." She raised an eyebrow. "I'm the media director. Who do you think wrote all the publicity flyers leading up to last night's big event?"

"So you're the reigning expert on Harry Gabriel?"

"I don't know about expert, but I spent the past two weeks reading everything I could get my hands on about him. And let me tell you, for a guy that's just hitting forty, it was a lot. That's where I found out that before he was in the PhD program here, he went to Columbia on a track scholarship and that he completed two New York City marathons. His father was a high school principal and his mother was a social worker. Dad's half black-half Italian, mom's Jewish. And he has a weakness for pricy single malt scotch. Actually, it's more a problem than a weakness. But supposedly, he's got a handle on it."

"That's all very interesting but it's not proof.

"Well how about this? It also seems that our boy has a fuse the size of a sparrow's pecker and a penchant for fisticuffs."

"Really?"

She nodded knowingly. "He's been arrested twice for brawling in public. He got into it once with an African American blogger who called him a white wolf in black sheep's clothing. Another time he decked a paparazzo who followed him into the men's room of the 92nd Street Y after he gave a lecture there. And the rumor is that he and Berg once had a little knock-down-drag-out of their own when Berg was his dissertation director. People around here at that time said it was inevitable. That two arrogant, self-centered, egotistical narcissists can't play together in the same sandbox. That's when Gabriel decided that the academic life wasn't for him and decided to try his hand at popular fiction. His first book went to number one on the New York Times bestseller list and he wound up on the cover of the Book Review. There were features on him in New York Magazine and People and guest spots on the late night talk shows. It didn't hurt that he has the looks of a movie star, sort of a cross between Chris Evans and Michael B. Jordan."

"I never heard of either of them."

"What was the last movie you went to, Birth of a Nation?"

"Forget about that bullshit, get back to Berg."

"As you can imagine, all of Gabriel's fame and glory infuriated him."

"So if Berg hated him so much, why the hell did he invite him here?"

Lizzie shook her head. "He didn't. Angie did. She met Gabriel at some function in the city and she's been trying to get him to speak here ever since. You know Angie, she gravitates to stars. And Gabriel's a star."

"I bet that really pissed Berg off."

Lizzie smiled. "You could see the smoke coming out of his ears."

MacArthur grabbed his phone. "Angie's not gonna like this, a high profile murder investigation on campus, Suffolk County cops all over the place, students and teachers in a panic, and the pain-in-the-ass press, they're gonna be everywhere, taking pictures, asking all kinds of annoying questions. We'll have to cancel Homecoming, that's for sure."

Lizzie shook her head. "This isn't the kind of news we can give to her over the phone. Angie always wants to hear bad news in person. And when she hears that the university's most important faculty member was murdered and the prime suspect is Harry Gabriel, it'll be 'Katie bar the door.'"

"It's times like this I wish I was back on the street. Drug dealers, mobsters and thugs were a lot easier to deal with than Angelina Della-Rosa when she's throwing a fit."

Chapter 4

MacArthur walked up to the front desk, his chest heaving after bounding up four flights of stairs. Lizzie was still en route, having opted to wait for the elevator.

"We need to see the President immediately," he said with as much severity as he could muster. "It's extremely urgent."

Like the Great Sphinx that guarded the tombs of the ancient pharaohs, Edie Kaiser, the guardian of the Melville University Presidential Office Suite, was awe-inspiring, monumental, imposing, beautiful and timeless. No one could see President DellaRosa without going through Edie. Even seated behind her massive golden oak desk, she seemed to tower over her visitors. When she stood she was well over six feet tall, with long, slender, perfectly manicured fingers, thick wavy hair the color and texture of honey and steely gray eyes that belied a sensitive soul. Now in her seventh decade, from a distance she still appeared to be the beauty pageant finalist that she had been forty years earlier.

"We?" Edie cocked a quizzical eyebrow and gazed around in an exaggerated fashion. "We who? There's nobody here but you."

"Me and Lizzie, she's on her way."

"The President's in with the head of the Alumni Association. They're finalizing the details for the big event tomorrow."

"That's what we need to see her about. She has to call it off."

Edie glared at him like he just told her to eat a cockroach.

"Are you insane?" she shrieked. "This is Whale-a-Palooza, the biggest homecoming weekend ever. We've been working on it for six months. It's president's number one priority. There's no possible way it can be cancelled now."

Lizzie lumbered through the door. "So Mac, did you tell her?"

"Hello Lizzie, how are you?" Edie said with a skeptical smile. "Tell me what?"

"I'm fine, Edie. Now about your other question. Somebody cut off Spenser Berg's head this morning and stuck it on a spike on the second floor of the library."

Edie grimaced in horror. "Lizzie, that's disgusting. I know you have a bizarre sense of humor, but that's over the line, even for you."

"She's not kidding, Edie," MacArthur said. "Jordan Day, the Special Collections librarian, discovered Berg's head this morning. We found most of the rest of him back at his house."

"Most of the rest?" Edie was starting to lose her legendary composure. "What parts were missing?" She was feeling slightly sick to her stomach.

"You don't really want to know, kiddo." Lizzie smiled ruefully. "Now, can you let her highness know that we need to speak with her. Pronto."

Edie picked up the phone and pressed a key. Three seconds later she began to speak. "Lizzie Peltz and Gregg MacArthur are here." She hung up.

"Go ahead in." As they walked past her, Edie shook her head sadly, then took a white handkerchief out her handbag and dabbed her forehead where small droplets had formed.

The President's office was large but welcoming, like a nicely furnished living room. One wall was covered completely with books. Reference books, textbooks, business books, art books, literature, popular novels, cookbooks. Another wall was filled with photos of Angelina DellaRosa with some of the more famous Melville U guests. Hillary Clinton, Barack Obama, Ralph Nader, Luciano Pavarotti, Barbara Streisand and Mike Piazza. They were all hung together haphazardly, interspersed with shots of her children and grandchildren.

Except for one. Situated by itself, in a gold frame on the wall closest to her desk, was a yellowing black and white photograph of a little girl, about eight years old, in a plaid skirt and white blouse, standing next to a large black man wearing a Brooklyn Dodgers uniform. The faded inscription read, "Angelina, keep swinging for the fences. Your pal, Jackie Robinson."

"Gregg, Elizabeth, come in, sit down." President DellaRosa was seated at a round oak table in the middle of the room, writing on a yellow legal pad. Her dark brown hair was perfectly coiffed. Though past sixty, she looked trim and fit in her tailored blue business suit. Sapphire studs glistened in her ears. She wore the same serious expression as the little girl in the photograph and her eyes had the same confident gleam.

"Dr. DellaRosa," Peltz said. "Something terrible has happened. Spenser Berg was murdered."

"And that's not the worst of it," MacArthur blurted out. "That severed head I spoke to you about, the one they found on a spike at the library, it really was Berg's. We found the rest of him at his house."

The color drained out of DellaRosa's face. She absentmindedly picked up a pencil and squeezed it with both hands. Her chest heaved as her breathing intensified. She closed her eyes for several seconds. When she opened them, her composure had returned.

"Are you absolutely sure that what you saw at the cottage was Spenser's body?"

"Ninety-nine percent sure. We can't be positive until we can verify it somehow. The body was set on fire. Burnt pretty bad. I don't know if we can get his fingerprints off it. We can probably recover some DNA but it'll be complicated."

"That would entail getting more people involved, wouldn't it?"

"We'd have to send it out to a lab. We don't have those kinds of facilities here."

"Let's hold off on that and assume that what your officers saw was Spenser and not some elaborate hoax."

"Okay."

In a throaty whisper, she said, "Start from the beginning and tell me everything you know in as much detail as possible."

MacArthur methodically recounted the events of the morning, downplaying the grisliness whenever possible. But when he got to the part about finding Berg's charred, headless, mutilated body sprawled out on the billiards table, DellaRosa made a loud retching noise, covered her face in her hands and yelled, "Enough!"

"I'm sorry, Dr. DellaRosa, but you did ask for as much detail as possible," he said, softly.

"Well Chief," she said, her voice calm. "What do you propose we do?"

"Of course, first we have to cancel Homecoming, or Whale-a-Palooza, or whatever we're calling it this year. Then we'll have to call the local police, the Special Crimes Unit and possibly Homeland Security. This could be a terrorist act," he said ominously.

She shifted her gaze to the head of media relations. "Lizzie, do you agree with Chief MacArthur's analysis?"

Peltz bit her lip and nodded slowly. "That sounds about right. Of course the press'll be all over campus like locusts. They live for stories like this, the more gruesome the better. I may have to take on some free-lancers to help me keep them under control."

DellaRosa steepled her fingers in front of her and looked from one to the other. "I thank you both for your advice, but I have a different plan."

"I'm not sure I understand," MacArthur said.

"Whale-a-Palooza goes forward as scheduled," DellaRosa said emphatically.

"But..."

"No buts, Chief! Do you remember what this campus looked like before I arrived?"

Neither Peltz nor MacArthur said a word, they just nodded feebly.

"It was oppressive. The architecture was right out of a Russian prison. Some of the windows even had bars on them. Students hated being here. Once they graduated, they never came back. And would never dream of sending us a donation." She stood up and walked over to the window behind her desk. "Now they will. It's taken over five years and close to fifty million dollars to turn that dump into this." She gestured grandly at the panoramic view outside her window. Perfectly manicured lawns, lush trees and shrubs intermixed with vibrant plantings and fall flowers. Rustic cobblestone walkways and paths sported colorful benches and picnic tables as they led to the academic buildings, all of which had been refaced with russet colored brick, except for the library.

"Whale-a-Palooza is Melville University's coming out party," she continued. "We've invited thousands of people — senators, congressmen, the governor, CEO's of Fortune 500 companies. The most important and influential men and women on the east coast will be here. The last thing we need is an army of policemen, reporters and camera crews upsetting everyone and asking questions about severed heads in the library." She glared at both of them. "Am I making myself clear?"

MacArthur stared at his shoes and began to speak in a barely audible mumble. "With all due respect, what you're asking us to do is against the law. As a sworn police official, I would lose my badge and probably wind up in jail if I followed your orders." He met DellaRosa's eyes. "I don't know if I can do that, ma'am."

"I respect that, Chief MacArthur. But tell me, how long have you been with the University?"

"It'll be eight years in March."

"How do you feel about it?"

"You don't have to ask me that." He glanced towards the window then back at the president. "I love it."

"As much as you loved being a New York City detective?"

MacArthur thought for a moment, then said, "Pretty close."

"Well, by bringing in the local police, the press, Homeland Security and who knows who else, you very well may undo everything I've... we've done to bring Melville to where it is today." She looked penetratingly into his eyes. "I won't order you not to make that call, but I am asking you...as a friend, and as someone who loves this university."

MacArthur closed his eyes for a few seconds. "You know, when I was on the NYPD, we kept the Feds out of the loop whenever we could, we felt it was a matter of pride that we solved our own cases. I guess this is pretty much the same thing." He turned to Lizzie. "What do you think?"

She was still for a few seconds, then a puckish smile washed over her face. "We're just as smart as those bozos. No, I take that back," she said, her eyes twinkling. "We're smarter! We know this campus better than anybody. If we can't figure out what happened to Berg, nobody can. I say let's do it."

"Just to be clear, Dr. DellaRosa," MacArthur said. "You're asking us not to contact any other law enforcement agencies and to investigate this matter by ourselves."

"That's correct."

"What about my men? Can I use them in the investigation?"

"How many have been involved so far?"

"Just two. Wheeler and Suarez."

"Are they competent?"

"They're the best we have." MacArthur stared up at the ceiling, hoping the president wouldn't remember when they mistakenly arrested the student-manager of a rival football team for trespassing before a game.

"Try to limit university police involvement to yourself and those two officers."

"Yes, ma'am."

The President smiled benignly, ending the conversation. As they all stood, she walked over to MacArthur, and gave him a hug. "Thank you, Chief."

"I'll do my best," he said, then about-faced and marched out of the room. Lizzie winked at DellaRosa as she followed MacArthur.

While they were waiting for the elevator, Lizzie said, "When you talked about the NYPD your eyes got all dreamy, like you were remembering your first love."

"In a way, I am. All I ever wanted to be was a cop. I loved every minute of it."

"So, why did you quit?"

MacArthur took a gulp of air. A melancholy half-smile formed across his lips as he shook his head dolefully. "I was a lieutenant in the 112th Precinct, Forest Hills. I probably would have made captain by now."

"So what happened?"

"I got shot."

Lizzie's eye bulged. "Oh my God!"

"It's no big deal," he said with a shrug. "I was off-duty, on my way home, and this punk is sticking up a liquor store right around the corner from my house. So I go in, gun drawn, identify myself and tell him to drop his firearm. He turns, gets off a shot and runs like hell out the back. Hits me here." He pointed to his upper thigh. "It was a scratch, I was in and out of the ER in two hours."

"Wow, Mac, I had no idea." She thought for a second. "Did they ever catch the kid?"

"The moron actually turned himself in." MacArthur shook his head in disgust. "He thought he killed me and figured he would get the electric chair for murdering a cop. Figured if he came in on his own they'd go easier on him."

"A lot of cops get shot on the job. They don't leave the force. Why did you?"

He scowled. "My wife."

She gaped with surprise. "I never knew you were married."

"She was from Denmark. I met her in Copenhagen. She had flaming red hair and a body like..."

"What the hell were you doing in Copenhagen?"

"A group of us from the NYPD were there training the Danish police in crowd control. Some kind of reciprocal program between the two departments. I met her at Tivoli, the big amusement park there. She came back with me. Six months later we went to City Hall and got married. Crazy, huh?

"Mac, you old romantic," Lizzie gushed. "I didn't know you had it in you."

"Anyway, after I got shot, she showed up at the ER hysterical, screaming. She said if I didn't quit the force she'd leave me then and there and move back home, where people didn't shoot each other in the street like cowboys in the Wild West."

"So that's when you started working here?"

"Uh huh."

"That's so sweet. You chose the woman you loved over the job you loved."

"Yeah, real sweet. Six months later she was gone anyway. Left me a note that said she hated New York and couldn't stand being here another day. If I was ever in Aarhus, I should look her up."

"I'm sorry, Mac."

"It's okay," he said stoically. "It was never gonna work. Too much of a culture clash."

"After she left, did you ever try to get back on the force?"

"Yeah, a few of times. I kept getting a lot of bullshit excuses. Hiring freeze, budget cuts, I was the wrong color. After a while, I got the hint."

She winked at him. "After you solve this case they'll be plenty interested. You'll be a hero. They'll beg you to come back."

"You think so?"

"Absolutely. Spenser Berg is very well known. And Harry Gabriel's a famous American author." She thought for a second. "He's gotta be the prime suspect. If you bring him in, you'll be on the front page of every newspaper in America. Then the NYPD will be thrilled to get you back."

The dreamy look was back on his face. "Maybe."

Chapter 5

Josh Campanella hovered behind Jordan while she scurried around the main reading room of the Special Collections department, reshelving books, pushing chairs under tables, straightening pictures on the wall. "Are you sure you're all right? Let me get you a cup of tea or something. You look pale."

"No thank you, Joshua," she said rather sternly.

He always reminded her of a golden retriever, big, slightly ungainly, always eager to please, sometimes annoyingly so. His recently grown goatee and thinning hair that sprang haphazardly from his scalp in unruly tufts only added to his Scooby Doo appearance.

"You just had a close encounter with a severed head. I really think you should go home."

She stopped abruptly, turned and glared at him. "I don't want to go home. I don't want a cup of tea. If you want to help me, please stop following me around like a mother hen!"

Josh's head snapped back as if he'd been slapped. "Well, uh, I didn't mean..."

Jordan put a hand on his shoulder. "I'm sorry, Josh. I didn't mean to snap at you. It's been a very stressful couple of days — even before this morning."

"What happened before this morning?"

"I got some upsetting news."

"What do you mean? What's going on?"

"Do you remember the meeting I had with Dean Childress on Monday?"

"Of course. You said it was just business as usual."

"I know. I was trying not to burden you."

"Well, what did he say?"

"He told me that the state mandated that the university cut $130 million from this year's operating budget."

"We're not the budget office. What does that have to do with us?"

"Some people on the Board of Trustees think that a Special Collections department is an expensive luxury that has nothing to do with the university's core mission."

Josh threw his hands in the air and started yelling, "That's crazy! What we do is of immense value to the university. There are teachers, students and scholars in here every day doing important work."

"That's exactly what I told him."

"So what did he say?"

"He was noncommittal. But he was never a big supporter of our department. If you ask me, I think he'd be happy for an excuse to close us down."

"So what do we do?"

"We have to raise $500,000 to defray our costs."

"Five hundred thousand dollars!" he was yelling again. "Why not five hundred million? Where the hell are we going to get that kind of money?"

"I was hoping to get some or all of it from Lady Millicent DeVere. She's already the University's biggest benefactor and has indicated that she'd like to donate some volumes to our collection. I'm actually supposed to have dinner with her tonight and talk to her about our situation, but with all that's happened..." She shrugged. "Who knows."

"Why didn't you tell me what Childress said?"

"I was going to wait to see how my dinner with Lady DeVere went. I didn't see any reason for both of us being stressed out all week."

"What'll happen to us if they close the department?"

"I'm not sure. You're in the union, they'll find you another position somewhere in the library. I'm management, so..."

"Oh my God!" Josh shrieked. "They can't fire you can they?"

"It's possible. Now do you understand why I've been so edgy lately." She covered her face with her hands. "And knowing that that horrible thing is behind the curtain on the other side of the window." She clutched head with both hands. "I don't know how much more I can take."

Josh walked toward the window. "I'll take it down right now."

"Campus Police said not to touch anything."

Ignoring her, he drew back the heavy beige drape. He leaned in and looked around. "My God. It's gone!"

"What are you talking about? What's gone?"

"The head."

"Gone? How can it be gone?" She ran over and peered out the window. "It's not there. How can that be? Nobody's been here but you and me. Josh, when I was in my office, did you...?"

"Did I take that head off the spike? Are you crazy!" He gave an exaggerated shudder. "Ugh!"

"Then where did it go?"

"I have no idea."

"It couldn't have just disappeared?" she said, a little more stridently than she intended.

"When I went down for coffee. Did you hear anyone come in?"

"No. But I had headphones on and was doing some cataloging in the other room. How long were you gone?"

"Ten, maybe fifteen minutes. Someone could have snuck in, grabbed the head and ran out."

"I guess it's possible. But how could they be sure that I wouldn't come out of my office or that you wouldn't return?"

"I don't know. Or maybe it was the police."

"Yes it could be...if they climbed up a ladder and removed it that way."

There was a loud knock at the door. "We're closed," Josh shouted. "Come back tomorrow."

The knocking became pounding. "University Police," came the gruff response from the other side. "We need to talk to Miss Day."

Josh turned back to Jordan and whispered, "Do you want me to tell them you're not up to meeting with them?"

She thought for a moment. "No, you better let them in. I'm going to have to talk with them sooner or later. It might as well be now."

By the time she pulled the drape shut, Josh was back with Lizzie Peltz and Gregg MacArthur.

Lizzie sat down next to Jordan. She grabbed the younger woman by both shoulders and moved her face so close that they were almost rubbing noses. "Tell me, Jordie," she said, dripping ersatz sincerity. "Are you doing all right?"

Jordan, who despised being called Jordie and had a problem with people invading her personal space, drew back with a shudder. "I'm perfectly fine," she said, stiffly. "Do you need to talk to me about something? Or did you just want to see how I was feeling."

MacArthur stepped forward. "We need to speak with you about what happened this morning." He glanced over at Josh. "It's extremely confidential."

Josh shuffled awkwardly to his feet. "I'll go get the mail, then I'll be in my office if you need me." He walked out of the main room into the corridor, closing the door behind him.

MacArthur paced back and forth, his brow furrowed under the weight of his overly gelled hair. He opened his mouth once or twice to speak, then thought better of it and continued pacing. The two women stared at him as if watching an exotic animal at the zoo. Finally he stopped in front of Jordan and leaned over with his hands resting on his thighs. "We have a sort of situation here, Miss Day."

"A situation? What do you mean?"

"Have you spoken to anyone about what you saw this morning?"

"I told Joshua."

"You mean Campanella in there?"

"Yes."

"Anyone else?"

"No."

"You haven't called anyone or emailed or put anything on Facebook or Tweeter."

Lizzie cut him off. "That's Twitter, you blockhead. Stop badgering the kid. She said she didn't talk to anyone but Josh and that's that."

"Why do you want to know who I spoke to?"

"Angie wants us to keep what happened this morning under wraps, literally," Lizzie continued. "Our esteemed president doesn't want anyone to find out about your very unusual discovery until after the weekend."

"I don't understand."

"It's Whale-A-Palooza. Melville U's biggest event of the year. Maybe ever. Homecoming on steroids." Lizzie threw her hands in the air to punctuate her statement. "The campus'll be full of big shots and high rollers. She wants to show off all the wonderful things she's accomplished here. Having one of our star professors on display with his disembodied head on a spike won't impress the politicians and certainly won't encourage potential six-figure donors to be writing any checks to the Melville University Capital Campaign."

While Lizzie was talking, MacArthur was peering intently into a black leather notebook. He looked directly at Jordan. "Are you and Campanella the only ones who work in this office?"

"Yes."

"And one of you is always here?"

"No. Not necessarily."

"Don't you have a lot of valuable old books?"

"We have several volumes here that are extremely rare."

"What's to stop someone from stealing them?"

"The truly irreplaceable ones are kept inside the vault. All the books, though, are tagged with a microchip. There are sensors at every door. Anyone trying to remove a book without checking it out would set off the alarm."

MacArthur nodded. "I see. It wouldn't stop anyone from sneaking in here and sticking a severed head on one of those spikes, though."

His eyes were fixated on the curtain in front of the window.

"I'm sure one of us would have noticed that."

"Not if neither of you were here." MacArthur cleared his throat, glanced at his notebook, then turned his attention back to Jordan. "According to Officer Wheeler, everyone who comes up here has to sign in. Is that correct?"

"Yes."

"Can I see the sign-in sheet from yesterday?"

She walked into the vestibule, returned a few seconds later with a sheet of yellow paper and handed it to MacArthur, who perused it intently. After several seconds his head snapped back. "When was Harry Gabriel here?"

"Harry Gabriel! Never."

"Then how did his name get on the list?"

MacArthur thrust the paper at Jordan. Her eyebrows arched in surprise as she saw the name halfway down the page.

MacArthur pressed on. "Is that his handwriting?"

"I have no idea."

"So how do you explain it?"

"He may have been here when I was out of the office."

"Did Campanella see him?"

"He didn't mention anything to me. I'll call him and you can ask him yourself."

As she walked over to the phone on the main desk, Josh scurried into the room, holding a small, light blue envelope in his quivering hand.

"Good timing, Campanella," MacArthur said. "I want to ask you a question."

"Y-yes."

"Was Harry Gabriel here anytime yesterday?"

"No."

"Are you sure?"

"Positive." Still clutching the envelope, Josh turned to Jordan. "You better read this."

"Is it from Millicent DeVere? She's not canceling, is she?"

"It's not from Lady DeVere." He handed her the envelope. "Here, take a look." His voice had an urgent edge, bordering on panic.

She gently brushed his hand away. "I'm sure it can wait a few minutes. I think Ms. Peltz and Chief MacArthur are almost done."

He thrust it at her aggressively. "You really need to see this now. They should too."

Jordan twitched. The cuddly kitten turned snarling tiger. She took the envelope. It had already been opened. Inside was a note, typed on fine rag paper, the same robin's egg blue as the envelope. Embossed in bronze foil at the top of the page in an elegant Old English font were two words that brought forth from Jordan a small but discernible gasp. The words were "Spenser Berg."

Saying nothing, she handed it to Lizzie.

"Honey, what's wrong? What is it?" She looked at the paper. "Holy crap, it's from Berg...like a message from the great beyond."

"What are you waiting for?" MacArthur barked. "Read it!"

Lizzie read. "My Dear Jordan, It gives me consummate pleasure to inform you that I intend to make an extraordinary gift to the library. Whilst in London doing research, I was able to acquire one of William Shakespeare's original tables. It would please me greatly if the library were to become its permanent home. My only stipulation, Jordan, is that you take personal responsibility for it. Of all my colleagues at this university, you are the only person I trust with this priceless artifact. When you receive this missive, please contact me so that we may make arrangements as to how to transfer ownership. Remember, you and only you are to take possession of this precious gift. My only hope is that you receive as much joy in accepting it as I have in bestowing it. Fondly, Spenser Berg."

MacArthur glared at Jordan. "What's this all about?"

"I...I have no idea," she said, the color draining from her face.

"Berg never spoke to you about any kind of table he was going to donate to the library?"

"No, never."

"We were just at his house," MacArthur growled to no one in particular. He turned to Lizzie. "Wait a minute. What about that big old pool table in the living room."

"I'm not sure if they played pool in Shakespeare's time. Besides, that damn thing is huge. There's nowhere in the library where they could fit it."

MacArthur pointed to Josh. "What about you, Campanella? Do you know anything about this?"

"Me? No sir. I've never heard of any kind of table that belonged to Shakespeare, billiard or otherwise. I'll bet it's some sort of a writing table."

MacArthur turned to Jordan. "How much would something like that be worth?"

"A table originally belonging to William Shakespeare. Millions. Perhaps tens of millions. I'm sure there are people who would kill for something like that." As soon as she said it she covered her mouth and gasped for the second time in as many minutes.

"This makes things interesting," MacArthur said to Lizzie. "We were wondering about a motive. Here's ten million motives." He reached into his jacket pocket, pulled out a business card and put it in Jordan's hand. "If you remember anything else about this morning or Spenser Berg or about the table he was supposed to give you, call me." He turned to Lizzie. "Let's go. I think we're onto something." He walked to the door. Lizzie followed.

As soon as they left, Josh said, "See. Spenser Berg thought so much of you that you're the only one he was going to trust with the greatest literary find of the century. Do you have any idea what that could do for the library's reputation? And yours?"

"Yes, that would have been wonderful," she said glumly. "It would certainly stop anyone from closing the department."

"So why do you look so miserable?"

"Because we don't have the table. Dr. Berg is dead. And Chief MacArthur thinks I did it."

"No way. That's crazy."

"Did you see the way he glared at me after Liz Peltz read the letter? I'm sure he considers me a suspect."

"Why would you even think that?"

"I was the first one here this morning, which means I had plenty of opportunity. Maybe Dr. Berg told me about this Shakespeare table and I decided to sell it and keep the money for myself — like MacArthur said, that's a ten million dollar motive. And the board cutter we have back in the bookbinding studio, why do you think they call it a guillotine? That thing could easily decapitate someone. There's my means. Means, motive and opportunity, isn't that how they convict murderers?"

"They also need proof. Besides, Berg must have weighed at least 300 pounds. If you used the board shear to cut off his head, what did you do with the body?"

"Well, maybe he thinks I had help."

"Who?"

She said nothing, then raised her eyebrows at Josh.

After an uncomprehending few seconds he pointed to himself with both thumbs and said, "Me? How could you even suggest such a thing? I mean...I hardly knew Spenser Berg, why in the world would I want to kill him? Really Jordan, that's just crazy."

"Calm down, Joshua, I'm not accusing you. All I'm saying is that if MacArthur suspects me, he might suspect you too." She paused for a moment. "And you're very strong, the way you move the heavy furniture around here like it's made of Styrofoam. I bet you could have moved Berg's body without even trying."

"Jeez, now you're making me paranoid. You don't really think I had anything to do with this, do you?"

She gave him a tepid hug. "Of course not."

Chapter 6

The shrill ring of the phone on the night table shot through Harry Gabriel's head like a jolt from a cattle prod. He reached clumsily across the bed to grab it before it struck again. His heavy head and blurry vision, a result of the half a bottle of scotch he drank after his run-in with Berg the previous evening, conspired to sabotage his efforts. His wrist smacked into the phone, sending a shooting pain up his arm and the instrument careening onto the floor.

He struggled to extricate himself from the bed sheets and blankets that had cocooned around him during his restless night. Finally free, he lowered himself to the floor and picked up the phone. "H-hello," he said, his voice a throaty whisper.

"Dr. Gabriel, this is Alice, from the Melville University Department of Conferences and Events," came the nasally, sing-song voice from the earpiece.

"Yes, Alice." Harry Gabriel must have spoken to her well over a dozen times while the logistics of his lecture was being arranged, and yet every time she called him she introduced herself as if she had never spoken to him before.

"I hope I didn't wake you, Dr. Gabriel, but they want you to come to the office right away. It's very important."

"Are you sure?" he asked, trying to clear what felt like three layers of insulation from the inside of his head. The taste of sawdust mixed with bile permeated his mouth. "I'm supposed to talk at the Shakespeare colloquium at one o'clock this afternoon, nothing's scheduled before that."

"I know. I'm very sorry, but you're needed here now." She hung up before he could ask any more questions.

About a half-hour later, he lumbered through the door of the Conferences and Events office.

"Good morning Dr. Gabriel, it's so nice to see you again," Alice Palacio chirped from behind her desk.

"Not from where I'm looking," he said morosely. "You wouldn't have a couple of aspirin, would you?"

"Sorry, I'm afraid not."

"Oh." Harry grunted forlornly.

"I do have some Tylenol, though. Will that do?"

"That will be fine, Alice."

As she reached down into her desk drawer, Harry leaned forward. Suddenly her head popped up, nearly clipping his jaw. "I'm sorry, Dr. Gabriel, we're all out of Tylenol too."

"I'll be fine."

"I did see some Advil. Do you think that would be all right?"

"Perfect. Thank you." He forced himself to smile.

"You're very welcome, I'm sure." She reached into the drawer and withdrew two foil packets.

He grabbed it from her hand before she could think of doing something else to inadvertently torture him.

"Don't you feel all right, Dr. Gabriel? If you don't mind my saying so, you look a little green around the gills."

"I'm okay, just a little hung...headache. Once these kick in, I'll be fine." He tore open one packet, then the other, and threw all four pills in his mouth, dry-swallowing them with a grimace. "Is there a water fountain close by?"

"There's one of those tank things back in the kitchen."

"A water cooler?"

"Yes, that's right. Why don't you go back there, get your water, and I'll send them back when they come in."

"They?" Harry asked, confused. "I thought this was about last night's lecture. Exactly, who is it that wants to see me?"

"Oh, I thought you knew. Lizzie Peltz and Gregg MacArthur want to speak with you for a few minutes."

"Speak about what? I've never heard of either one of them."

"Oh. Lizzie's in media relations and Gregg is with the campus police."

"What do they want with me?"

"I'm sure I have no idea, Dr. Gabriel," Alice said sweetly, "But they should be here soon and then you can ask them yourself. Why don't you have a seat in the kitchen." She gestured toward a door on the opposite wall.

The small, cramped offices of the Conferences and Events department were tucked away in the basement of the Student Union building, a far cry from the well appointed space allotted to the university's most illustrious faculty, the Language and Literature department.

The room that Alice referred to as the kitchen was a storage room with a sink. Books, napkins, paper plates, empty file folders and coffee filters were strewn haphazardly along shelves and on the floor. In the back was a small refrigerator with its door slightly askew, a dripping water cooler and an unplugged Mr. Coffee atop an old metal file cabinet. In the center of the room four white resin chairs surrounded a round glass-top table, stained and sticky from months of spilled coffee. Remnants of jelly and sesame seeds, escaped from donuts and bagels long since eaten, had wedged themselves under the glass.

Harry had just settled into one of the chairs when Alice walked in followed by Peltz and MacArthur. "Lizzie, Gregg, this is Dr. Harry Gabriel. He was the Presidential guest lecturer last night."

"We know," MacArthur grumbled.

Gabriel stood up slowly, his legs still a little wobbly from the previous evening, and offered his hand. "I'm Harry Gabriel. I understand that you want to speak with me."

Lizzie stepped in front of MacArthur and grabbed Gabriel's hand with both of hers. She shook it warmly and vigorously for about ten seconds. "I'm Liz Peltz, director of media relations here at Melville. This is Gregg MacArthur, he's the Chief of University Police. We'd just like to clear up a few things."

MacArthur scowled at Harry, saying nothing. His fists were clenched at his side.

Gabriel stiffened. He looked nervously from one to the other. "I don't understand. What things? What needs to be cleared up?"

"Your lecture ended at around half past nine last night," MacArthur said curtly, facing Gabriel from the other side of the table. "Could you tell us where you went after that?"

"I went to the University Club Lounge with Ike Semansky."

MacArthur wrote something in his notebook, looked up and asked, "Could you tell us what time you left?"

"It was after midnight."

"Can Dr. Semansky verify that?"

"No. He left earlier."

"Oh? What time was that?"

"About ten, ten-thirty."

"You remained alone in the bar for almost two hours after Semansky left?"

"I joined some grad students."

"Can they verify that you were with them?"

Gabriel stood, glaring down at MacArthur. "What's this all about? Why are you treating me like some sort of criminal? Did Berg put you up to this? It's not enough he tried to humiliate me last night? Now he gets the campus Gestapo to harass me. Well, you tell Spenser Berg that it's not gonna work. He can't intimidate me and neither can you." Anger and adrenalin cleared his head. He stood and started to walk toward the door. "If there's nothing else..."

"Were you at Berg's house any time last night?" Lizzie asked matter-of-factly.

"No, of course not. He hates my guts and the feeling's mutual. I wouldn't go to his house at gunpoint. I came to Melville as a personal favor to Dr. DellaRosa. As far as I'm concerned, Berg can drop dead."

"That's very interesting to hear you say that," MacArthur said, his eyes now boring in on Gabriel. "Because he is dead. Murdered. Right after more than 300 people saw you threaten to put him out of his misery."

Gabriel stopped abruptly and doubled over like he'd been kicked in the stomach. "Spenser Berg's dead? That's impossible. I don't believe it."

"It's true," Lizzie said softly. "One of our librarians found the body early this morning."

"That's why, Doctor Gabriel." MacArthur spat the word doctor. "We're interested in your whereabouts last night."

"You really think I killed Berg because we disagreed about Shakespeare?"

"I was there," MacArthur said, his voice rising. "Your argument with Berg had nothing to do with Shakespeare. He insulted you, humiliated you, threatened you. That wasn't intellectual, it was personal. And it was vicious."

"It was an old man ranting."

"You said last night that you wanted him dead. Was that just a young man ranting?"

"I said I didn't care if he was dead. It's not the same thing."

"It's pretty close."

Harry turned to Lizzie. "What about you, Miss Peltz, do you think I'm a murderer, too?"

"Of course not...and neither does he." She poked MacArthur in the ribs. "Do you?"

"I don't think anything," MacArthur said. "I know Spenser Berg was in good health last night. And the last time anyone saw him alive, he was threatening to destroy your career. This morning his severed head was discovered on a spike in front of the library. You're the hotshot writer, Gabriel. Where does this story end?"

Harry glowered at MacArthur. "With a puffed-up campus security guard who thinks he's Dick Tracy trying to make headlines, and making a fool of himself instead. Now, if there's nothing else." He stood up and turned towards the door.

"There is something else," MacArthur said sternly. "What do you know about a table that was once owned by William Shakespeare?"

"I have no idea what you're talking about."

"We have a letter from Berg saying he found a table belonging to Shakespeare and he was donating it to the library. Now the table's missing and Berg's dead."

"What does that have to do with me?"

"You were in the library yesterday."

"You're crazy! I was nowhere near the library."

"Then how did your name get on the sign-in sheet in the Special Collections department?"

"Who said it was?"

"We saw it. Jordan Day, the head of Special Collections showed it to us."

"Jordan Day, how is she involved in this?"

"She's the one who found..."

"Let's all calm down," Lizzie interjected. "The fact is, we're at a very early stage in this investigation. President DellaRosa asked Chief MacArthur and me to quietly try to find out what happened without alarming the campus. So until we get some answers, please let's keep this conversation amongst ourselves." She flashed a conciliatory smile. "And the President wants to know if you could extend your visit here for a few more days."

"So I am a suspect."

"Until we find the killer, everyone's a suspect," MacArthur growled.

Gabriel turned his gaze toward Lizzie.

"Am I free to go now?"

"Of course."

Harry stood up and stormed out of the room. As he passed Alice's desk she looked up and said, "Good bye Dr. Gabriel, have a nice..."

He was out the door and up the stairs before she could finish.

Back in the kitchen, Lizzie was yelling at MacArthur, who was pacing around the detritus. "What the hell is the matter with you? You practically told Gabriel he was our number one suspect."

"He is. He's lucky I didn't haul his ass to jail."

"Whoa." She held up her hands. "Slow down there, cowboy. Harry Gabriel's not just anybody."

"He doesn't look like much to me, just a tall pretty boy."

"You don't read a lot, do you?"

"So he's a writer, big deal. Half our faculty have published books."

"Get a clue, Mac. You ever hear of Othello Jones?"

"No. Who is he, some sort of rap hoodlum?"

Lizzie shook her head in exasperation. "It's not a who, it's a what, you numbskull. It's a book. It was on the New York Times bestseller list for two months."

"Big deal. That doesn't make him innocent."

"No, but it makes him someone to be careful with. We've got to be 100 percent sure he's guilty before we even suggest that he might have done it. Especially since he's black."

"Black? If he's black, I'm six-foot-six. I have relatives darker than him on my Sicilian grandmother's side." MacArthur shook his head skeptically. "Light brown hair, gray eyes. Maybe you could call him olive skinned, but black, no way."

"His father's mother was African American."

"So because this guy's got some black blood and he's written a book, he gets away with murder? Not on my beat."

"Gabriel's a celebrity author and Angie's a huge fan. That means we have to tread very, very lightly. If she thinks we're harassing him, we'll both be out on the street."

"I don't care if he's Angie's long lost grandson. I've already put my reputation on the line by not reporting this to the authorities. If he's guilty, I'm going after him with everything I've got."

"Absolutely. And I'll be right behind you. But first let's make sure he did it."

"I am sure. And I'll prove it."

"Well until you do, don't do anything crazy."

"Crazy?" MacArthur shouted. "This whole situation is crazy! We find a head in one place, a body in another. We're keeping it a secret. And the guy who did it gets a 'get out of jail free' pass because he has a couple of drops of black blood and our president thinks he's a cool dude."

"I didn't say he gets a free pass. I just said let's be careful."

MacArthur hammered his fist against the table. "I'm sick of being careful. All I've been since I started here is careful — playing nursemaid to a bunch of asshole professors who think who they are and busting spoiled eighteen-year-olds for smoking pot or drinking beer." His voice rose with each syllable. "I'm a cop goddammit — and this is the first piece of real police work I've had in eight years. My gut tells me it's Gabriel and I'm gonna prove it. Then I'm gonna nail his ass to the wall. And I don't care what Angie DellaRosa or anyone else has to say about it."

42

Chapter 7

"So how'd it go last night last night after I left?" Ike Semansky said with a lascivious grin as he sat down opposite Harry in the Coffeteria, the campus coffee shop. "Those grad students sure seemed to appreciate your work. Especially that redhead in the tight sweater"

Professor Isaac Semansky looked more like an aging folk rocker than one of the nation's leading Elizabethan scholars. He stood 5'8" and weighed 150 pounds. His long, curly salt-and-pepper hair pulled back in a stubby ponytail was mismatched with his reddish goatee. He wore a faded blue denim shirt, open at the neck, and cuffed corduroy pants. On his feet were weathered leather sandals, which he wore year round, even in snow. He and Gabriel were PhD students together and had remained friends ever since.

"Forget about the redhead, Ike, this is serious," Harry said, his voice barely louder than a whisper. "Berg's dead."

"Dead?" Ike blurted as he sprayed coffee across the table. Then, lowering his voice. "What the hell are you talking about?"

Harry wiped his face. "I just got finished being interrogated by Gregg MacArthur and Lizzie Peltz. It seems your heartthrob, Jordan Day, found Berg's body somewhere in the library early this morning. They're pretty sure he was murdered and they think I did it. At least MacArthur does."

"What! Hold on. Somebody killed Spenser Berg last night and the campus police think it was you?" He took another sip of coffee. "Start from the beginning."

"After you left, I stayed in the bar with those girls for awhile and had a few more drinks. Maybe more than a few. Then I went back to my room and fell into bed. I was unconscious as soon as my head hit the pillow. The next thing I know, the phone rings. It's that ditzy Alice from Conferences and Events telling me I have to come to her office immediately. When I get there MacArthur buttonholes me, tells me Berg is dead and I shouldn't leave the area. He glared at me with utter contempt the whole time. I was waiting for him to cuff me and read me my rights"

"What are you going to do?"

"I've been thinking about that all day. MacArthur is convinced I'm guilty. He's not looking at anybody else. All he's going to do is try to find evidence against me." Harry rolled his eyes. "Which right now looks pretty strong." He took a sip of espresso. "I have no alibi and half the campus saw Berg threaten to ruin my career and me say that I'd be more than happy to aid in his demise."

"I remember. I was there."

"MacArthur called it a threat. And maybe it was. I was so angry I could have strangled that bastard right there on stage. If I didn't know otherwise, I'd think I was guilty too."

"But you're not guilty." Semansky raised his eyebrows. "Are you?"

"No I'm not. But if even my friends have doubts, there's only one thing I can do."

"And that is?"

"Find the guy who did it."

"You're kidding, right?"

"No. I'm dead serious."

"What do you know about solving murders?"

"I spent a lot of time with the police while I was researching Othello Jones and Makki B.

Semansky slowly shook his head. "I spend a lot of time at the movies, that doesn't make me Steven Spielberg."

"Steven Spielberg's a genius. The cops I met with were morons and they solve murders every day. How hard can it be?"

"It still sounds like you've been watching too many reruns of Murder She Wrote. Besides, you don't know this campus or most of the people here. How are you gonna get them to talk to you?"

"That's why I need your help. Whaddaya say, are you up for solving a murder?"

Semansky sat up in his seat. "You want me to be Robin to your Batman, Watson to your Holmes, Cagney to your Lacey. Or should it be Lacy to your Cagney? I could never figure out who was supposed to be the main character in that show?"

"Who cares? Are you with me?"

A broad, toothy smile overspread Semansky's face. "Why the hell not. Count me in."

"All right then. Can you think of anyone else who might want to see Berg dead?"

"I could probably name you a couple of dozen people who would first on line to volunteer to drop a guillotine blade on the old bastard's neck."

"Really? Who?"

"Peter Foote, for one."

"Foote? Why would he want to kill Berg?"

"Peter is brilliant. He was developing an international reputation as one of the top scholars in the field and was a lock to be named the next Chair of our department. Then Berg showed up and all Peter's hopes and dreams went into the crapper. Not only that, Berg treats him like his butt boy. Humiliates him at every opportunity."

"Can you get him to talk to me?"

"I can do better than that."

* * *

Four times a year, the contributing editors of Yorick's Brain, Melville University's widely acclaimed Shakespeare journal, met with Spenser Berg to review submissions and plan the upcoming issue. Berg started the journal and appointed himself publisher and editor-in-chief. Peter Foote, Natasha Ferette and Isaac Semansky did most of the real work of reviewing abstracts, editing papers and publishing the 120 page quarterly.

Foote was seated on an upholstered chair at a round cherrywood coffee table in the English Department Faculty Lounge when Semansky and Harry walked in. He looked every bit the prototypical professor in his brown tweed blazer, pale blue oxford shirt, striped tie and khaki trousers, which all fit him perfectly when he bought them a decade earlier, but lately strained at the seams due to the fifteen extra pounds he had gained. His expertly coiffed hair was a buttery ash blonde, courtesy of Clairol Natural Instincts for Men. "You're late, Isaac," he said without looking up. "Of course, Natasha is later and even Spenser, who is always on time, hasn't arrived yet." Then he saw Harry and stiffened. "What is he doing here?"

"He's my special guest."

After a disconcerted glare, Foote offered his outstretched hand. "It's a pleasure to meet you, Dr. Gabriel. I attended your talk yesterday evening. It was quite...illuminating."

"Well, Peter, you're about to be illuminated some more," Semansky said. "Spenser Berg is dead."

"That's not a bit funny," Foote said huffily. "Especially after what happened last night."

"It's not meant to be funny," Harry said. "Chief MacArthur spoke to me this morning, shortly after they discovered Berg's body."

At that moment Natasha Ferette breezed into the room. Her jet black hair was cut short. She wore a tailored blue pinstriped business suit with a fitted knee-length skirt more suited to a middle manager of a Fortune 500 company than to a professor of women's literature. Deep-set dark eyes and full red lips gave her a more intimidating air than her slender frame would suggest.

"Hello, gentlemen," she said. Then she noticed Harry. "Harry Gabriel," she said, extending her hand. "Natasha Ferette." As Harry took it, she gripped his hand tightly and shook it ferociously. "It's a pleasure to meet the man who finally put Spenser Berg in his place. It's just too bad you didn't punch him in the mouth. Then he'd have an inflated lip to go with his inflated ego."

"Natasha, please," Foote said, his voice cracking with emotion. "We just received some horrifying news." He paused for effect. "Spenser's dead."

"Really?" she said with a rueful smile. "You wouldn't say that just to make me feel good."

Foote shook his head. "Natasha, that's over the line, even for you."

"You mean you're serious."

"Serious as the grave," Semansky said. "And it gets worse. They found his disembodied head impaled on a spike on the front wall of the library."

Both Ferette and Foote gasped and recoiled, as if on cue. Foote's already pallid complexion turned pasty. He slumped in his chair, looking ill.

Ferette brightened immediately. "Do they have any suspects?"

Semansky turned towards Harry.

"Gregg MacArthur thinks I did it," Harry said.

Ferette said, "You? Because of that little dust-up last night. Big freaking deal. Everyone in our department has more reasons to kill Berg than you do." She looked over at Foote. "Aren't I right, Peter?"

"What is that supposed to mean?"

"It means that all of us hated Berg. He was an equal opportunity abuser but you had the most to gain from his death."

"Are you insinuating that I had cause to kill Spenser?"

"It sure wouldn't hurt your job prospects if he were suddenly out of the picture."

"That's ridiculous." Foote stood and glared at Ferette. "Spenser was my friend. He and I were collaborators. We were on the verge of one of the greatest discoveries in the history of modern literature."

"I heard that fairytale before," Harry said. "Last night, in fact. It's the one where Spenser Berg proves that William Shakespeare never wrote any of the works attributed to him."

"It's true. I've seen the proof."

Harry said, "I don't believe you. And even if you did see something, knowing Berg, it was probably a fake."

Foote shook his head. "I saw it and it was absolutely authentic."

"How can you be sure?" Harry pressed.

"Harry, if Peter says it's the real thing, it is," Semansky interjected.

"He's one of the leading experts on literary forgeries. In fact, he wrote the book on it." He walked over to a bookcase and pulled a thick volume from the shelf and handed it Harry. Ersatzery — The Art and Science of Literary Forgery by Peter R. Foote, Ph.D.

"Thank you, Isaac." Foote bowed with an exaggerated flourish. "Now, if you will excuse me, I have to prepare for a class." He left the room.

"He did it," Natasha said. "Did you see how nervous he was?"

"We came in here, ganged up on him and practically accused him of murdering Berg," Semansky said. "Of course he was nervous."

"That doesn't mean he didn't do it," Natasha said.

Chapter 8

Jordan looked up as Josh Campanella walked shakily into Jordan's office. His skin was clammy.

"Josh, what's wrong?"

"Officer Wheeler was just here. I think he thinks I had something to do with Berg's beheading. He's going to arrest me. I know it." His entire body was quivering.

Jordan had been shelving books. Now she was cataloging new acquisitions. Basically doing anything she could to keep her mind off the gruesome events of the morning. She walked over to him and gently guided him to a chair.

"Sit down. I'll get you a glass of water."

Josh can be such a child sometimes, Jordan thought as she walked over to the cooler. She filled two paper cups. "Here, drink this," she said, handing him one.

He drank it in a single gulp and crumpled the cup in his hand.

She sat at her desk, facing him. "Okay, what happened. What did he say?"

Josh squirmed in his seat, cleared his throat and began, "Wheeler came to collect the head." He twitched slightly, took a breath and seemed like he was about to burst into tears. "He had this bag with him, about the size of a small garbage bag. I kept wanting to tell him that the head wasn't there anymore but I was so nervous I couldn't speak. Then, when he opened the curtain and saw that the head was missing. I almost fainted."

"What did you tell him?"

"The truth. That it disappeared."

"How did he take it?"

"Not very well." Josh shook his head slowly and bit his lower lip.

"What did he say?"

"He asked me what happened to it and I said I didn't know."

He paused, looking like he was about to cry. "Then he accused me of taking it. He said that tampering with evidence made me an accessory to murder and that I could go to jail if I didn't give it to him immediately. I really thought he was going to arrest me. Or worse."

"Then what?"

"I told him I didn't touch it and I had no idea where it was. He glared at me for a couple of seconds and said MacArthur was going to be pissed. Then he asked about you."

"Me?" Jordan bolted upright in her chair. "What did he want to know about me?"

"How well you knew Berg. If you knew about this table Berg was supposed to have given you." He wiped his head with a mauve hankie. "That's about it. Then he gave me his card and said if I happen to find the head to give him a call and he'll come pick it up — no questions asked."

"That's it?"

"He reminded me not to say anything to anybody and said he might be back later if he had any more questions." Josh gnawed nervously on his thumb. "Do you think they actually suspect that we had something to do with all this?"

"They're cops. They're suspicious of everybody."

The outside doorbell rang.

"Josh please, whoever it is, send them away. There's no one I want to talk to right now."

He waddled slowly to the door.

Jordan bristled when a few seconds later she heard the door open and Josh saying, "Come on in."

She was about to read him the riot act, when a smallish twelve-year-old boy wearing baggy khaki painter's pants, a New York Yankees baseball jersey and black and blue plaid Converse Chuck Taylor high-tops ambled into the room.

"Hey Jor."

"Tristan," she shouted, running over to the kid. "With everything going on, I forgot that you were on campus today." She gave him a quick hug and kissed him on the cheek. When their faces met the resemblance was striking. Though his skin and hair were a shade darker, they shared the same almond eyes, slightly retroussé nose and full lips.

The boy stepped back, stared intently into her face and said, "Whatsa matter, Jor? What's going on? You don't look right."

Before she could say anything, Josh walked into the main room coughing loudly and noisily clearing his throat. He wasn't alone. A beefy young man in his mid-twenties was beside him. Around six-feet tall with a pockmarked face that could use both a shave and a wash. His long, coarse, greasy brown hair was pulled back in a ponytail. He was dressed all in black — t-shirt, leather vest, jeans and motorcycle boots. He had thick arms and pudgy fingers with bitten, grime encrusted fingernails.

Josh said, "This is Drew Wolcott. He arrived with Tristan."

"Oh yeah." Tristan turned to Jordan. "Drew's my new campus friend. He's a real good chess player. You know how hard it is for me to find anyone to play with. We've had a couple of awesome games."

Jordan found it difficult to believe that this Hell's Angels reject could spell chess, much less master the intricacies of the game.

Tristan turned to Wolcott. "This is my sister, Jordan. She's in charge of the Archives and Special Collections department here at the Library."

"Nice to meet yuh," he said in a nasally voice, higher than his large body would indicate. "Your brother's a cool little dude."

"Thank you." She patted Tristan on the shoulder. "I think so too."

"Tell me about it. I've been playing chess for years, spent a whole summer hustling blitz chess in Washington Square Park, made a couple of hundred bucks — and this kid blows me away. Beats me every time, no sweat. Unbelievable!"

Jordan eyed Wolcott suspiciously. "What brings you to our department?"

"I work with the Department of Instructional Technology. They got me on a project about the book business in England during Queen Elizabeth's time...the first one, not the one who just croaked. The catalog says you got a couple of books about it. I figured I'd have a look."

Jordan eyed him quizzically. "You're a student here?"

"Nah. I work for Spenser Berg. I'm basically his full-time tech guy."

"I was under the impression that Professor Berg hated technology."

"He does. But these days, you can only get some stuff with a computer, that's what I'm there for."

Jordan glanced furtively over at Josh, then turned back to Wolcott.

"We have a number of books that touch on printers and stationers of Renaissance England." She walked over to the front desk, took a small square of white paper from an index card caddy and handed it to Wolcott, along with a stubby little pencil. "Write your email address here. We'll contact you when the volumes are ready to be viewed."

"I'm ready now."

"Oh, I'm afraid that's out of the question," she said brusquely

Wolcott glared at her. "Whaddaya mean?"

"We have procedures here and the books you require are quite old and very fragile. Either Josh or I will have to handle them while you view them."

Wolcott scowled. "Forget it." He shook his head in disgust. "Berg's gonna be majorly pissed."

Jordan struggled to maintain her composure. "You saw Professor Berg today?" Her heart began to pound.

"Naaa, it was a couple of days ago. We were supposed to meet early this morning in his office but he left me hanging. Then I heard he didn't show up for his big magazine meeting and I started to wonder where the hell he was."

"And you thought he might be here?"

"Yeah, maybe." He leered at her. "Couldn't blame him if he was."

Jordan felt a wave of nausea travel from her stomach up to her eyes.

"Dr. Berg didn't use Special Collections very often, but when he did, he followed all procedures. I'm sure he'd want you to do the same."

She stood, then gently guided Tristan towards the door.

"Now if you'll excuse us, my brother and I have an appointment." She grabbed Tristan's wrist, walked him out the door and slammed it behind her, leaving Josh to deal with Wolcott.

She hustled her brother down the corridor. "Who is that horrible person?"

"He's just a guy I met at the Student Union playing video games. One day I had my chess set with me and he asked me for a game. He's really not bad, came close to beating me once."

She grimaced . "He's not the kind of person you should be associating with."

"Oh, he's okay. Just maybe a little rough around the edges."

"I don't mind rough around the edges, but he seems vile to the core. Plus, he's twice as old as you, maybe more. I don't trust him. Please Tris, stay away from him."

He looked soulfully into her eyes. "Something's bothering you besides Drew. What is it?"

She had been debating with herself whether or not to tell her brother what happened that morning. He was just getting over their mother's death and didn't want to set him back. But she thought he was bound to hear about it one way or the other and it was better for him to hear it from her.

"Okay, sit down." They sat on a teak bench at the far end of the hallway. "You have to promise me you won't say a word about this to anyone."

"Sure, sure, I promise."

"Tristan, you know who Professor Berg is, right?"

"Of course. I've even been to his house a couple of times."

"What!" She sat straight up, eyes wide, mouth agape. "What were you doing in Spenser Berg's house?"

"I went there with Drew. Berg wasn't even home."

"Oh my God. You could've been killed!"

"What are you talking about?" He stared at his sister as if she had taken leave of her senses.

She turned to face him and in a breathy whisper said, "This morning when I arrived at the library, I saw Spenser Berg's head impaled on a finial outside the second floor window."

Tristan's eyes bugged open. "Are you serious?"

She nodded emphatically. "Very."

"You're sure it was...?"

"I didn't think so at first. I thought it was one of those silly Halloween pranks. But it was real."

"Holy crap! That's unbelievable! What did you do?"

"Please Tris, keep your voice down," she said in hushed tones. "I called University Police."

"And...what did they do?"

"They told me not to say anything to anybody. That's why I was so amazed that your friend Wolcott knew."

"He didn't say anything about a severed head. He just said that Dr. Berg was missing and he thought he might be here."

Jordan shuddered. "The way he leered at me when he said it made my skin crawl. I'm sure he knows Berg is dead. I think he used those Elizabethan books as an excuse to come here and assess the situation." Her face turned solemn. "I wouldn't be surprised if he had something to do with it."

"No way, Jor! This isn't one of those old time mystery books you're always reading. Drew might not look it but he's pretty smart. Professor Berg trusted him and so do I."

"I hope you're right." She put an arm around him. "Let's go to the Food Court. I'll buy you some pizza."

Chapter 9

Uncle Moishe's Matzoball Bistro was located on the second floor of the Melville University Student Union building. Modeled after the legendary Katz's Deli on Manhattan's Lower East Side, behind its counter hung a row of various sizes of Hebrew National bologna around a red neon heart-shaped sign, inside of which were blue letters that spelled out "Give Your Honey Some Kosher Baloney." When someone pointed out that it didn't rhyme, Uncle Moishe, whose real name was Morris Gittleman, said, "Yeah, I know. But it should."

Harry walked in and looked around. The place was empty. His first thought was that someone had pranked him, sending him on a wild goose chase. A waitress approached him, young, with dark hair and features. "We're closed until 3 pm," she said, disinterestedly and began walking away. Then, as if jolted back to reality, said, "Wait! Are you here to see Professor Foote?"

Harry nodded. "Yes."

"Oh...okay, follow me." She ambled through a door marked 'Private' into a smaller room. Harry followed.

Seated alone at a table for four, drinking a cup of tea and munching on a bialy, was Peter Foote.

"Thank you for meeting me, Gabriel," he said in a conspiratorial tone. "I wasn't sure you'd come."

"What is it you wanted to speak with me about?" Harry said warily.

The waitress who showed Harry in came to their table. "Can I get you anything?"

"Just a cup of coffee."

"Have a bialy," Foote said, his face brightening. "It's a cross between a bagel and a crumpet and a vast improvement over both. They ship them in every morning from Kossar's Bakery on the Lower East Side, the only authentic bialy bakery this side of the Biala River. I discovered them when I was a visiting scholar at NYU."

Harry smiled at the waitress. "Sure, I'll have a bialy."

As the waitress left, he turned to Foote, his smile gone. "I have to admit I was surprised to get a text from you, much less to have you invite me to a clandestine meeting in a deserted deli for a lecture on esoteric Jewish baked goods. I distinctly sensed some hostility in the editorial meeting."

"That was for the benefit of my colleagues. I didn't want them to suspect my true feelings."

"Oh?" Harry's eyes widened. "And what feelings are those?"

"That one or both of them may be involved in Spenser's murder."

"That's ridiculous!" Before Harry could say anything else, the waitress arrived with his bialy and coffee. He waited until she was out of earshot, then said, "What possible reason could either of them have for killing Berg?"

"In addition to the fact that Semansky hated him with a venomous passion, Spenser had been blackmailing him for quite some time."

"I don't believe it. What could Berg possibly blackmail him about? Ike has always been very open about his radical past."

"Yes, but not about his criminal history."

Harry smiled. "You're kidding. Everybody knows that he's been arrested for disorderly conduct at a couple of protest rallies. He brags about it. It's a point of honor for him."

"I'm not talking about disorderly conduct at some silly left wing demonstration. I'm talking about domestic terrorism." Foote paused for dramatic effect, sipped some coffee and had a bite of his bialy. "When he was an undergrad at Harvard, your friend Dr. Semansky was arrested by the Boston police for attempted murder."

Gabriel stood and shouted, "You're lying! Ike is the least violent person I know."

"Please sit down and hear me out."

Harry sat stiffly.

"Perhaps you don't know him as well as you think you do," Foote said smugly. "Have you ever heard of the Red Panthers?"

"Some sort of revolutionary group, weren't they?"

"They were a band of Harvard student radicals. Their hope was to revive the violent activism of the sixties. They idolized the Black Panthers and the Red Brigades, hence the name."

"What does that have to do with Ike?"

"Semansky was one of them. He and his fellow domestic terrorists blew up a military recruitment office in Boston. An army recruiter lost his leg, almost died."

"Yes, I remember reading about that. I thought they all went to prison."

"That's correct. All except your friend Ike."

"That's probably because he had nothing to do with it."

"On the contrary. He was arrested and charged. I've seen the records."

"How?"

"I'd rather not say."

"It was Berg, wasn't it?"

Foote was silent but his sly grin was all the answer Harry needed.

"So what happened?"

"His uncle was a New York State senator. He pulled some strings and got him out of it and had his record expunged."

"How did Berg find out?"

"The rumor is that he has a private investigator on retainer. Or should I say had."

Harry shook his head. "Even if it's true about Ike, it still doesn't make sense. Berg was a wealthy man, with book deals and lecture fees more than doubling his exorbitant salary. Ike is a single father with an autistic child. He lives from paycheck to paycheck. Blackmail just doesn't fit into that scenario."

Foote spoke slowly, as if explaining the answer to a complex problem to a slow student. "It wasn't his money Berg was after. It was his mind."

"What are you talking about?"

"Semansky was Spenser's ghostwriter."

"I don't understand."

"Spenser's literary journal pieces denouncing Shakespeare as the true author of the works were all written by Semansky."

"You're telling me Ike wrote all those Oxford authorship articles in the Shakespeare Quarterly?"

"Every one."

"But Ike fervently believes that Shakespeare is the true author. We've had many discussions about it while I was researching my book."

"He believes more strongly in keeping his job...and his son. A revelation about his past transgressions could certainly jeopardize his custodianship of his son Nicholas. "

"But why Ike? Berg could have asked any one of several people in the department to write those pieces for him."

"Because Spenser took pleasure in making other people suffer. He knew Semansky was a strong adherent of Shakespeare's authorship. Ike hated writing those pieces and he hated Spenser for making him do it. That made the entire enterprise all the more enjoyable for the odious Dr. Berg."

Harry shook his head slowly. "Even if everything you say is true, I just can't see Ike as a murderer. He doesn't have the temperament"

"What about Natasha Ferette? Does she have the temperament?"

"She has the guts to do it, but what's the motive?"

"There have been vague rumblings about a sexual incident between her and Spenser when she was a student at Barnard."

Harry grimaced. "Ferette and Berg together, that's hard for me to imagine."

"I didn't say fling, encounter or relationship, from what I heard, the incident was brief, ugly and far from consensual."

"Where did you hear this?"

Foote smiled slyly. "Little birdies are constantly tweeting in my ear. In fact, I have one more person of interest to add to your list of suspects."

"Go ahead."

"Angelina DellaRosa."

"Now you're just pulling names out of your..."

The waitress returned. "Would either of you like anything else?"

Harry looked up. "No thank you."

Foote shook his head curtly.

"C'mon Foote, Angie loved Berg. A lot of people thought it bordered on unseemly, the way she fawned over him."

"That's just the point. If Spenser were to leave Melville, our esteemed president would not be very pleased."

"Who said Berg was leaving?"

Foote grinned. "He did. He showed me the letter he received from Tufts offering him an endowed chair in language and literature. If he showed that letter to Angie, who knows how she might react."

"This is all very interesting, if it's true. But why tell me?"

"Self preservation. I assumed, after you mentioned that the police considered you their prime suspect, that you'd be conducting an investigation of your own. As successor to Spenser as department chair, I knew you'd be looking at my culpability. I simply wanted you to know that there are several people on this campus who would benefit from his untimely demise far more than I." Foote stood. "I have to go. Finish your bialy and chew on what I just told you."

Chapter 10

MacArthur's phone buzzed as he and Lizzie walked across campus "This is Chief MacArthur," he barked into the mouthpiece."

"It's Suarez, sir." His nervous voice betrayed a slight Hispanic accent that wasn't there when he was calm. "We're just leaving. Berg's house. The...um...item you wanted us to pick up is in the trunk of the cruiser and to tell you the truth, it's making me a little sick. Where should we take it?"

MacArthur was silent for a few seconds. "I'm not sure. It'll have to be someplace where it'll hold for a couple of days without anybody finding it. What about the hospital morgue? They have all kinds of dead bodies there."

Lizzie shook her head vigorously and said in a muffled but urgent voice, "Not the morgue. They have to record every stiff that goes in and out of there. And there's lots of traffic, doctors, pathologists, custodial staff. We need quiet place where nobody will be around to ask awkward questions."

"I'll get back to you." MacArthur returned the phone to its holster and turned to Lizzie, "A quiet place to hide a headless corpse? Any suggestions?"

Lizzie stopped walking, shut her eyes, clasped her hands in front of her and stood silently still. After half a minute she eased into a wide grin. "Yeah, I know just the place."

"Let's hear it. I could use a good idea right about now."

"The gross lab. It's where the medical students cut up cadavers for practice."

"What about it?"

"A couple of years ago one of the would-be Dr. Kildares stole a penis, took it to a party and dropped it in the punch bowl. Freaked a lot of the girls out. Boys too. I had to do some fancy footwork to keep that one out of the papers."

MacArthur grimaced. "I was the first one on the scene, remember. I'm the one who had to tag and bag the damn thing."

"So you're familiar with the gross lab?"

"Not really. The crime scene was the frat house. The kid who did it was still there, scared shitless he was going to get thrown out of school. We took him in, gave him a good scare and let him go. Don't want to let a stupid prank ruin a kid's life."

She nodded with approval. "Look at that, you're not the hard-assed fascist everybody says you are."

A sheepish grin broke through his permanent scowl. "Don't spread that around. In my job it pays to have people think you're a son of a bitch." The smile vanished as suddenly as it had appeared. "You're sure the gross lab is the right place?"

"I'm positive. They have bodies and body parts scattered all over the place. It's like a zombie smorgasbord. Nobody'll notice one more stiff."

MacArthur grabbed his phone and hit push-to-talk. "Are you still there Suarez?"

"I'm here Chief."

"Get Wheeler and meet us at the rear entrance of the Medical School, by the loading dock. We figured out a place to put your uh....bundle." He turned to Lizzie. "Okay, let's go."

"One more minute." She reached into her handbag, rummaged around for a few seconds, pulled out her phone and punched a few keys. "Hello Donnie, it's Lizzie Peltz, I have a really big favor to ask you. They found a homeless guy dead by the co-generation plant last night. They don't want us to report it until after the big Homecoming to-do on Saturday, you know, bad publicity and all that. Could we store it in your lab?" She waited a few seconds, then said, "Thanks, you're a doll."

Across the road from Melville's main campus were what looked like two eighteen-story Chinese lanterns made of concrete, steel and glass — the two towers of the Melville University Medical School and Hospital, the tallest buildings in all of Suffolk County. Many residents would also tell you they were the ugliest.

When Lizzie and MacArthur arrived at the loading dock, Suarez and Wheeler were waiting in their University Police cruiser. Donnie Scotallaro, the Gross Anatomy lab tech, was leaning against the car chatting with the two campus cops. Stockily built, with thick, tattooed arms, he wore pale blue hospital scrubs and kept his long, oily, thinning hair in a ponytail.

"Hi Donnie, how are you?" Lizzie said as they approached.

"Terrific, terrific, Ms. Peltz. It's great to see you again." He spoke with the animated earnestness of a man who spends most of his day having one-way conversations with dead people and was thrilled to have a live person to interact with.

"Donnie, this is Chief MacArthur of University Police, and I see you've already met officers Wheeler and Suarez."

"It's great to meet you sir." He offered MacArthur his latex gloved hand. The Chief shook it gingerly, trying not to think about what kind of cadaver ooze it had already touched that morning.

"Thanks for helping us out. I'm sure I don't have to tell you that this is highly confidential."

"Don't worry Chief." Donnie chuckled awkwardly. "Who am I gonna tell, the cadavers?"

"What's the best way to transport the...material?"

"I brought a lab trolley. Just have your guys pop the trunk and I'll take care of the rest." Donnie wheeled what looked like an oversized laundry cart to the back of the cruiser. He leaned into the open trunk.

"Whoa, that's a really big bag!"

Dr. Berg had been a large man, six-foot-four and well over 300 pounds. Wheeler and Suarez borrowed some black extra-duty leaf and refuse bags from the landscaping crew. They put one bag over the top of the body, pulled a second up from the bottom and sealed the middle with duct tape.

"Officers, give Donnie here a hand," MacArthur ordered.

Suarez and Wheeler climbed half-heartedly out of the cruiser, annoyance and disgust etched on their faces. After much groaning and cursing, the three men lifted the unwieldy bundle carefully out of the trunk and dumped it unceremoniously into the trolley.

MacArthur turned to the two patrolmen. "Remember, you're to talk to no one about this. For the next 36 hours you're on special assignment, reporting only to me."

Wheeler said, "What do you want us to do now?"

"Right now, nothing. Go home, take a nap, whatever. Just be ready when I call." He paused for a few seconds. "And one more thing..." Wheeler and Suarez exchanged looks of dread. "You're both on double-time pay until further notice."

Their expressions morphed instantly from revulsion to joy.

"Thanks, Chief."

They hustled into the cruiser and drove off before MacArthur had a chance to change his mind.

Donnie wheeled the trolley down the ramp to the basement of the medical school, whistling happily. He motioned for Peltz and MacArthur to follow. As they moved down narrow corridors and through swinging doors into the bowels of the building, the lights grew dimmer, the walls dingier and the air thicker and more pungent.

"Are you sure this is a good idea?" MacArthur whispered to Lizzie as his imitation Gucci loafers began to stick to the linoleum floor.

"I'm positive."

They went around one more dark corner and stopped in front of an unmarked blue door.

"Here we are," Donnie said as he opened it to a room the size of a small middle school gym.

It was filled with dozens of stainless steel dissecting tables, each about seven feet long and two-and-a-half feet wide with five-inch wheels under tubular legs. Most had white zippered vinyl bags lying across the top. They looked like extra long garment bags and had numbers and letters scrawled across them in black marker. Other tables were strewn with dirty lab coats, cardboard boxes, plastic buckets — some empty, some filled with variously colored liquids. A few red plastic containers labeled 'Sharps' were scattered around the room, as well as several large refuse bins filled with trash.

"This is where you want to stash the body?" MacArthur asked, looking around the room with horror and disgust.

"You think Berg's gonna complain about the accommodations?" Lizzie turned to Donnie. "What do you think?"

"I don't know how long you want to store it. But if we keep it in here it'll start to decompose in a day or so."

MacArthur's face went pale. "So we went through all this for nothing?"

"No way," Donnie said, grinning like the only kid in class who knew the correct answer to the teacher's question. "We'll put it in the cold room."

He walked to the rear of the lab. The entire back wall was paneled in quilted aluminum, as was the wide door in the middle of it. Donnie opened it to reveal a room as spotlessly clean as the other was filthy. Five four-tiered steel racks jutted out from the four walls. Each rack supported four stainless steel body trays. Cadaver bags occupied most of the trays.

Donnie led Lizzie and MacArthur inside. "It's three degrees Celsius in here. We can store it for a couple of weeks, no problem."

While Donnie was looking for a vacant shelf, MacArthur stood rigidly in the center of the room, trying not to touch anything.

"Jesus, it's f-f-freezing. You could keep meat in this place," he said as he began to shiver.

"They do." Lizzie grinned.

"Found one," Donnie shouted gleefully. "Okay, let's go get the body."

While he went to retrieve the trolley, the other two exited the frigid cadaver closet.

"What's with that guy? He's a little off-kilter, no?" MacArthur whispered.

"If you spent all day surrounded by stiffs and inhaling formaldehyde, you'd be goofy too."

As if on cue, a smiling Donnie rolled the trolley up to the cold room door with the partial remains of the former Distinguished Professor of Humanities and Chair of the Melville University English Department. "Excuse me, Chief, could you give me a little hand?"

MacArthur looked beseechingly at Lizzie, who just shrugged and grinned, for once not saying a word. "You know my back has really been giving me a lot of trouble lately. I don't know how much assistance I'd be."

"That's okay. I just need a little help getting it out of the bin. It'll just be for a few seconds."

Steadying himself in front of the trolley, MacArthur took a deep breath and said, "Okay, here we go."

Grasping the top end of the taped-together bags, MacArthur strained to lift it. Donnie easily hoisted his end up and out of the cart. As he did, the bags began to separate and finally, pull apart.

The charred, headless corpse of Spenser Berg rolled slowly onto the floor as Donnie, Lizzie and MacArthur looked on in horror.

"Hey, there's no head on that body!" Donnie exclaimed. "And it's all, like, barbecued."

Lizzie put a hand on Donnie's shoulder. "What I'm about to tell you is top secret," she said in hushed tones. "There's been a murder on campus. They set fire to the body so we couldn't identify it."

"Of course you know, if word of this got out, what kind of panic would spread around here," MacArthur added.

Donnie nodded his head several times. His mouth opened but no words emerged.

"The Chief wasn't sure that this was the safest place to store the remains while we pursue this case," Lizzie continued. "But I assured him you were the man we could trust to keep this incident under wraps."

"Can we count on you?" MacArthur asked, solemnly.

"Yes, sir," Donnie said. Then he saluted.

MacArthur returned the salute smartly and said, "Okay. Now if you can cover it back up and put it on one of those shelves, you'll be doing this university a great service. There's a good chance you'll receive a commendation."

Donnie beamed proudly, then scooped the torso into a fresh white body bag and zipped it up. He took a black Sharpie from his pocket, wrote "M.G." on the bag, then heaved it over his shoulder, carried into the cold room and placed it carefully on the empty tray.

"M.G. Is that some kind of code?" MacArthur asked.

Donnie grinned. "Yeah, sort of. It stands for Murdered Guy."

"Donnie, you're a real hero." Lizzie kissed him on the cheek. "I don't know what we would have done without you."

"Anytime I can help, just give me a call," he said proudly. "You too, Chief."

MacArthur smiled weakly. "Roger that. Now we really have to go."

Chapter 11

Ike Semansky sat uncomfortably behind his desk, chomping on a piece of Nicorette gum, staring at a pile of papers purporting to discuss the twenty-first century political and social implications of Dickens' Little Dorrit.

His office had been recently redecorated on orders from Dr. Della-Rosa. About a month earlier, she came in to see if he had any Reese's Peanut Butter Cups, which they both shared an addiction to. He said he thought he might have one squirreled away in the back of his desk drawer but when he tried to open it, the drawer-front came off in his hand and landed with a crash on the floor, inches from her foot. She jumped back, choked off a tiny scream, shook her head angrily and said to no one in particular, "This is unacceptable!" Then stormed out of the office.

Two weeks later at nine a.m., the furniture movers arrived. His office was completely refurnished by noon. He missed his comfortable chair with the indentation that perfectly conformed to his butt. The new ergonomically designed one gave him a backache. And the cherrywood desk that now stood where his old ink-stained, cigarette-scarred writing table used to be, had too many drawers and not enough open space, forcing him to keep his papers in neat piles instead of spreading them out the way he liked.

Natasha Ferette walked furtively into his office and closed the door. She looked around, whistled softly and said, "Nice digs. When did this happen?"

"A couple of days after Angie decided I needed new furniture whether I wanted it or not."

"She's right." She looked around to see if anyone was in the hall. "At least now you've got a door that locks." She slammed it shut behind her.

Semansky noticed tiny beads of sweat high on her forehead. "Are you okay?" he asked with genuine concern. "What's wrong?"

"They think I did it." She sat down stiffly in one of his two new brushed chrome guest chairs.

"Who thinks you did what?"

"I'm sure those campus police bozos think I killed Spenser."

"You're not serious."

"Do I look like I'm joking?"

"Well, if you are serious, then you're seriously insane."

"What if I told you that Berg sexually harassed me when I was at Barnard?"

"I wouldn't believe it."

"Why not? Don't you think he's capable of it?"

"I'm sure he's capable of it. I just don't think he'd survive after you cut his nuts off with a rusty nail file and jammed them down his throat."

"Is that the kind of person you think I am?"

"I think you're the kind of person who stands up for herself and doesn't take any crap from anybody. So, more or less, yeah. The nut cutting business was an embellishment."

"Well, then I have you fooled, along with everybody else. I'm not the tough cookie everyone thinks I am — and back then I was an absolute weenie."

"I find that hard to believe."

"It's true. In high school I was the smart, pudgy girl with horn-rimmed glasses, a face full of zits and Raggedy Ann-inspired clothes. My prom date was my cousin Marvin, who was a year younger than me. I was hysterically clever with my friends but excruciatingly shy and awkward with everyone else. Things got even worst when I went to college. In high school the girls who smoked and wore heavy makeup were the tough chicks. The smart girls, me and my friends, were dorks. At Barnard a lot of the girls were from private schools. They smoked, wore a lot of makeup and dressed slutty — but they were incredibly smart too. I never realized you could be both. It was a revelation."

She leaned back, pulled a pack of Gitanes non-filter cigarettes out of her handbag, her fingers caressing its distinctive blue box emblazoned with the defiant silhouette of a gypsy dancer. "Speaking of smoking I could really use a cigarette right now, you don't mind, do you?"

"I'd love it. Since I quit, second-hand fumes are ambrosia to me."

She lit the stubby cigarette, took a deep drag and exhaled slowly. As the smoke wafted out of her nose and mouth, her arms and legs loosened and her shoulders sagged.

"So you were a little nerdy in high school, so what. A lot of us were. I know you might find this hard to believe, but I wasn't exactly Joe Cool in eleventh grade either," he said with a grin. "I still don't see what any of this has to do with you and Berg."

"I was in my junior year at Barnard and Berg was a superstar English professor across the street at Columbia. He had just been named America's Preeminent Man of Letters by the New York Review of Books. Every English major on both sides of the street was dying to take his class."

"Berg's a good scholar," Semansky said, shaking his head. "But he's no super genius. How the hell does he keep getting all those awards?"

"He has a P.R. firm on retainer."

"Of course." He slapped his forehead. "Now it makes sense. Every time he farts it gets into the Chronicle of Higher Education." He held up a hand. "But we digress. You were going to tell me how Berg sexually harassed you."

"Right. It was in my junior year. By that time I figured out how to dress, talk and act like the cool girls. On the inside I was still the shy nerd from Larchmont but my outside persona was East Village hipster-punk. My diet consisted of black coffee and tobacco. I lost twenty-five pounds and gained half of it back in makeup. When I finally started hanging out with the in-crowd I realized that it wasn't just me, everyone was insecure. We all idolized Patti Smith. We'd take the subway downtown and hang out at CBGB's and The Limelight. We wore black jeans, black hair and black boots, wrote bad punk poetry, drank cheap wine and smoked unfiltered French cigarettes that smelled like cowshit." She took a long, slow drag on the Gitanes and smiled languidly. "Some old habits are hard to break."

"So what happened? You were in one of Berg's classes and he hit on you?"

"I never made it that far. I registered for three of his courses but got closed out of every one. Even through Barnard is part of Columbia University, Columbia undergrads always got the first crack at the great classes. They treated Barnard women like their ugly stepsisters. So I decided to take matters into my own hands. I sent him a couple of my short stories just to see if he would even bother to read them.

"So far I'm not seeing a motive for murder."

"It's coming. Two weeks later I received a note from him, saying that my work demonstrated verve and insight into the human psyche, and asking me to meet him for dinner at a Spanish restaurant near the campus so we could discuss it further."

Semansky raised an incredulous eyebrow. "And you went?"

"Are you kidding, I would have gone to Saskatchewan to eat poached whale blubber for a chance to talk about my work with Spenser Berg. My dream was to be the next Gertrude Stein. Or at least, Dorothy Parker."

"Okay, so what happened?"

"I had no idea what to do. I had never been on a date with anyone, much less a man I idolized who was more than twice my age. I was twenty years old and still a virgin for Christ's sake."

Semansky opened his mouth to say something snarky, thought better of it, and just said, "Keep going."

"I grabbed two packs of Certs and hoped I wouldn't humiliate myself."

"Well, did you?"

"Totally." She grimaced at the memory. "I borrowed a black dress from a friend that was a little too tight and changed my makeup to something I thought was sophisticated. I was sick to my stomach by the time I walked into the restaurant. The great man was sitting at a small table. When I walked over he leered at me. I think he actually licked his lips. The maître d' sat me next to him."

"Then what happened?"

"Not much. He spent the next hour talking about himself. Ranting about literary theorists, college administrators and book reviewers. Complaining about how frustrating it was to deal with barely literate students and totally incompetent colleagues. I don't think I said two words."

"So far it sounds just like the Berg we all know and despise, a totally self-absorbed, egotistical asshole. But where's the harassment?"

"Calm the fuck down, I'm getting there." She lit a second Gitanes with the smoldering tip of the first. "I finally asked him what he thought of my story."

"And?"

"His eyes went blank. He started mumbling about clever balance of plot and character, intriguing wordplay, keen insight into the human condition. In other words, total crap. I'm sure he never even looked at it. Then he put his hand on my thigh and kept moving it up."

"What did you do?"

"Nothing."

"Nothing?!"

"I was petrified. I just stared into space like some sort of brain-dead zombie. This was the man I idolized. Someone whose approval I yearned for. When I thought he liked my writing I was ecstatic. Then, when I realized he was just looking for a quick lay, it made me sick, literally."

"So what happened?"

"He went on talking and moving his hand slowly up the inside of my leg. My head was spinning. When he was just about at my crotch, I puked."

"You what?"

"I threw my guts up. All over the table, the paella, my roommate's little black dress and on the cashmere sweater of America's Preeminent Man of Letters."

"Oh my god! Then what?"

"I was mortified, humiliated, disgusted with myself, the world and especially Spenser Berg. I ran out of there, blind with rage and revulsion, and somehow made it back to my dorm room in one piece, though I almost got hit by a gypsy cab."

"Did you tell anybody?"

"My roommate. She found me huddled cross-legged in the corner of our room, sobbing, retching and ranting incoherently. She was great. She calmed me down, walked me to the shower and put me to bed. She didn't even make me pay to dry clean her dress."

"So you've got nothing to worry about. Nobody knows about the incident except you, me, Berg and your former roommate, wherever she is."

"Right now, I wish she was in Antarctica. Unfortunately she's an editor at Vanity Fair. She's been begging me for years to write the story and expose Berg as the bastard he is."

"Don't tell me you did it."

She nodded.

"Why now?"

"The sonuvabitch tried to blackmail me."

"Blackmail? How?"

She shook her head with disdain. "He said he had some pictures that I wouldn't want published and he'd give them all back to me, including the negatives if I wrote an essay for him."

"How is that blackmail? You already write for his magazine."

"You don't understand. He wanted me to write a piece about Shakespeare's villainesses so he could submit it in his name and show the world his sublime understanding of the feminine psyche."

"Did you do it?"

"Are you kidding. I'm no whore. If I agreed to something like that I'd be just as despicable as he is."

Semansky flinched, then quickly regained his composure. "What did you do?"

"I sent him a note telling him what he could do with his story. And what I'd like to do to him. It was vicious."

"This is bad. If the police find that letter, it'll sound like a threat, maybe a murder threat."

"No maybe about it. I threatened to murder him in several gruesome ways."

"When did you mail it?"

"A couple of days ago."

"It might still be in his mailbox or laying around his house."

"You're not making me feel any better. The police will probably find it."

"Not if you find it first."

"You mean break into his house? I don't think I can."

"Then I don't know what to tell you."

She smiled sweetly, gazed into Semansky's eyes and said, "Could you do it?"

He grinned back at her. "Trust me, I'm a much bigger coward than you are. And besides, with all those protests I take part in, those fascist cops would put my head on a spike if they caught me in Berg's place."

"Well, will you at least visit me in prison?"

"I will...if I'm not there too."

Chapter 12

"I can't believe I let you talk me into this," Lizzie said as she stood behind the antique oak billiard table in the great room of Spenser Berg's house. Though the windows were left open by Wheeler and Suarez when they removed the body, there was still an acrid whiff of burnt flesh.

Ten feet long and five feet wide, each of the table's ornately carved legs were eight inches in diameter. The massive rough hewn frame was scored with cascading filigreed designs that encircled its ten-inch rails. A large amoeba-shaped stain, the color of merlot, marred its emerald green felt top.

Lizzie leaned over the table, oblivious to both the beauty and the blood. "My first studio apartment was smaller than this thing. It must weigh at least a thousand pounds."

"Show some respect," MacArthur scolded. "Shakespeare could have actually played on this table, maybe between writing Hamlet and Macbeth."

"If Shakespeare played pool on this table, I'll strip naked and skinny dip in the admin fountain at high noon."

MacArthur cringed and rolled his eyes. "I don't know if the campus, or the world, is ready for that. I know I'm not." He took off his jacket, folded it neatly and placed it carefully on a nearby chair. Coming back to the table, he bent his knees and hooked his arms under the thick crossmember. "All right, on the count of three, are you ready?"

Lizzie inhaled slowly, grabbed her side of the table with both hands and sighed. "I guess I'm as ready as I'll ever be."

"Here we go," MacArthur shouted. "One...two...three."

His face red with strain, he emitted a loud sound somewhere between a grunt, a groan and a yelp as he tugged with every fiber in his body. He managed to lift his end a half-inch off the ground before it thudded back to the floor.

Lizzie, though she tried gamely, couldn't budge her side. When she looked up, MacArthur was doubled over, grimacing in pain, awkwardly messaging the small of his back.

"Are you all right?" she asked with real concern.

"I'm fine." He straightened up slowly. "I had no idea a pool table would be so heavy."

"Are you kidding? These things weigh a ton. There's a big slab of slate under the green canvas top. That's what keeps it from warping. And I'm sure that the wood is solid oak."

"When did you become such a billiard expert?"

"In college, I had this boyfriend who thought he was a real pool shark. After most of our dates, we wound up in the student lounge playing eight-ball. I think he broke up with me when I started beating him."

"Do you still play?"

"I haven't touched a cue stick in twenty years. Looking at this beautiful table, though, gives me the urge to rack 'em up."

"Do you think there's any way to disassemble it and take it out in pieces? Let's have a look." He took a pen-sized flashlight out of his pocket and kneeled down to look under the table. "Hey, what's this?

"What?"

"It some kind of metal plate about the size of a business card."

"Does it say anything, like 'William Shakespeare played here?'"

On his knees, his eyes inches from it, he strained to focus. "It's hard to see. It's really dirty." He reached into his pocket, pulled out a handkerchief, spit on it and began vigorously rubbing the medallion. After a few seconds he shouted, "I'm beginning to make out something."

"Anything helpful?"

"I think...yes. I can see a 'B', maybe an 'L'."

"You think maybe it's spelling 'billiards?' "

"Could be."

"Keep going."

"That's all there is. It's too faint."

"Great work Sherlock, you proved it's a billiard table. Keep looking."

He shined the flashlight around the underside of the table.

"I see something."

"What?"

"I'm not sure. It's taped to the bottom." He grunted, crawled under, reached as far as he could, grabbed whatever it was, and yanked. He pulled out an envelope covered with dust and started coughing.

"Are you okay?"

MacArthur wriggled out from under the table, still coughing. "I'm fine. It's a damn dustbowl under there," he said, clearing his throat.

"So, what did you find?"

"Here, you look. I don't need anymore dust." He handed her the envelope.

She opened it and pulled out a stack of newspaper and magazine clippings, some yellowed, others recent, and started leafing through them. "These are all about Harry Gabriel."

She began to read. " 'Gabriel has the unique ability to break down ethnic, educational and social barriers, blending high culture with hip-hop culture, liberating Shakespeare out of the lofty perches of the academy and bringing him onto the streets.' "

She picked up another. " 'Best-selling Author Arrested After Barroom Brawl.' " She put down the clippings. "You think Berg was stalking Gabriel?"

"I don't know about stalking, but he was collecting a lot of information."

"What do you think it means?"

"My guess is that Berg was either trying to take Gabriel down or getting ready to blackmail him."

Lizzie grinned. "Our boy Harry wouldn't have reacted very well to something like that. Like I told you, he's the kind of guy to punch first and ask questions later."

He nodded. "Put that together with the altercation last night and I think we've got a case."

"Enough to arrest him?"

"Probably. People have been arrested on less."

"But are you ready to arrest someone of Gabriel's stature with 'probably'?"

"Stature has nothing to do with it," MacArthur said firmly. "Like I said, if he's guilty, he's guilty. I don't care who he is."

"Maybe you don't, but Angie does. We'd better keep looking for that table. That's why we came here. Those clippings are just a bonus."

"I guess you're right," MacArthur said with no enthusiasm.

"Check out everything in this room. I'll look in there." She headed to a large alcove that housed an antique roll top desk and hundreds of books stacked on shelves from the floor to the ceiling. Students' papers, Berg's hand-written notes to himself, official Melville University documents, utility bills and shopping lists were all strewn about on top of the desk in no particular order.

Lizzie went through them all. "There's nothing here." She walked back into the great room. "I think we're done. Did you find anything?"

"No." He thought for a second. "I still think the table is the key. But if it's not here, where could it be?"

"I'm guessing the library."

"Maybe the blonde librarian isn't telling us all she knows."

"You don't really think she could have something to do with Berg's murder, do you?"

"That table's supposed to be worth tens of millions of dollars. That's enough to tempt anybody."

"She didn't know about that table until she got that letter."

"Maybe. Maybe it was just an act."

"You think she and Campanella had that scene all rehearsed and ready to go so if we happened to show up, they could fool us?"

"It does sound pretty farfetched when you put it that way. But I'm not ruling anything out."

"Where to now?"

"Back to campus. But first I have to reset the house alarm."

Chapter 13

"Are you sure it was him, Dr. Berg, I mean?" Tristan's voice echoed up into the high domed ceiling.

"Tristan, please!" Jordan hissed in an emphatic whisper. "We can't discuss that here."

She glared at her brother, then gazed around the Rotunda, the glass-enclosed, oval-shaped building that was the University's main eatery. Though it was still a half-hour before noon, it was filled to capacity. Solitary students sat at tables strewn with empty coffee containers, getting in some last minute studying. Others in groups of three or four were laughing, relaxing, flirting. Most of the tables were homogeneous. Whites sat with whites, Asians with Asians, blacks with blacks. The only integrated table was filled by some hulking guys from the football team. Some of the older professors were also enjoying each other's company. The young faculty never ate there, not deigning to mix with the their young charges.

Jordan couldn't help feeling that the entire room was surreptitiously listening in on their conversation. She was sure that everyone there, in fact everyone at the university, would be more than happy to see her leave the Melville campus. She was convinced that they all thought that the only reason she was the head of Archives and Special Collections was because of her mother's influence, when the truth was that she earned that position, graduating with honors with a Masters of Science in Library and Information Science from one of the top-ranked programs in the nation. She arrived at Melville well before her mother ever set foot on campus. No one pays attention to the goings-on at the library, but when a celebrity comes aboard to chair the new TV and Video Production program, everyone notices.

Tristan was oblivious to his surroundings. He was focusing all his attention on an enormous slice of the Rotunda Gigunda, a gargantuan pizza, topped with extra cheese, extra sauce, meatballs, sausage, pepperoni and mushrooms. He was determined to eat it without using a knife and fork. He read a story in one of Jordan's Vanity Fair magazines that said that real New Yorkers never ate pizza with anything but their hands. And though he now lived sixty miles from the city, he considered himself a real New Yorker, having spent the first five years of his life there.

Using both hands, his left executing the legendary New York fold, his right, cradling the bottom, keeping all the toppings in place, he maneuvered the slice to his mouth. After a triumphant swallow, he turned back to his sister. "How can you be sure it was him? Wasn't it still dark outside?"

She leaned in towards him and whispered, "It was light enough. I saw his face as clearly as I'm seeing yours right now. It was Spenser Berg. I'm positive."

Tristan said in a hushed voice, "Why are we whispering like this?"

"Because the police said it would start a major panic if word got out."

"Wow. You must have been totally freaked out. Are you okay?"

"Of course I'm not okay. Finding the...finding what I found this morning was only the beginning. While they were interviewing me, a letter arrived saying that Dr. Berg was giving a priceless Shakespearian artifact to the library under the stipulation that I and only I would be responsible for it."

"So why are you so worried? It shows that he trusted you."

"I doubt that. I have no idea why he wrote that letter but it certainly wasn't because of his high regard for me. In all the times he's been to the library, he hardly ever acknowledged my existence. And when he did, he spoke to me like I was a servant not a trusted colleague."

"He made that gift to the library and he put you in charge of it. That must mean something."

"Right now, it means I'm a prime suspect in his murder."

"What! How can that be?"

"Because it's missing. I'm sure the police think I stole it and murdered Dr. Berg in the process."

"What!" Tristan screamed. "That's so freakin' messed up."

Now everyone in their vicinity really did stop what they were doing to stare at them.

She shot her brother a withering glare. "Thanks, Tris." Her voice dripped with sarcasm.

He covered his mouth for a second, then said contritely, "I'm sorry. It's just that I can't believe that they think you're a…"

"Sssshhhhh. Let's change the subject."

"All right, what do you want to talk about?"

"How about your friend Wolcott?"

"I think he's cool."

"Cool?" Jordan grimaced. "He's repulsive. Aren't there any kids your own age you can hang around with?"

"I'm home schooled, remember. I never get to meet anyone my own age. Anyway if it wasn't for Drew, I wouldn't have seen Harry Gabriel's lecture last night."

Jordan recoiled slightly. "You were there! I thought you said you were hanging out with a friend."

"Drew is my friend."

"I heard that it was completely sold out. How did you get in?"

"Drew got us in. He's good friends with Spenser Berg. Or was."

"I find that hard to believe." She curled a wisp of hair with her fingers. "He's a uncouth pig and Dr. Berg was the most snobbish, priggish and supercilious person I've ever known."

Tristan shrugged. "Whatever. Drew got us in and it was awesome, like a rap battle with really smart people."

"Comparing a scholarly lecture to a hip-hop confrontation isn't making me wish I was there. It just doesn't sound very interesting."

"You're wrong. Harry Gabriel was awesome!"

"He writes those imitation Shakespeare novels, doesn't he," she said, disinterestedly. "I'd much rather read the real thing."

"I bet you didn't know that Shakespeare killed Christopher Marlowe."

"That's ridiculous." She shook her head disdainfully. "Nobody believes that."

"That's what Harry Gabriel's new book is about. He said it's just as possible as anything else written about Shakespeare. And that's not even the best part. Dr. Berg came in and started yelling at him and cursing him and calling him all kinds of horrible names. He said Shakespeare was a fraud and so was Gabriel. And he said he had proof."

"I don't believe it."

"It's true," Tristan said emphatically. "You can ask anyone who was there."

"Did he say what kind of proof?"

"No. He said he wasn't ready to reveal it, but it was something that was going to rock the world.

Jordan leaned forward. "Did he mention anything about a table?"

"A table?" Tristan thought for a moment. "I don't think so. How could a table prove that Shakespeare wasn't Shakespeare?"

"I don't know, but that was the Shakespearian artifact that Berg said he was giving to me...I mean to the University."

"A table, huh." Tristan considered this new piece of information. "Maybe there are some clues inside it. Does it have drawers?"

"I don't know."

"You mean you've never even seen it?"

"No."

"And he never said anything to you about it?"

She shook her head. "I never heard of it until I got Berg's note today."

"What are you going to do?"

"I guess I'll have to try to find it. As of now, that table is my responsibility."

"Maybe when we find it we'll find out who chopped Spenser Berg's head off."

Jordan shot him a dirty look and put her finger to her mouth.

"Oops, sorry. I forgot."

Suddenly the din of the Rotunda subsided and heads turned towards the entranceway.

Harry Gabriel walked in. He was with a slender man of early middle-age with thinning salt-and-pepper hair and a goatee to match.

"Jor look, it's Harry Gabriel," Tristan said, excitedly. "I bought his new book at the lecture and it's still in my backpack. Do you think he'll sign it if I bring it over to him?"

"You're not bringing anything anywhere! It would be extremely rude and totally inappropriate for you to bother him here."

Several swooning female students ran over to Gabriel and handed him their copies of his book, which he seemed very happy to autograph.

"See, they're all doing it."

"I don't care."

"That guy he's with, isn't that your boss?"

"No, he's not my boss," she snapped. "That's Phil Bergstrum, the Assistant Dean for Acquisitions and Library Events. He's probably trying to convince Gabriel to come back to the library for another reading."

Bergstrum, craning his neck searching for a place to sit, noticed Jordan and her brother at a table with two vacant seats. He waved and walked towards them with Gabriel in tow.

"Jordan, this is Harry Gabriel," Bergstrum said as he approached. "I'm trying to convince him that our library ballroom is a very congenial venue for an author appearance."

Gabriel stepped forward, smiled broadly, and said, "It's great to see you ag..."

Jordan sprung to her feet, thrust out her hand and said, very formally, "Jordan Day, head of Melville University Library Special Collections, a pleasure to meet you, Dr. Gabriel. This is my brother Tristan. He's a great fan of yours."

Gabriel gingerly shook the proffered hand. The strength of her grip surprised him.

Tristan was out of his seat in an instant, a hardcover copy of Alas,

Poor Shakespeare in his hand. He handed it to the author. "Do you think you could sign my book?"

Gabriel beamed. "That would be my great pleasure, Tristan." He glanced at Bergstrum, then at Jordan. "Would anyone have a pen?"

Jordan fished around in her handbag, came up with one of the library's promotional pens, and handed it to Gabriel. He thanked her and wrote, "Tristan, thanks for your support. I can use all the fans I can get. Harry Gabriel." He then handed the book to the boy.

There was a brief moment of awkward silence, then Bergstrum blurted out, "Have you heard about Spenser Berg?"

"Heard what?" Jordan said, a little more intensely than she had planned to. She glanced over at Gabriel, who looked edgy.

Bergstrum assumed a mock conspiratorial tone. "He's gone missing. Presumed dead. There are rumors flying all over campus. Murdered by an angry student? A jealous colleague? A former lover? You know, he was supposed to have been quite the lothario in his day." He looked at Harry. "Of course, after the way he ambushed you last night, he's lucky you didn't shoot him on the spot."

There was no reaction, just blank stares.

Undaunted, Bergstrum blabbered on. "Are the rumors true about Childress eliminating your department?"

Jordan stiffened. "Who told you that?"

He shrugged. "Just water cooler talk. I didn't think there was anything to it. I have no idea why they made that man Dean of Libraries. He's a computer geek. He has no more regard for books than I for...ugh...video games, which I hear he might be adding to our collection." He looked over at Tristan. "What do you think about that, young man?"

"I like video games but libraries should be for books."

"What about you, Dr. Gabriel, books or video games?"

"I write books. What do you think?"

Before Bergstrum could reply, his eyes darted to the other side of the room. "Oh my God, it's Ed Strauss. I've been trying to get hold of him for days." He moved away from the table, toward his quarry. "I'll see you folks later." He winked at Jordan. "Be extra nice to Mr. Gabriel, I want him to come back for a reading."

No one said anything for a minute, then Tristan asked, "Did you model Makki B. after yourself?"

"An author puts something of himself into all his characters."

"Even Othello Jones?"

"Maybe him most of all."

"But he was a murderer."

"He was a black man put on a pedestal by white society, tempted with the trappings of privilege, then vilified and persecuted by the same people who anointed him."

Jordan bristled. "It sounds to me that you are justifying an act of murder committed by a member of an oppressed minority solely on the basis of racial discrimination."

"I wasn't saying that, exactly."

"What were you saying?"

"That America has a habit of putting its media-created heroes of color, mostly athletes and entertainers, on a pedestal, then joyfully knocking them off."

"And that's how you see yourself?"

"I didn't say that I was Othello Jones. I said that he and I have things in common."

"What could you and a thug like that possibly have in common."

"Well, for one thing, we've both been falsely accused of a crime we didn't commit."

Jordan froze. "You were questioned about Spenser Berg, weren't you?" Her voice was barely more than a whisper.

"How did you know?"

In the few seconds of silence that it took her to compose a response, Tristan blurted out, "Jordan found Dr. Berg's head this morning. It was on a spike outside her window. She's a suspect too."

Harry turned to Jordan. "You? Why would anyone suspect you of killing Spenser Berg? I'm the one who nearly came to blows with him."

In hushed tones, she told him about seeing Berg's severed head early that morning. And about Berg's letter saying he was donating a table that belonged to William Shakespeare to the library on the condition that it would be under Jordan's, and only Jordan's, care. Then she talked about her subsequent questioning by MacArthur and Peltz.

After she finished, Gabriel took a deep breath. "I guess we both have something in common with Othello Jones."

"So who do you think did it?" Tristan asked, breathlessly.

"Right now I don't have a clue," Gabriel said resolutely. "But I'm going to find out."

"What do you mean?" Jordan said.

"The only ones investigating Berg's death are Lizzie Peltz and Gregg MacArthur. And they're putting most their effort into proving it was me. And the rest of it on you."

Tristan blurted, "While the real killer gets off scot-free! That's so bogus."

"Except that I'm not going to let it happen."

"How do you propose to stop it?" Jordan asked.

"I know a thing or two about how to conduct an investigation. My last two books were police procedurals. I spent a lot of time talking with police officers and detectives. I even went on a couple of ride-alongs in patrol cars. While MacArthur and Peltz are spinning their wheels investigating us, I'm going to find the actual murderer." He winked at Tristan. "It might even be fun."

"Fun! For a minute I was starting to believe that you were serious." Jordan stood up, her chair squealed as she pushed it back. "Let's go, Tristan."

"What's wrong?" Gabriel asked, taken aback.

"You may think it's all a big joke, but this is real life. That they might think I'm responsible for Spenser Berg's murder makes me sick. And you..." she pointed a shaky finger at him. "You seem to feel that this is just one big adventure, grist for your next novel." She grabbed her brother's hand and yanked him up. "Forgive me if I don't feel that way."

Gabriel quickly stood up in front of them, blocking their way. "Jordan please. I'm taking this whole situation very seriously, believe me. I know this is no game. I was just trying to lighten the moment."

Tristan looked up wide-eyed at Gabriel and said, "You really think you can find the real murderer?"

"If I don't, no one will, certainly not MacArthur and Peltz. They're too busy trying to convict your sister and me."

Tristan said, "Can I help?"

Jordan glared at her brother. "You most certainly cannot."

He looked up at her, defiantly. "I'm not going to let them arrest you for murder. If Dr. Gabriel needs me to help him, I will."

Jordan turned to Harry. "Do you see what you've done? Now, on top of everything else, I have to worry about him too."

"There's no need to worry. I'd never let him get involved in something that would put him in harm's way." Harry turned to the boy and held out his hand. "Thanks for your kind offer. You've a brave young man. It was a pleasure meeting you."

Tristan beamed and shook his hand. "Me too,"

"Now if you'll both excuse me." Harry stood up and walked out of the Rotunda, stopping once or twice to chat with some young fans and sign a few books.

"I can't believe how rude you were," Tristan said to his sister.

She looked at him dolefully. "I know you think he's wonderful. A hero. But there's another side of Harry Gabriel that you know nothing about. Chief MacArthur has been a policeman for a long time. If he suspects him, there's probably something to it."

"He suspects you too. Is there anything to that?"

"I know that I didn't murder Spenser Berg. Whether or not Harry Gabriel did, I'm not 100 percent sure."

"Well I am." Tristan jumped up and stormed out of the Rotunda.

Chapter 14

As he walked past the small fountain on the lower level towards the parking garage, Harry tried to formulate a plan. He knew damn well that writing a murder mystery is a far cry from solving an actual murder, especially one where he was the prime suspect.

Standing at the garage entrance, trying to remember where he had parked his car, he heard a young voice calling, "Mr. Gabriel, Mr. Gabriel."

Harry looked up. "Tristan?"

"I want to help you find the guy who killed Dr. Berg."

He tousled the boy's hair. "Listen, you're a great kid and I really appreciate that you believe in me and want to help me. But it's really not a good idea."

"Why not?"

"A lot of reasons. The campus police chief thinks I'm a murderer. It's only a matter of time until he arrests me. If he does, you shouldn't be with me."

"Why not. He's not gonna arrest me."

"He's a fascist. He'll probably add kidnapping to the murder charge."

"But that wouldn't be true."

"He won't care. But that's not the only reason. There's a real killer out there. Who knows when he'll decide to kick it up a notch and murder me. If things get scary I don't want you in the middle of it. And one more thing. Your sister didn't want you to even think about looking for Berg's killer. I'm sure your mom and dad wouldn't be too pleased either."

"My mom passed away a few months ago. And I never met my dad."

Gabriel's expression morphed from annoyance to compassion. "I'm sorry, I didn't know. You mean it's just you and Jordan?"

He gazed down at the boy, paused pensively, then said. "That's tough, having your big sister as your only parent."

"Jordan's always been like my second mother. My mom was an actress. She worked crazy hours. Most nights Jordan made dinner, helped me with my homework, all the stuff that moms usually do."

"Now's your chance to be there for your sister the way she was always there for you. I can deal with figuring out who the real killer is. Your job right now is to take care of Jordan. She's involved in this mess too and may be in danger."

Tristan shook his head. "Jordan's a lot tougher than you think. She doesn't need me to help her." He looked up at Harry with a sly smile. "But you do."

"Oh? And why is that?"

"Have you ever been in Dr. Berg's house?"

"No."

"Well I have. The place is like booby trapped. There are secret passages, hidden rooms, all kinds of weird stuff like that. If you want to find out who killed him, you need to know where to look."

"Booby traps? Secret rooms?" Harry said skeptically. "Nice try, but we're talking about Spenser Berg's house, not the Haunted Mansion in Disneyland."

"It's true, really. My friend Drew Wolcott knows all about it. He's sort of like Dr. Berg's right-hand man. He does all kinds of jobs for him. He has a key and everything. He told me that Dr. Berg had his house built to be an exact copy of the one Shakespeare grew up in. He said that in those days a lot of houses had that kind of stuff."

"Okay, I'll buy that, but even so, how do you know where they are?

Berg hated kids, I find it hard to believe that he let you roam around his house."

"I went there a couple of times with Drew when Dr. Berg was out of town."

"Oh." Harry paused for a few pensive seconds. "You really think you know your way around the place?"

"Absolutely. Drew showed me the hiding place where Dr. Berg keeps his secret papers. He even showed me how to bypass the alarm."

"There's an alarm?"

"Yeah. One of those keypad things."

Harry sighed, gazed up to the sky, then back at Tristan, alternately nodding and shaking his head. "Your sister hates me already. If anything happened to you, there'd be another murder on campus. Mine."

"Jordan doesn't hate you. Why should she?"

"She never mentioned that we dated a couple of times?"

Tristan jumped as if from an electric shock. "You went out with my sister? No way!"

"It was a long time ago. I was a Graduate Teaching Assistant for a summer class she was in. We had coffee a few times. I thought we really connected. Then all of a sudden she stopped returning my calls. I never knew why."

He paused for a moment. "Whatever it was I did, it must have been bad, because it looks like she still can't stand the sight of me."

"Well she's wrong! And once we find out who killed Dr. Berg she'll realize how wrong she is."

"WE aren't doing anything of the sort. YOU are going back to your sister."

"Please let me just ride with you to the house. I won't even get out of the car."

Harry shook his head slowly. "Not gonna happen."

"You'll never get into the house without me."

Harry ruminated for a few seconds. "You're sure you know Berg's alarm code."

"Positive."

Harry sighed, rolled his eyes and said, "Okay, come on."

He led the way up to the third level of the Admin parking garage. They walked over to a cream colored, low slung sports coupe.

"What kind of car is this?" the boy asked, wide eyed.

"It's a Karmann Ghia," Harry said as he opened the passenger door for his young companion.

"I've never seen one before, sounds Italian," Tristan said as he got in.

"It's a Volkswagen."

"A Volkswagen? This doesn't look like any Volkswagen I ever saw."

Harry walked around to the other side, slid into the driver's seat and started the engine. "Volkswagen never made anything like it before or since. Actually it's of dual parentage."

"Dual parentage?"

"It was designed in Italy and built in Germany. Maybe that's what attracted me to it in the first place. My car and I are both mutts," he said as he drove around the spiral turns down the three levels to the garage exit.

"What do you mean?"

"My mother's white and my father's part black — dual parentage, two different breeds, two different cultures, just like this car."

"Like Othello Jones?"

"That's right. And Derek Jeter, Tiger Woods and President Obama."

"That's why you bought this car?"

Harry laughed and shook his head. "No. Actually, it was love at first sight. I was about your age, maybe a drop older, when I saw a Karmann Ghia for the first time. I thought it was the most beautiful thing I'd ever seen. I had to have one. To be inside it and be in control." A dreamy expression overspread his face. "By the time I was seventeen I had saved enough money to buy one. It was eight years old, creamy yellow, with a couple of dents and the heat didn't work, but I didn't care. I loved that machine."

"And you kept it all that time?"

Harry laughed again. "No, that one's long gone. I had this beauty shipped in from California. It's only about two years newer than my first but the owner kept it in perfect condition. It cost me ten times as much, but when I got it I felt like I got back part of my soul."

They drove through campus, then after a quick turn they were on College Avenue. The railroad station ran for several blocks on one side of the street and assorted shops occupied the other.

Tristan stood on that Long Island Rail Road platform dozens of times, waiting for the train to Penn Station. It was the territory north of College Avenue, down the ominously named Dark Hollow Drive, that always gave him quivers. Though it was an exclusive area with huge, old gated mansions that had names like Suncrest and Oakmont, the rumor among the neighborhood kids was that one of the unoccupied houses was haunted. Of course, Tristan didn't believe in such things, but still...

As they drove down the long serpentine road toward Spenser Berg's cottage, Tristan gripped the armrest so tightly he left small dimples in the vinyl.

"What's the plan once we get inside?"

"The plan is you stay in the car."

"But..."

"No buts. If I get caught rummaging around Spenser Berg's house with you, I don't know which would be worse, facing the police or your sister. "

Tristan started to say something, then slumped and said a timid, "Yes sir."

When they arrived at the house, the street was deserted.

"I'm going to park around the corner just in case the police cruise by," Harry said, "If they see a strange car in front of Berg's house they might get suspicious."

After they parked Harry said, "Now stay here until I get back," he said, exiting the car. He turned back and wagged a finger at Tristan. "I mean it — don't leave the car."

Berg's house was made of brick, with twin gables in front. Harry turned the knob but the door wouldn't budge. On the wall next to it was a small white keypad. A red dot glowed at the bottom of the screen and the LED read 'ARMED.'

"Goddamn!" he muttered as he walked back to the Karmann Ghia. He knocked on the passenger-side window, startling Tristan, who was deep in thought.

"What's wrong?"

"It's the alarm. What's the password."

Tristan grinned mischievously. "Only if I can go inside with you."

"I thought we settled that."

"Sorry. Let me come and you get the password. Or you can try to break the code."

"I told you, I can't bring you inside." he yelled. "Now are you going to give me the password or not?"

Tristan shook his head defiantly.

After five seconds of thought and an exasperated sigh, Harry said, "Okay, c'mon."

Tristan bounded out of the car and raced around the corner with Gabriel following. Standing in front of the alarm pad, he pressed, '2B-ORNOT-2B.' There was a short beep, the LED screen went blank and the red dot turned green.

Harry pushed the door open, let Tristan in ahead of him, then closed the door. They found themselves in the great room with the massive billiard table in the center.

Tristan gasped. "That's blood all over that pool table, isn't it."

"I think so," Harry said, placing an arm gently on his shoulder. "Are you okay?"

"I'm fine." But his unsteady gait and sweaty forehead told Harry otherwise.

Harry surveyed the room, shaking his head. "It looks like MacArthur's men were here already. If there ever were any clues, they're not here now."

"I bet I know some places where they didn't look."

"You were serious about those secret hiding places?"

"Watch this." Tristan walked over to the fireplace, constructed of randomly shaped stone slabs. The hearth, also stone, was raised about a foot off the wood floor. He bent over a rectangular slab, grabbed it and lifted.

"Be careful," Harry cautioned.

"Don't worry, it's hollow. See." Tristan smiled proudly as he lifted it easily.

"You were serious, Berg really did build this like Shakespeare's birthplace."

Peering inside, Tristan said, "I think there's something in here."

"Can you see what it is?" Harry walked over to the hearth.

"It's a box."

Harry squatted next to him. "Let's see if we can get it out." He reached in, and after a little maneuvering, managed to lift the box up and out, setting it down on the floor next to the hearth. It was a shirt box sealed with packing tape. He slit the tape with his Swiss Army knife. Inside were several thick manila envelopes, also sealed.

"Is that what you were looking for?" Tristan asked eagerly.

"It might be." Harry picked up one of the envelopes, slit it open and pulled out what looked like a handwritten note and some photos. The note was from Natasha Ferette threatening Berg with a few creative methods of torture. The photos were of a much younger Ferette in various stages of undress, posed artfully with strategically placed pieces of produce. Harry quickly shoved the letter and the photos back into the envelope.

Tristan looked eagerly at Harry. "Well..."

Before Harry could answer, the screeching of brakes echoed through the room. "Holy crap!" he yelped. "Somebody's coming."

Chapter 15

Harry looked frantically around the room. "Where's the back door?"

"In the kitchen," Tristan said as he headed to the rear of the house.

Harry followed, then stopped short. "Wait, if it's the police, they probably have someone stationed out back."

Tristan turned and ran past Harry, back into the great room. He stopped in front of the fireplace.

"Climbing up the chimney only works for Santa Claus. We have to find someplace for actual humans to hide."

"That's what I'm doing."

There were floor to ceiling bookcases on either side of the fireplace. Grabbing a shelf, Tristan swung the bookcase open. "Come on!"

Clutching the box against his chest, Harry followed the boy into a small room hidden behind the bookcase and pulled the door closed behind him. He spotted a white handkerchief on the floor and nonchalantly scooped it up and stuffed it in his back pocket. It had red splotches and was monogrammed with the letters 'A.D.' in blue.

They heard footfalls coming up the cobblestone walkway.

"How do you know about all this?" Harry asked in hushed tones.

"Drew showed me," Tristan said softly. "He said Professor Berg would spy on his guests from here. See, we can look through the spaces between the stones and see and hear everything."

The front door opened slowly. Natasha Ferette, a cigarette dangling from her lips, tiptoed in and flicked the light switch. Peter Foote followed cautiously.

"This really stinks," she said.

"You're right. It's a terrible idea. I don't know how I let you talk me into coming here."

"I didn't mean that. I meant the room, it reeks. It smells like somebody barbecued dead rats in here."

"One of your culinary specialties?"

"Very funny, Peter. Are you here to help or just annoy me?"

"I told you I'd help you and I will. Just make sure you fulfill your part of the bargain. By the way, what exactly are we looking for?"

"It's a letter, handwritten, plain white paper in a plain white envelope."

"That narrows it down considerably," he said sarcastically.

She pointed to a small antique oak taboret cabinet on the other side of the room. "If you really want to help, start opening drawers."

Foote ambled over, opened the top drawer and began casually shuffling papers. Ferette made her way to Berg's massive roll-top desk on the other side of the room and quickly rifled through the compartments, her hands working with the speed and dexterity of a sushi chef.

"What's this?" Foote took something from one of the drawers.

"You found the letter?"

"No. A tin of tea."

"Tea?" she smirked. "If you find some crumpets, we'll invite the Queen."

"You mock, but this could be significant. I happen to have a passion for tea and this is extraordinary. Fortnum & Mason Darjeeling Loose Leaf Tea. Extremely pricey." He held up the purple tin. "Somewhere around a hundred dollars for this."

"So Berg splurged on tea. He had plenty of money, he could spend it on whatever he likes."

"That's true. But I happen to know that Spenser didn't drink tea. Coffee either. Hot cocoa was his morning beverage. And, as I'm sure you know, he was quite parsimonious. I can't imagine him spending fifty cents for tea, much less a hundred dollars."

Back in their hiding space, Tristan whispered, "Who are they?"

"They're professors from the English department," Harry said under his breath.

"What are they doing here?"

"Same as us, looking for clues."

"Why? Do you think they had something to do with the murder?"

"I don't know. It's possible."

Ferette walked towards the fireplace.

"Holy crap!" Tristan whispered frantically. "She's coming over here."

Harry put his hand on Tristan's shoulder, calming him. Ferette was inches from the mantel. They stood motionless, holding their breath. She reached up, took something off the oak shelf and examined it. "Ugh!" she shrieked and jumped back, shaking her hand.

"What's is it?" Foote said, startled.

"A disgustingly moldy Ritz cracker. It must have been up there for months. I knew Berg was a pig, I didn't realize he was a slob too."

Before Foote could comment his head jerked towards the front window. "I think I hear a car pulling up" he said, his voice etched with panic. "It's probably the police."

"Why should they be coming here?"

"Because this is a crime scene. To be exact, this is where Spenser was murdered. Didn't you see that billiards table? All that blood? Ughhh! We should go now."

"One more minute." Ferette walked to Berg's desk, grabbed a file folder out of the open top drawer and started rifling through it. She picked up a single sheet of paper and read it carefully. "This is interesting."

"You found your letter."

"No. Something else."

"What?"

"Never mind." She folded the paper and threw it in her handbag. "Okay let's go. Good thing we parked in the back."

Foote walked quickly towards the kitchen, followed by Ferette, who flicked off the lights and closed the door behind her. Seconds later, the front door inched slowly open.

Behind the façade, Tristan gripped Harry's arm. "I'm scared. What should we do?"

Chapter 16

"There's nobody here," Josh Campanella whispered as he tiptoed into the house.

"Of course there's nobody here," Jordan said, striding past him. She flicked on the light. "Who did you think would be here?"

"I don't know. The police. The killer. Berg's ghost."

She turned back to glare at him, her hands on her hips. "Now you're just being childish."

From behind the fireplace, Tristan grabbed Harry's wrist and whispered, "It's my sister."

Harry nodded, put a finger to his lips and placed his other hand reassuringly on the boy's shoulder.

"Maybe we should go," Josh said. He still hadn't moved from his spot just inside the door. "Suppose the police find us here?"

"We'll tell them the truth, that we're looking for Shakespeare's table, the one Spenser Berg donated to the library and entrusted to my care. Technically, it belongs to the library. We have every right to try to find it. What are you so afraid of?"

"They could arrest us for trespassing, breaking and entering, who knows what."

"We're not trespassing because nobody owns this house to make that accusation. And we didn't break anything, the door was unlocked and we entered. There's no such crime as 'entering.' "

"Even if you're right, I still think we should go," Josh said nervously.

"It was your idea to come here in the first place. Now you want to leave. What's the problem?"

"Being in his house...the house where he was killed." Josh shuddered. "It's just creepy."

"Well, we're here. We might as well look around. If we find the table, we'll put it in the back of your Jeep and leave. Okay?"

"Okay." Josh trudged in like Marley's ghost. The only thing missing was the clanging of chains. He stopped at the pool table. "Oh God. That stain. It's Berg's blood." His legs wobbled. He grabbed the rail for support.

"Are you all right?"

"I'll be fine," he said, straightening up. "Seeing all that blood knocked me for a loop."

"If you want to leave, we'll leave."

"I just need to sit down for a few minutes."

He sat in one of the high-backed upholstered chairs while Jordan walked carefully around the room, stopping at each of the tables, none of which looked like it might have once been the property William Shakespeare.

"You know," she said. "Childress wouldn't dare close Special Collections if it housed the most important literary artifact in the country."

"I think we'll be fine even if we don't find it. You'll charm old Lady DeVere into donating the money we need. That'll shut Childress up."

"I'm glad you're so confident. I haven't felt very charming lately."

"I'm sure you'll be fabulous. Just like I'm sure Gabriel's the one who killed Berg."

Jordan turned to him. "How can you say that? There's no reason to believe he's any guiltier than I am."

"Come on, Jordan, don't tell me you still have a thing for him."

"What are you talking about?"

"Weren't you and Gabriel an item at one time?"

"We saw each other once or twice a long time ago. Nothing came of it. I haven't seen him since, nor do I care to."

"When they found his name on the sign-in sheet, I thought maybe he came to see you."

"I have no idea how Gabriel's name got there. I certainly never saw him in the library," she said indignantly.

He walked over to her. "I'm sorry. It's just that I don't want anything to happen to you when he gets arrested."

"I still don't understand why you're so sure he did it."

"Look at the facts. Gabriel has a history of violence and he had a huge fight with Berg the night before he was murdered. And you can just see that he's one of those jerks who think the law doesn't apply to them."

"Since when are you such an expert on Harry Gabriel?"

"I'm no expert, but I read the papers, and trust me, he's evil."

"You don't even know him."

"I know everything I need to know. He's rich, good looking, arrogant. Probably never had to struggle for anything in his life."

Jordan gestured around room. "If there ever was a table here that belonged to William Shakespeare, it's gone now. We might as well leave."

"Are you sure? If you want to keep looking, we'll keep looking."

"No. Let's go. I have to get ready for my dinner tonight with Lady DeVere and then prepare for the Scholars Showcase tomorrow."

"Shit!" Josh clapped himself on the forehead. "With everything that's happened today, I forgot all about the Showcase."

"I'm sure President DellaRosa didn't. If I'm not prepared for tomorrow's presentation, I won't have to worry about Special Collections closing down, she'll fire me on the spot."

Jordan headed for the door. Josh followed and slammed it behind him.

As soon as he heard the car pull away, Harry pushed to bookcase open. "I'm glad you knew about this secret compartment."

"Me too," Tristan said, gulping air. "It was pretty crowded in there. I don't know how much longer I could've stayed cooped up."

"You did great. I'll share a foxhole — or a priest hole — with you anytime."

"What's that?"

"It's that secret room we were just hiding in. It was built for fugitive priests."

Tristan looked confused. "Fugitive priests?"

Harry slipped into his professor persona.

"When Queen Elizabeth came to power, England was in the middle of a religious civil war. Instead of North versus South, it was Catholic against Protestant. Elizabeth was Protestant. It was against the law to be Catholic. Catholic churches were torn down or transformed into Protestant ones. And Catholic priests were public enemy number one. Hundreds were executed. Catholic families had to hide their allegiance or they would be prosecuted. The wealthier ones built secret chambers in their houses, like the one we were just in, to hide priests from the Queen's secret police."

"What happened if they found them?"

"Pretty much the same thing that happened to Berg."

Tristan cringed. "You mean they chopped off their heads and…"

"They did all kinds of horrible things to them."

"Just because they were Catholic?"

"I'm afraid so, kid."

"I was worried what the police would do if they found us, but compared to those priests, I guess it's not so bad."

"I'm more concerned about what you sister will do to me when she finds out I brought you here."

"Don't tell her."

"I have to. I have some questions for Josh and once I ask them he'll know I could only have heard him if I was here."

"You could say you were here alone, not mention me at all."

"I don't think that's a good idea. Sometimes little lies like that come back to bite you. Suppose I get interrogated and they ask how I knew about the priest hole. Or the alarm code. Or whatever. Once they catch you in a lie all your credibility is shot. It's better to get everything out in the open.

"Jordan's gonna be majorly pissed."

"Yeah but she'll be pissed at me, not you. And since she already hates me, it's no big deal." Harry clapped Tristan affectionately on the back as they walked to the Karmann Ghia. "But don't worry, we'll still be pals."

They drove in silence for a few minutes when Tristan said, "I can't believe Josh saying all those terrible things about you. I thought he was a good guy."

"When you're successful, there are people who are going to resent you. Josh probably hates me because I'm a best-selling author and he spends his days shelving old books. I'm sure he'd love to see me go down for murder, whether I did it or not."

"At least Jordan stuck up for you."

"That surprised me."

"See, she doesn't hate you."

"She will soon."

Chapter 17

"Can I help you, madam?" Edie Kaiser said authoritatively, rising up in her chair.

"I'm certain you can," the elderly lady said in a firm, confident voice that had the slightest hint of a British accent. Barely over five feet tall and no more than a hundred pounds, she wore a beige tweed blazer over a white dress with black polka dots. A kaleidoscopically multicolored Hermes silk scarf hung loosely around her neck. "Will you please inform Dr. DellaRosa that Millicent DeVere has arrived."

"You're Lady DeVere?"

"Yes, I'm aware of that."

Edie pressed the red intercom button on her phone. "Excuse me, Dr. DellaRosa, Lady Millicent DeVere is here to see you. Let me know when you'd like me to bring her in?"

"That won't be necessary, I'll come out," the voice crackled over the speaker.

"All right ma'am."

Puzzlement wafted across her face. Many influential people came to the office, college presidents, prominent politicians, business leaders, and Edie had to escort them all back to the inner sanctum. She thought it was rude of the president not to come out and personally greet these important guests. And now, after letting senators, congressmen, and

CEOs cool their heels in the front room, she decides to give special treatment to this old crone. It didn't make sense.

Edie didn't have much time to try to solve the enigma because in less than a minute the President walked up to Millicent DeVere, a huge smile draped across her face.

"I've been looking forward to meeting you for a very long time, Lady DeVere." DellaRosa enveloped the dainty outstretched hand of her guest in both of hers. "We have so much to talk about."

A faint upcurl of the lip was her only acknowledgment of the president's effusive greeting.

DellaRosa led her into her office to a glass-top coffee table. They sat facing each other. "Thank you so much for coming. And please allow me to express my sincerest sympathy in regards to the untimely death of your brother and sister-in-law.

"It was a great shock to us all." Lady DeVere inclined her head slightly and smiled benignly. "The flowers from the university were quite exquisite."

"It was the least we could do. Your brother was extraordinarily generous." After a few seconds of awkward silence the president asked, "Would you like some coffee or tea?"

"Tea would be lovely. Darjeeling, if you have it." She gazed around the room, nodding approvingly at the many plaques and citations.

DellaRosa pressed the intercom button on her telephone. "Edie, will you please bring us two cups of tea, Darjeeling if we have it."

"Yes, ma'am," came the electronically amplified answer. Edie was sure that the president knew that Lipton was the only brand of tea they kept in the office. She would now have to spend the next ten minutes trying to find a box of Darjeeling.

"I'm surprised you didn't invite professor Berg to our little tête-à-tête," Lady DeVere said, creasing her eyebrows. "I should have thought that the prospect of a ten million dollar gift would have excited even the blasé Lion of Literature."

DellaRosa sat up stiffly in her chair, then quickly composed herself and said, "Mea culpa. I haven't informed Spenser yet. After we finalize the details, I thought you would like the pleasure of giving him the news yourself."

"That's very thoughtful but wouldn't Spenser want to play a role in the disbursement of the funds?"

"I highly doubt it. Spenser has no patience for the financial side of things."

"That's not been my experience," she said pointedly. "I've been acquainted with him for many years and as long as I've known him, the subject of money has always fascinated him. In fact, I remember him once remarking that if he hadn't been bitten by the literary bug, he would have enjoyed investment banking."

DellaRosa demurely placed her hand over her mouth to stifle a subtle chuckle. "Spenser Berg, an investment banker, that's one I hadn't heard before."

"Why do you laugh?" Lady DeVere said indignantly. "The man possesses one of the great intellects of our time. There's no endeavor at which he wouldn't excel."

"I couldn't agree with you more," the president said, imagining with horror the specter of ten million dollars escaping her grasp. "Of course Spenser is absolutely brilliant, but as you know, he can be extremely indolent as well. It's picturing him in the frenetic investment banking lifestyle that I found amusing."

"I always considered him to be a man of boundless energy."

"Well, yes, when his interest is piqued."

"If ten million dollars isn't enough to arouse his interest, I'm sure I don't know what is."

"Of course, you're correct, Lady DeVere."

"Yes, I'm sure I am."

DellaRosa gazed out the window for a moment, then busied herself rearranging some papers on the table. "You mentioned in your note that you wanted to discuss some parameters of the endowment," she said without looking up.

"That is correct. I have some very specific guidelines."

"Guidelines?"

"As you may or may not know, my late brother and I are direct descendants of Edward de Vere, the 17th Earl of Oxford. I'm sure you are aware that for a long while, many highly credible experts have believed that Oxford did, in fact, create the plays and poetry attributed to the man who called himself William Shakespeare. Spenser Berg confided in me that he is on the verge of announcing to the world that this is true. A major portion of this endowment must be set aside to ensure that his work continues and that my ancestor will be universally recognized as the peerless genius that he was."

Before DellaRosa could respond, Edie walked in, carrying a polished silver tray. On it was a plate with a half dozen small puff pastries and several packets of Twining's Darjeeling teabags, also a teapot, two cups, a creamer, and sugar bowl — all in white porcelain with delicately rendered flowers and butterflies — hastily snatched from the president's residence. She placed the tray in the middle of the coffee table and a cup in front of each lady, filling them halfway with hot water from the pot. Throughout this ritual Edie's mien was stiff and formal. When she finished she bowed slightly and walked briskly out of the room.

Lady DeVere eyed the tray with distaste.

"Bag tea," she said scornfully. "I guess it will have to do."

DellaRosa ignored the comment, picked up her cup and sipped in silence. Then she said, "You know, most Shakespearian scholars are quite sure that the works were, in fact, written by the Stratford man, while still others are proponents of Marlowe, Bacon and various assorted candidates, including Queen Elizabeth, herself. Suppose Dr. Berg's research concludes that the author was someone other than Oxford, will the endowment remain in force?"

Lady DeVere smiled serenely. "Spenser assured me that he has definitive proof."

DellaRosa raised her eyebrows in dismayed surprise. "Oh. He never mentioned anything to me about that. Did he say what sort of proof he had?"

"He didn't. But I hope for the university's sake that he's correct."

"I'm sure he will be proven to be the genius we know he is."

"And when that happens, the DeVere name will be elevated to the exalted position that we have been denied for several centuries."

"That will be an exciting time for you and for this university," DellaRosa said, glancing at her watch. "Speaking of time, I'm afraid I have another meeting I mustn't be late for. It's been a great pleasure to finally meet you."

Lady DeVere stood. "Thank you very much for the tea, Dr. DellaRosa."

"No. Thank you for all you're doing for this university," the president said as she escorted her back into the anteroom.

As she passed Edie on her way out, Lady DeVere said, "Thank you, my dear."

"You're quite welcome," Edie said as the slender old lady strode purposefully into the elevator.

As soon as the elevator door closed, DellaRosa barked at Edie, "Get MacArthur and Peltz in here now!"

Chapter 18

Jordan remained at her desk for most of the afternoon, staring blankly at the frontispiece of a 73-year-old Northern Chinese cookbook. It would eventually take its place next to the library's 2,600 other such books (the library boasted the largest collection of English language Chinese cookbooks in the world), but she couldn't bring herself to catalog it.

Josh broached the subject of their foray into Berg's house but Jordan's only response was a silent frown and a curt shake of her head. He busied himself reshelving books in the archive stacks, trying to stay out of her way.

When the doorbell rang, they both ran for it, nearly colliding in the main reading room. "We almost had a Three Stooges moment there," Josh said with a sheepish grin.

Jordan nodded back, her lips tilting slightly upward. It wasn't exactly a smile but it was the closest she had come to one all day.

"I'll get it," Josh said.

He opened the door to Tristan and Gabriel.

The boy hurried quickly past him.

Harry and Josh stood in the doorway facing each other for several awkward seconds.

Harry broke the strained silence. "Harry Gabriel."

The handshake that usually followed was not forthcoming.

"Josh Campanella, I work here with Jordan."

He turned and walked back to the office. Harry followed.

They walked through the dimly lit anteroom, decorated with vintage Daniel Patrick Moynihan campaign posters (the library was the repository of Moynihan's collected papers) and found Jordan and Tristan sitting at a large table in the main reading room, already in the middle of a heated discussion. Josh sat down at an adjacent table while Harry stood with his hands clasped in front of him.

Jordan glared up at him and bristled. "Tristan just informed me about your little escapade. How dare you drag my brother into the middle of a crime scene, especially after I specifically asked you not to."

Tristan raised his hand and said "But..."

Jordan scowled at him. "You be quiet."

She turned her ire back at Harry. "How irresponsible can you be! Don't you realize that you exposed him to grave danger? The police might have been watching the house. The maniac who murdered Dr. Berg could have been lurking." She paused for a breath, then yelled, "Are you insane or just idiotic!?"

Harry's jaw dropped open but no words emerged.

Tristan jumped up. "Harry didn't want me to go with him. I made him take me."

She faced her brother. "And how did you do that? With a gun? A knife?"

"C'mon, Jor. You know it wasn't like that."

"What I know is...you're still a twelve-year-old boy who is capable of making some very dumb decisions, no matter how high your I.Q. is."

"I know...and I'm sorry. But don't blame Harry, it was all my fault. He didn't want me to go inside the house. I begged him. He even warned me that you'd be really angry when you found out."

"He was absolutely correct." She turned to Harry. "Stay away from my brother or I'll have you brought up on kidnapping charges."

Gabriel was silent for a few seconds, then he erupted. "Hold on a minute. I know you've had a rough day. So have I. In the last 24 hours, I've been threatened and insulted in front of hundreds of people. Then I got the third degree from the campus Keystone Kops, who did everything but clap me in irons and lock me up for murder. The last thing I need are threats from you."

"I'm not interested in what you need." She glowered at him. "I'm interested in my brother's well-being. And you put him in a perilous situation."

"I didn't put him anywhere. He came of his own free will. In fact, I did everything but throw him out of my car to keep him from coming with me."

"He's a twelve-year-old boy and you're a grown man. Don't tell me you couldn't have stopped him if you wanted to."

"I could have and I probably should have. But I'm glad I didn't. Your baby brother has more brains and more guts than most adults I know. Maybe you should have taken him with you when you broke into Berg's house today instead of this loser." He jerked his head derisively at Josh, then turned quickly back to Jordan.

Jordan's eyes widened. "How did you know we were there?"

"We saw you. Both of you."

"You're lying. The house was empty."

"You were searching for Shakespeare's table while your friend over there was doubled over in fright. The only thing he had the strength to do was to tell you that I'm a monster and a murderer."

"You heard that?" Jordan said. Josh stiffened in his chair.

"Every word." Harry glared at Josh.

Josh stood and faced Harry. "I'm glad you heard it. I stand by everything I said. There's been nothing but misery and death at this university since you arrived."

"What the hell are you talking about?" Harry shouted.

"Everywhere you go trouble follows. You're in this room for two minutes and Jordan and Tristan are screaming at each other. I've never seen them fight in the three years I've known them." Inhaling through his clenched teeth, he wagged a finger at Harry. "And then there's the murder. Everyone knows you did it. They're just afraid to say it out loud cause you're a big hotshot writer from New York City. Well, to me you're just a two-bit killer and I can't wait till the police put you away for the rest of your life."

Harry seethed with rage. "You're lucky I'm not a murderer or there'd be two dead bodies on campus right now." He stormed out of the room.

Jordan, Josh and Tristan sat uncomfortably, glancing back and forth at each other until Josh broke the silence.

"I can't stand people like that. They think they don't have to follow the rules that the rest of us live by just because they've gotten lucky and had a little success in life. Well, let's see what happens when they arrest him for Berg's murder."

"He may be a pompous, self-centered jerk." Jordan shot a quick glance over at Tristan, who was glaring at both of them. "But that doesn't mean he's guilty."

"Peltz and MacArthur think he is."

"Harry's not a jerk and he didn't murder anyone." Tristan shouted emphatically. "When we find out who did, and it won't be Harry, I want you to apologize."

"If you do, I will." Josh stood and offered his hand. "Deal?"

Tristan hesitated, then grasped Josh's hand and shook it. "Deal."

Josh turned and said to Jordan, "Why don't you take your brother home and get ready to meet Lady DeVere."

"Actually, Tristan and I are both going. It seems that she is an ardent follower of the New York Yankees. When I mentioned that Tristan is also a huge fan when I spoke to her on the phone, she got very excited. She said she rarely gets an opportunity to talk about baseball and insisted that I bring him along."

"Great!" Josh said, as he started towards his office. "I'm going to stick around here for a little while. I'm supposed to meet someone."

"Just make sure you lock up before you leave." Jordan turned to her brother. "Come on, Tris."

Chapter 19

Angelina DellaRosa's withering stare had been known to turn fearsome administrators jelly-legged in seconds. The people who worked closely with her called it "the glare" and strove to avoid it at all costs. At the moment, it was focused directly on Gregg MacArthur as he sat in the small chair in front of her mammoth desk. He was surprised to feel himself trembling slightly, like a second-grader on his first unscheduled visit to the principal's office.

"Where's Liz?" she said sharply. "I'm sure I asked to meet with both of you."

"She had to meet a reporter from Newsday. They're doing a big spread about Whale-a-Palooza."

"Are you sure she's not talking to him about Spenser Berg's murder?"

"What?"

She turned up the voltage on the glare and leaned forward. "Everyone around here seems to know all about it. We might as well give press briefings."

MacArthur squirmed in his seat, shifting his shoulders back and forth. "I'm sure that's not true, ma'am. We've been very discrete."

"Really? Our most important donor, Lady Millicent DeVere, was in here a little while ago and practically accused me of murdering Dr. Berg myself."

"DeVere? He's the one who got killed in that car crash outside campus a couple of months ago."

"That's right."

"I thought his wife died with him."

"She did. Her name was Annie, Annie Macaluso. She was on the faculty, a political science professor, wonderful teacher, the students loved her. Millicent DeVere is his spinster sister, his only survivor and only heir."

"So this sister, this Lady DeVere, she said that she knew Dr. Berg was murdered?"

"Not in so many words, but she knew. She kept asking about him, wanting to know why he wasn't here. Believe me, Chief, she knew. "

He sat stone still in his chair for a few seconds, staring at a spot a few inches above DellaRosa's head. Then he cleared his throat. "How would you like us to proceed, ma'am?"

"I want you to find the person who did this terrible thing. Quickly. How close are you to a solution?"

"We've interviewed several people and searched Dr. Berg's cottage, which we believe is the location where the original crime was committed."

"Do you know who the murderer is?"

"We have a very strong suspicion."

"Wellllll?" She managed to sound both skeptical and disdainful.

"We're looking at Harry Gabriel."

For several seconds, though to MacArthur it felt like millennia, DellaRosa was silent. Her gaze remained fixed on him as she slowly brought her clasped fingers up under her chin, resting it upon them, her head rocking slightly, almost imperceptibly, back and forth.

"So you and Ms. Peltz, after spending the better part of a day investigating the matter, have concluded that Harry Gabriel murdered Spenser Berg, decapitated him and placed his severed head on a spike outside the library sometime before six this morning."

"That is correct, ma'am." His voice cracked for the first time since Junior High.

"And his reason for perpetrating this horrific crime? I hope it's more than the fact that they disagreed on who wrote the plays attributed to William Shakespeare."

"We believe that Berg was blackmailing Gabriel, or at least was planning to."

DellaRosa folded her arms in front of her and eyed him disdainfully. "How did you arrive at this conclusion?"

"We found an envelope hidden in Berg's house filled with newspaper clippings of Gabriel."

"You know, of course, that Harry Gabriel was once a student of Dr. Berg."

"Yes ma'am."

"And that many professors keep up with the accomplishments of their students, especially ones as illustrious as Dr. Gabriel."

"Not all the clips were positive. Most put Gabriel in a bad light."

"If these are newspaper clippings, they're already in the public record. How can they be of use in a blackmail scheme?"

"We haven't quite worked it all out yet. But that's not all we got."

The glare was back. "I'm waiting."

"We think Gabriel had it in for Dr. Berg from the time he was rejected by him for a position on the Melville English faculty."

"Chief MacArthur," she said slowly and deliberately, as if talking to a ten-year-old. "Do you have any idea how many job applications we get here every day?"

"No ma'am," he said sheepishly.

"Hundreds. And almost all of them are rejected." She paused and stared down at MacArthur who said nothing, concentrating on keeping his lip from quivering. "How many of those people do you think murdered the person who turned them down?"

MacArthur hesitated. Not answering would make him look insubordinate or stupid, maybe both. Answering made him feel ridiculous. "None, ma'am," he said in a whisper.

"That's right, none. So far, your evidence is very weak. Have you anything else?"

The tie around his neck suddenly felt tighter. He reached up to loosen it, then thought better of it and put his hands back in his lap.

"We also found a hundred dollar bottle of single malt Scotch in Dr. Berg's house. Berg doesn't drink single malt but Gabriel does."

"Along with millions of other people, including my husband. Is he a suspect too?"

"No ma'am." The whisper grew fainter.

"So you're ready to accuse one of America's rising literary luminaries of murder and eradicate this university's reputation on the basis of a couple of newspaper clippings, a ten year old job rejection and a bottle of pricey whisky?"

"And other things." His voice broke on the word 'other.'

"Such as?"

"The manner in which the murder was carried out indicated that the perpetrator had knowledge of old English execution methods. Harry Gabriel has such knowledge."

DellaRosa shook her head. "So do most of the English faculty, Renaissance scholars and everyone who has seen the movie, 'Elizabeth I.' If you want to convince me that Gabriel is the murderer, you'll have to do better than that."

MacArthur sat up a little straighter, reached into his shirt pocket and handed her a sheet of baby blue notepaper, folded in half.

She opened it hesitantly. It was undated and typewritten.

My Dear Chief MacArthur,

I'm extremely concerned that my safety will be in jeopardy when Harry Gabriel arrives on campus. He is a violent drunkard, who for some reason believes that I am responsible for derailing his erstwhile academic career. He has threatened me with physical harm a number of times and has indicated to me on several occasions that should he ever return to Melville University, he would wreak his vengeance upon me. As you know, this homicidal miscreant is scheduled to speak here. Please be forewarned that if any ill shall befall me during his stay, Gabriel is most assuredly the perpetrator.

Yours very truly,

Spenser Berg

She refolded the sheet and handed it back to MacArthur. "When exactly did you receive this?"

"The day that Gabriel arrived on campus."

"Don't you find it odd that there is no signature?"

"Not especially, Ma'am. A lot of people don't sign their correspondence."

"Had Dr. Berg ever written to you before?"

"No."

"He has written to me many times. And his notes were always handwritten, never typed, and always signed and dated. Don't you find it a bit odd that this one time he would type his note and not write it?"

"I don't know, Ma'am."

"Well I do." She shook her head slowly. "I'm sorry Chief, but I just don't believe that this is credible. Anyone could have written it."

"But..."

"Have you shown this to anyone else?"

"No ma'am."

"Not even Ms. Peltz?"

"Absolutely not."

"Good. Please don't. If it turns out to be false it could be very embarrassing to the university."

She paused, gazed wistfully up, then back at MacArthur. "When I first arrived at Melville I had several goals. It pleases me to say that I've been able to achieve most of them. Unfortunately, one thing I haven't been able to do is to make our faculty more diverse. Some of the more strident civil rights organizations have even accused us of being racist."

"That's ridiculous."

"Of course it is. But once you get that reputation, it's nearly impossible to change it."

"Yes, ma'am."

"So how do you think they would react if we falsely accused one of the nation's foremost African American writers of murder?"

"African American? He's what, a quarter black!"

"He's black enough to galvanize the entire African American community against us if your accusation proves to be false."

"I understand," he said sheepishly.

"So no more talk about Gabriel. Now, do you have any other suspects?"

MacArthur sat up a little straighter, trying to regain some semblance of professional dignity. "We are investigating several leads and are considering other potential suspects."

"Oh really." She smiled sardonically. "Who?"

"Jordan Day, the librarian who first called it in."

"What reason could Miss Day have for killing Dr. Berg? As far as I know they hardly knew each other."

"They knew each other better than you think. While we were talking to her she received a note from Dr. Berg, apparently written before he was killed."

"That's very astute of you, Mr. MacArthur," she said derisively. "You're positive that he didn't write it after his death?"

He ignored the dig. "It indicated that Dr. Berg found some sort of table belonging to William Shakespeare and left it to the library under the provision that it remain strictly under Ms. Day's care."

"A table? What kind of table?"

"The letter didn't say. But I would think it would be very valuable if it belonged to Shakespeare, probably worth millions to whoever had it in their possession."

"Let me see if I have this right. Your theory is that Ms. Day, who couldn't be much more than 110 pounds, murdered Spenser Berg so that she could obtain this priceless table. Then she managed to decapitate him and impale his head on a spike outside her window, thereby positioning herself as a likely suspect. Is that it?"

"Yes, ma'am."

"I'm sure it takes a considerable amount of strength to actually sever a head. Do you have secret knowledge that Ms. Day is also a closet weightlifter?"

"No." He stared at his hands clasped in his lap, then at the pictures on the wall, finally he looked into Angelina DellaRosa's penetrating glare. "We're also looking at her assistant, Joshua Campanella."

"Josh Campanella? Why would he want to do away with Dr. Berg?"

"He and Day could be in it together."

"Oh, so now it's a conspiracy?" DellaRosa stood, keeping her eyes riveted on MacArthur. "I don't know whether to laugh or cry." She paced back and forth behind her chair. "Melville University is on the precipice of a cataclysmic disaster and you seem to think it's all a game."

"Not at all, ma'am."

"Oh no?" Now standing directly behind her chair, she grabbed the back of it, leaned over, squinted her eyes and pursed her lips in a derisive imitation of MacArthur. "It's Harry Gabriel, no it's Jordan Day, no it's Josh Campanella, maybe all three."

"That's how you conduct an investigation," he said forcefully. "You put together a list of suspects, then collect the evidence. That's what we're doing. It takes time. If you think someone else can do it better or faster, feel free to bring them in."

She walked over to MacArthur. "The point is Chief, we're running out of time. The largest event in the history of Melville University happens tomorrow. Thousands of alumni, dignitaries and students will flood the campus, along with dozens of reporters."

"I know that, ma'am," he said quietly. "I've been working on the security arrangements for six months."

"Well then, you know what will happen if a headless torso turns up in the reunion tent." She began pacing around her office, suddenly very interested in straightening pictures and rearranging the volumes on the bookcases.

"Don't worry, it's not going to turn up in the reunion tent or anyplace else. The body's in a safe place. We put it…"

"I don't want to know," she said before he could finish. "Just make sure no one finds it until Whale-a-Palooza is over."

"The body will stay hidden. Trust me." He didn't think it necessary at that moment to mention that the head in question did not accompany the body to its new hiding place.

"Trusting you is what's giving me this knot in my stomach." She turned and looked severely into MacArthur's eyes. "Just get on with your investigation but be careful. I don't want you accusing anyone, especially Harry Gabriel, until you are 100 percent certain of the suspect's guilt. " She waved her hand dismissively. "Now go and find out who did this terrible thing. And don't come back until you have proof. Ironclad proof!"

As MacArthur walked out of the office he noticed Peter Foote sitting in the reception area nervously picking at his cuticles. He mumbled a perfunctory hello on his way out.

"You can go in now, Peter," Edie Kaiser said without looking up from her computer.

"Thank you Edith." Foote trudged past her to the President's office.

"Peter, thank you for coming," DellaRosa said from behind her desk. "Please sit down."

He eased himself into the chair that Gregg MacArthur had just vacated.

Almost matter-of-factly, she said, "What do you know about Spenser Berg's disappearance?"

Foote shot bolt upright in his seat. "He wasn't at our monthly editorial meeting this morning and nobody's seen him since his altercation with Harry Gabriel last night."

"You haven't heard anything else?"

"Nothing I'd put any credence in."

"Please tell me what you heard that you believe isn't credible."

He paused for a few seconds, then said, "Ike Semansky brought Gabriel to our editorial meeting. He mentioned that the police questioned him about Spenser's disappearance."

DellaRosa clasped her hands in front of her and gazed severely at Foote. "There is an investigation ongoing and I'm hoping beyond hope that Spenser turns out to be fine. However, with the largest event in the University's history taking place tomorrow, we must prepare for the worst, even as we hope for the best. That is why I am naming you acting Chair of the English department effective immediately and placing you in charge of your department's Scholar's Showcase presentation."

Foote sat motionless in his chair, his eyes vacant.

"Dr. Foote, are you all right?"

"I'm sorry, Dr. DellaRosa, I was just processing." He looked up at the ceiling. "Spenser dead? It's unfathomable."

"I didn't say he was dead. Just missing. When did you see him last?"

"I was at the Gabriel lecture last night when Spenser confronted him. I've seen him ambush quite a few faculty members, myself included, but this was different. With the others, he was more or less tweaking their noses, but his time he was venomous. After it was over he was flushed, his hands were shaking and he was mumbling. Perhaps he had a heart attack."

"I don't think so, Dr. Foote."

"Why not?"

"Because if what we suspect is true, Spenser was decapitated."

Foote grimaced, covered his face with his hands and shouted, "Oh my God, you can't be serious!"

DellaRosa shook her head sadly. "I wish I wasn't."

"What are you going to do?"

"Right now we're just going to try to keep things as normal as possible, at least until Whale-a-Palooza is over."

He stiffened. "So there's a murderer roaming around campus and you're not doing anything about it?"

"On the contrary. Chief MacArthur and his team are doing everything possible to find out exactly what happened and apprehend whomever is responsible."

"I see." He nodded solemnly. "I'll do whatever you think best."

"I know Ike Semansky and Natasha Ferette are scheduled to do a book reading and signing in the Showcase. Make sure they do. As for tomorrow evening, Spenser is supposed to give a major presentation about the true author of the works of Shakespeare, I believe you worked with him on that."

"Yes, we collaborated."

"Will you be able to go on if Spenser is really..." Her eyes welled up. She couldn't finish her sentence.

"I'll be ready," he said softly.

"Thank you, Dr. Foote." She grabbed a tissue and began dabbing at her eyes.

Foote stood up slowly and eased out of the room without saying another word.

Chapter 20

The walls of the front lobby of the Humanities building were adorned with brass panels embossed with quotes from Shakespeare, Milton, Wordsworth, Keats and Tennyson. A small brass plaque next to the information panel read, "The Humanities Building restoration was made possible by a gift from the DeVere family."

Gabriel found Ferette's room number, then went up the circular stairway to her office. He was about to go in when he heard a voice behind him.

"What brings you to our little corner of purgatory?" It was Ike Semansky.

"I want show something to Dr. Ferette."

"I better go in there with you."

"Why?"

"Several men have never been seen again after entering Natasha's office when she's in a bitchy mood. And lately she's been bitchier than I've ever seen her." Semansky said with a sardonic smile. "You're a famous writer and an honored guest, we can't afford to lose you."

"Lead the way."

Semansky pushed the door open and marched into Ferette's smoke-filled office with Harry behind him. "Mr. Gabriel here wants to know why you killed Spenser Berg and what you did with the body."

The room went deathly silent. Ferette glared daggers at Semansky from behind her desk. Harry stood by the door, motionless.

"Come on, Tash, I'm joking," he said with a nervous laugh. "Harry has something he wants to show us." He turned to Gabriel. "So, let's have a look."

Semansky had already made himself comfortable on one of the chairs facing Ferette's desk, while Harry remained standing, shuffling uneasily from side to side, holding the manila envelope with both hands.

"So...do you know who the Campus Police's prime suspect is?"

Ferette jumped to her feet, her lip quivering, the cigarette dangling from her mouth Bogie-style. "I can't believe those puffed up mall cops think I did it. Well let them try to prove it. I had nothing to do with Berg's death, but I want to shake the hand of whoever did."

"What are you talking about?" Gabriel said, taken aback. "It's not you, it's me."

"You?" Ferette and Semansky said in unison.

"You hardly knew the old bastard," Semansky said. "It's those of us who work with him on a daily basis who have every reason to kill him. Is it because of what happened last night?"

"Yes, partly."

"We have those kinds of psychodramas several times a month. If someone was killed after every academic disagreement, this campus would be littered with corpses."

"Except last night, Berg was killed," Harry said. "Right after he threatened to ruin my career and I said that I would be happy to help him into the great beyond. And besides, Berg and I also had some history."

"Everybody had history with him," Semansky retorted. "He was the most despised man in academe."

"Harry," Ferette said. "If you didn't come here to warn me about being a suspect, why are you here?"

"I thought you might want these back." He handed her an envelope.

She spread the contents over her desk. There were four black and white glossy photos of a twenty-year-old crew cut Natasha Ferette and two other women about the same age, one with spikey hair dyed jet black, the other wearing a long, shiny blonde wig. They were posed, nude, in front of a giant wooden fruit bowl with huge plastic bananas, oranges and apples.

She perused the shots and smiled wryly. "The series was called 'Still Life With Barnard Babes.' My friend Olga took these. She was a double-major in Biology and Photography. She became a gastroenterologist. What a waste. She was a really talented photographer and the last thing the world needs is another gastroenterologist." She picked up one of the prints and examined it, then peered down at her chest. "My boobs are still perky, thank goodness."

Semansky grinned. "To quote the great Mae West, 'Goodness had nothing to do with it.' "

She looked over at Gabriel. "By the way, where did you find these?"

"In Berg's house."

"You were there? When?"

"The same time as you."

"So that was you we heard driving up?"

"No. I was there the whole time you were there. You and Peter Foote."

Semansky, who looked like he was still thinking about Mae West, jumped up. "You went to Berg's house with Peter? You said he was the second most insufferable person on campus."

"Actually with Berg dead, he's number one. But when I mentioned that I would love to have a quick look at Berg's cottage, he practically dragged me over there."

Harry said, "What was he looking for?"

"Nothing I could see. He just ran around the cabin like a headless chicken."

"And what were you looking for? It obviously wasn't the photos. You don't seem to care who sees those."

"What's with the third degree, Dirty Harry?"

"Just looking for the truth."

"The truth is, it's none of your goddamn business."

"Was it this?" He handed her the letter.

She grabbed it, read it quickly, ripped it into several pieces, then violently crushed her cigarette in a ceramic ashtray on the desk. "You bastard! I've been nauseous all day, worrying about this goddamn letter.

How long were you going to string me along until you showed it to me?"

"I could have left it there for the police to find. Then you'd be the prime suspect and not me."

"Don't give me that crap. You could have showed me the letter first. Instead you decided to try to humiliate me in front of Ike with those pictures. Well, it didn't work. Now get the hell out of my office and take Sancho Pansy with you."

"Just what I need, another enemy," Harry said as he and Ike left Ferette's office.

"Don't worry. She's thrown me out of her office dozens of times. She never stays mad for too long."

Harry shrugged. "I could use a drink. Can I get a decent single malt anywhere around here?"

Semansky looked at his watch. "Five- thirty. I didn't realize it was that late. There's a place over in Port Jefferson has the best scotch selection on Long Island. I planned to take you there last night to celebrate your triumphant return to campus but after what happened with Berg, I didn't think it was such a good idea."

"I think tonight it's a very good idea."

Chapter 21

Jordan waited until the young sailor-suited waitress was out of earshot. She and Tristan were seated at a table in the White Whale Inn, a historic bed and breakfast a few miles from campus. Ship's wheels, bells, harpoons and small anchors provided the decor. Each table had a miniature lantern at its center. Many of the other "early-bird" diners in the room looked as though they might have been present at the Inn's grand opening, reputed to have been a few years before the start of the Revolutionary War.

The last thing Jordan wanted to do at that moment was eat, which could pose a problem. She wasn't sure she could even speak coherently. Her stomach was roiling, her head clanging. Multiple immanent catastrophes swirled in her brain like thunderheads. Losing her job. Being arrested for murder. Seeing her brother in thrall to a man who was at best an irresponsible, egotistical alcoholic prone to violent outbursts and at worst a vicious killer.

She took a sip of water and tried to pull herself together. Falling apart at this moment would be a disaster. She would not only lose her best chance at keeping her job, she could lose the any influence she had over her brother.

She leaned in over the white damask tablecloth and said in a half-whisper, "Remember, not a word about any of what's been going on today. About Harry Gabriel, Dr. Berg, what you saw this afternoon, nothing." She lowered her voice even more. "The lady we're having dinner with is very wealthy and very important."

"We're wasting time," Tristan snapped. "We should be trying to find out who killed Spenser Berg, not having dinner with some stupid old biddy."

"Keeping my job depends on this 'stupid old biddy.' "

"What are you talking about?"

"I haven't told you, but the dean is considering eliminating Special Collections unless we can provide our own funding. Lady DeVere is donating her family papers to the library. I have to convince her to donate a lot more. If I can't, they'll close the department down and I'll probably be out of a job."

"If you get arrested for murder you'll definitely be out of a job."

Jordan looked around furtively. "Please keep your voice down," she whispered. "You never know who might be sitting at another table, listening"

Tristan smirked. "Come on, Jor, look at these geezers. We're probably the only ones in this room who can hear anything at all. And the ones who aren't hard of hearing are probably blind."

Jordan shook her head and sighed. "You spend a little time with Harry Gabriel and you're already turning into a major wise-ass." She tried to keep the anxiety out of her voice. "Do you think I want to be here after everything that's happened today?"

Tristan reached across the table and grabbed Jordan's hand. "I'm sorry. I'm being a brat. I'll do whatever I can to help."

"Just be your sweet, charming, intelligent self."

She looked up and saw Lady DeVere walking toward the table with the hostess.

The spry septuagenarian stopped to say hello to diners at several tables on her way. As she approached, Jordan stood. Tristan also rose awkwardly to his feet.

"Jordan dear, you look lovelier than ever," Millicent DeVere said. She stood on her toes to kiss the much taller woman on the cheek.

She turned to Tristan. "And this must be your brilliant brother about whom I've heard so much." She thrust out her hand. "Pleased to meet you, young man. I'm Millicent DeVere."

Tristan grasped the hand and shook it gently. "I'm Tristan. It's nice to meet you too."

"Lady DeVere, thank you so much for your wonderful gift," Jordan said after they settled into their seats, "I can't tell you how excited I was when Dr. Childress told me about it. For the Melville University Library to be the home of the DeVere papers elevates our collection to top tier status."

Lady DeVere smiled demurely. "That's very flattering, my dear. But your collection is quite prestigious in its own right. For my money you're already one of the nation's top libraries." She reached across the table and clasped Jordan's hand in both of hers. "The fact that you have agreed to house some of our musty old papers does more for the DeVere family's reputation than your library's."

"You're very kind."

DeVere glanced up at the interlocking NY on the baseball cap sitting slightly askew on Tristan's head. "Judging by your cap, I see you follow the New York Yankees. So what do you think they need to do to get back to the post-season. This is the second year in a row that they didn't make the playoffs. I believe either a top of the rotation starter or a thumper in the middle of the lineup would do the trick. Perhaps both if they're willing to pay the luxury tax."

Tristan's jaw dropped. He gaped at the elderly woman with the slight British lilt in her voice as if she was a creature from another planet. "Y...you're a Yankee fan?"

"Have been since the days of Rizzuto and DiMaggio. Now those boys had heart, especially the Scooter. I'd take him on my team over any of the Yankees playing today."

"You saw Joe DiMaggio play?" he said with wonder.

"Oh yes, many times. What an outfielder! Back then it was 460 feet to left center and he got to every ball hit out there. And graceful, like Nureyev."

Tristan squinted in concentration as he tried to remember the name. "Who did Nureyev play for?"

"The Kirov Ballet, the Royal Ballet and the American Ballet

Theater," Jordan interjected. "He was only one of the best ballet dancers who ever lived."

"Yes, a lovely dancer, but not a very lovely man." Lady DeVere's eyes had a far-away gleam and her head shook slowly as she lapsed into a quick reverie.

"You knew Rudolph Nureyev?" Jordan asked, awestruck.

"I didn't know him, really, but we did meet on several occasions." Her dreamy expression became a grimace. "For a dancer of such supreme grace and elegance, he was an extraordinarily crude and uncouth boor."

Before Jordan could reply, the waitress arrived for their orders. When she left, Lady DeVere turned to Tristan. "Didn't I see you at the Rogers Theater last night?"

He nodded. "Yes. I thought Harry Gabriel was awesome."

"I thought his theory was interesting but extraordinarily farfetched. Shakespeare as Marlowe's assassin? Preposterous. What do you think, Miss Day?"

"I'm sorry, but I wasn't able to attend." Jordan slumped back in her seat.

"You missed a fascinating evening, my dear. I thought I heard every possible theory about Shakespeare, but Gabriel's was by far the most inventive."

"You're a Shakespeare scholar?" Tristan asked.

"Not exactly. A family interest. My late brother and I are direct descendants of the Earl of Oxford, the true author."

"You believe Oxford wrote works attributed to William Shake-speare?" Jordan sat up a little straighter.

"I'm absolutely positive of it. In fact, Spenser mentioned to me that he found definitive proof during his last visit to London."

"Proof?" Jordan stiffened. "What kind of proof?"

"He didn't actually mention what it was. He was being quite mysterious."

"If he had proof, why didn't he let us see it last night instead of going after Harry the way he did?" Tristan said, practically jumping out of his seat.

"I have no idea," DeVere replied. "Spenser's ad hominem attack upon Mr. Gabriel was most unfortunate. I believe there was some bad blood going back to when Gabriel was his student."

The waitress arrived with their food. Tristan attacked his hamburger immediately. He was halfway done before either of the women touched their salads.

The two perfectly round balls of white goat cheese in Jordan's plate stared up at her like Little Orphan Annie's eyes. She mashed them with her fork but didn't eat anything, then looked up at Lady DeVere. "Do any of the documents in your collection pertain to the Shakespeare authorship issue?"

"Not directly." The older woman picked at the green beans in her salad. "I believe the earliest document is dated around the mid-1700's, whereas my ancestor Edward de Vere lived in the last half of the 16th century."

"Then how can you be so sure that the Earl of Oxford was really the one who wrote the plays?" Tristan demanded.

"The man from Stratford had very little education, had never traveled outside of England and had no way of acquiring the very detailed knowledge of history, botany, geography, law, courtly behavior, or any of the other disciplines that the person who wrote the plays would have to have been very familiar with. Oxford, on the other hand, was well traveled, superbly educated and known to be a gifted writer. He was also part of the Earl of Essex's inner circle, giving him intimate knowledge of the royal court."

"Shakespeare was a genius," Tristan said. "Maybe the greatest genius of all time. A man with that kind of awesome intellect could have learned those things from books or from talking to people."

"Yes, he could have done," DeVere acknowledged. "But he would have to have been one of the most brilliant men who ever lived."

"A lot of people think he was."

"If William Shakespeare was the greatest genius of all time, why is it that his titanic intellect concealed itself until he was well into his twenties? Minds that brilliant almost always reveal themselves in childhood, or at least adolescence. Mozart was composing symphonies at five, daVinci painted masterpieces at fourteen. Shakespeare was twenty-five before he had written anything of note. And then, why did a man with so much wit, eloquence and brilliance hide his genius under a bushel? All the other notable playwrights and poets of that time — Marlowe, Jonson, Spenser — were highly sought after for their commentary and analysis of other plays, poems and events of the day. Shakespeare is never heard from. In fact, other than the plays and poems, the only other writing established to be by William Shakespeare of Stratford are a few lines of doggerel on his headstone and some legal papers, all of which appear to be written by a semi-literate bumpkin, not the greatest wordsmith who ever lived."

"Then I'll ask you the same question Harry asked Dr. Berg." He paused for emphasis. "How can Oxford have been the author of the thirteen plays that were written after he died?"

"I'm impressed, young man," DeVere said earnestly. "You really do know your Shakespeare. The answer is simple. The chronology of the plays is anyone's guess. The dates are only estimates. All of them could have been written before 1604, which would make it perfectly feasible for Oxford to have been the author."

Jordan, desperate to change the subject, said, "Now about your collection, if I may ask, exactly how large is it?"

"Oh, several boxes at least. Except I'm afraid that many of the papers are not in a very good state of repair."

"Don't worry. We have a climate controlled vault and other equipment designed to preserve fragile documents."

"I see. And I assume they will be well protected. "

"You have nothing to worry about there. We have an outstanding security system. You're welcome to come up to Special Collections any time and examine our facilities."

"Really? Any time I want?" A mischievous grin spread across Lady DeVere's face.

"Of course."

"How about right now?"

Jordan's head snapped back. "Now?"

"Well, we can finish our dinners of course, but yes, tonight."

"Why?" Jordan rustled nervously in her chair. "I mean, what's the hurry?"

"I'm a person who likes to strike when the iron is hot. You young people today are always so busy, who knows when we'll have another opportunity. You say 'why now?' I say 'why not?' "

"Well, yes, I guess now would be okay." Jordan turned to her brother. "You don't have to go back to the library with us if you don't want to."

"I'd love to go." He grinned. "I've never been in the vault."

Lady DeVere clapped her hands gleefully in front of her. "Well then, it's settled. As soon as we finish dinner, we'll go back to the library and see this wonderful archive of yours."

Though it was the last place she wanted to go, Jordan smiled sweetly and said, "It'll be my pleasure."

Twenty minutes later Jordan unlocked the door of the Melville University Department of Archives and Special Collections. She flicked the light on and held the door for Tristan and Lady DeVere, who looked around at the Daniel Patrick Moynihan posters and said, "You know I met the senator several times, very sweet man. I didn't care for his wife, though," she said with a scowl. "Extremely overbearing."

Jordan nodded noncommittally. All she wanted to do was get this over with and go home.

Located at the far end of the main reading room, the vault had a thick steel door with an impressive combination lock.

"This is where the DeVere papers will be kept," Jordan said, forcing a smile. "As you can see it is very secure. It's climate controlled and has its own dedicated alarm system."

Lady DeVere smiled contritely. "I'm sorry to put you to all this trouble, dear. But may I have a quick look inside?"

Suppressing a scowl, Jordan said, "Of course." She dialed the three-number combination, pulled the door open and disappeared inside the room-sized chamber. The next sound Tristan and Lady DeVere heard was an ear-piercing scream.

They rushed in to find Jordan propped against the wall, hands covering her eyes, shaking uncontrollably. Next to her on the vault floor was the lifeless, twisted body of Josh Campanella. A yellow nylon rope was tied tightly around his neck.

Chapter 22

Ten minutes later, Chief MacArthur walked through the Special Collections door with Lizzie Peltz trailing behind him. He went into the vault and took some pictures with his phone. Then he began questioning Jordan. After he established when and how the body was discovered and that nothing in the vault was touched, he started grilling her about Josh.

"Did Campanella have any enemies?"

"None that I know of."

"Was he depressed? Suicidal?"

"No. Not at all."

"Did he gamble?"

"I don't think so."

"Was he dating anyone?"

"No."

"Any jilted lovers or irate husbands around who might have it in for him?"

That actually elicited a tiny smile.

"Did I say something funny, Ms. Day?"

"No, of course not. It's just that Josh never seemed to be interested in women. I think he may have been gay, but we never really discussed it."

"His sexual orientation may or may not be pertinent to the case," MacArthur said sternly. "Can you think of anyone who might have a grudge against him? Has he fought with anyone recently?"

"Well, uh, no." She looked away from MacArthur for several seconds. "Not really." She glanced quickly at Tristan.

"What do you mean, 'not really'? Either he has or he hasn't."

"No, he hasn't fought with anybody." She looked over at Tristan again.

"Why do you keep staring at your brother. Does he have anything to do with this?"

He turned toward Tristan, pointing his finger at him like a gun. "Young man, do you have anything to tell me about what happened to Mr. Campanella?"

Tristan shrank into his chair. "No sir."

"Mr. MacArthur," Millicent DeVere spoke as if she were talking to a slightly slow second-grader. "There's no reason to interrogate this young man as if he were a common thug. He's been through enough today just seeing..." She motioned with her head towards the vault room. "That."

"I appreciate your concern, ma'am, but there have been two murders on campus and I don't have time to baby anyone who might help us find the maniac who is responsible. We may be dealing with a serial killer."

"Two murders...my God!" DeVere shrieked and covered her eyes. You mean someone else was killed on these grounds today. I haven't heard anything about a second murder."

MacArthur turned to Liz, who sat uncharacteristically demurely on the couch. "Could you take Lady DeVere for a walk outside and fill her in on what's been going on?"

She cocked an eyebrow. "Are you sure that's what you want?"

"I'm positive. She's a key witness to the second murder. She needs to know the whole story."

The feisty old lady jumped to her feet, her hands defiantly on her hips. "I'm not leaving these two young people to fend for themselves."

"It's okay," Jordan said.

Lady DeVere glared over at MacArthur, then turned to Jordan. "Are you sure you'll be all right, dear?"

"We'll be perfectly fine," she answered.

Lady DeVere reached into her handbag and produced a vellum calling card. On it in embossed gold foil lettering was written 'Annabelle Millicent DeVere' and a phone number. She handed it to Jordan. "Please call if you need my assistance."

Lizzie put her arm around Lady DeVere and walked her out of the room, saying, "Let me start from the beginning..."

Then she shut the door.

MacArthur sat down on the couch, took a deep breath and, stared directly into Jordan's eyes.

"I understand that this has been a really tough day for you. For someone to come upon a dead body is extremely traumatic. To discover two in one day is more than anyone should have to endure. If I were a religious person I would say that God put that burden on you because he knew you could handle it. Now I need you to share some of that burden with me."

He paused, glanced over at Tristan, then back at Jordan. "Who did Campanella fight with?"

She said nothing.

"Ms. Day, if the person you're shielding had nothing to do with it, we'll rule him out and be done with it. But if he is the murderer..."

Just as she was about to speak Tristan yelled, "Don't say anything."

"I have to. We can't be sure that he's not involved."

"I'm sure!" Her brother screamed.

"Sorry, Tris." She turned to look at MacArthur. "It was Harry Gabriel. He and Josh had some words this afternoon."

"Gabriel." A self-satisfied smile snaked across his thin lips. "I should have known."

"Harry didn't have anything to do with this," Tristan said, quite agitated.

"You may be right, young man, but the evidence disagrees," MacArthur said.

"What evidence?" Tristan snapped back.

"Gabriel fought with Spenser Berg last night and with Josh Campanella this afternoon. Now they're both dead. How do you explain that?"

"I don't have to explain anything to you. You made up your mind that Harry is guilty and nothing I say is going to change it."

He stormed out of the room.

"Tristan, stop!" Jordan stood and shouted after him.

MacArthur, now also on his feet, held up a hand.

"Let him go," he said calmly. "The kid's had a rough day. He idolizes Gabriel and he's upset thinking that his hero might be a murderer. Let him walk around for awhile and clear his head." He opened his notebook, grabbed a pen from his shirt pocket and said, "Now, tell me exactly what went on between Gabriel and Campanella?"

Jordan recapped Harry's argument with Josh.

MacArthur nodded his head periodically. "By the way, this location is now a crime scene. I'm afraid we're going to have to cordon off the area. You won't be able to work here for awhile."

"Believe me, I don't want to be here any longer than I have to." She shuddered, glancing quickly at the vault room. "But could you give me a few minutes? I need go back and get some things from my office for the event tomorrow."

MacArthur nodded. "Of course. Just don't disturb anything."

"Thank you, Chief," Jordan said, and walked to the front door.

"Hey, I thought your office was that way," MacArthur pointed towards the rear.

She stopped in the doorway and turned. "It is. There's another way to get to the back offices." She glanced at the vault. "I'd rather not go through there again."

"I understand."

Chapter 23

Jordan opened her office door to find her usually meticulous office a shambles. Drawers were flung open, books and papers strewn around the room, furniture displaced.

The exhibition case was toppled over, it's tempered glass shattered. The first edition of Herman Melville's Typee, signed and inscribed by him to his cousin Maria Peebles, was gone. Though quite valuable in its own right, it had special significance for Jordan. She acquired it for the university at auction, an accomplishment she considered one of the highlights of her tenure as head of Special Collections.

The murderer was here, she thought. He was looking for something. What? Then she realized it was the table that Berg wrote her about. How could he know about that? Only MacArthur, Peltz and Jason knew about it. Her head swirled. That's why he was killed. She gasped for air as she walked clumsily to a chair, gripping the arms with both hands as she sat. Her first instinct was to run back to the main office but what would she tell MacArthur? That her office was a mess? He wouldn't interrupt his work at the murder scene for that. And she was sure that the murderer was long gone. What should she do?

Her office was a crime scene. She didn't know when she'd be allowed back here again or what kind of damage there was or would be after the police got through processing it. She went over to a pile of books and papers that were dumped haphazardly in the corner. The Typee first edition was there. Undamaged, thank God. She carefully put it in an acid-free padded envelope and left it on the credenza.

She then spent the next few minutes trying to tidy up her office. She set aside several rare documents, pamphlets and papers to take with her for the next day's Scholar's Showcase exhibition. She had also been told to bring the ceremonial gold-plated shovel used at the university's initial groundbreaking ceremony for the 'Melville U Through the Years' exhibition. It was stored in Josh's closet.

Stepping into Josh's office, she felt his presence everywhere. His faded blue Mets cap hanging on a hook by the door, the 'Frank Zappa Live at Melville U' poster taped to the wall, his Star Trek coffee mug with grounds of the last few days still caked at the bottom, along with the papers, sticky notes and folders were scattered haphazardly all over his desk.

She began straightening the mess as she always did when suddenly, the shock of his murder hit her all over again. She crumpled into his chair and wept.

Wiping her eyes after a minute, she was about to look for the shovel when she noticed a yellow sticky note stuck to the handset of Josh's telephone. "STRAREFRAG" was scrawled on it with black magic marker. She peeled it off the phone, folded it in half and put it in her back pocket as a memento, sadly realizing that it may have been the last words he had ever written.

There was a storage closet, more like a super-sized walk-in junk drawer, at the rear of Josh's office. She was pretty sure that the ceremonial shovel was in there, along with various boxes and storage containers filled with items considered not important enough to put in the display cases in the main room, not valuable enough to take up space in the vault, but not yet ready to be discarded.

Jordan opened the door and tugged on the chain dangling from the ceiling to turn on the bare overhead bulb. Nothing happened.

"Crap!" she muttered. "I'll have to get Josh to change..." Then she remembered that Josh wasn't going to change anything ever again. She sighed, her shoulders slumped and she teared up again. The last time she saw the ceremonial shovel it was propped up against the left-hand wall towards the back of the closet. Carefully stepping over and around the assorted boxes, bundles and bags, she rummaged in the dark and found it. Holding it with both hands, she slowly turned around, not wanting to trip over the junk littering the floor.

Two strong hands gripped her throat, squeezing hard. Pain and panic shot through her like an electric charge. She tried to scream but only a muffled croak emerged from her constricted windpipe.

Feeling faint, gasping for air, she struggled futilely to break free. Then she realized that she had a weapon. The shovel. Summoning her last ounce of strength, she swung it blindly behind her and felt a thud.

"Ughhh!" Came a groan just inches from her ear as the stranglehold loosened slightly.

She swung one more time, again connecting, this time the sound was more a ping than a thud. Steel on bone? Then she heard a yelp of pain as the grip on her throat was released. She felt a sharp sting as her attacker grabbed hold of the slim gold chain around her neck and ripped it off as she ran out of the dark closet.

Dropping the shovel, she sprinted through Josh's office and into the corridor. She raced to the rear exit and ran down two flights of stairs. She pushed the exit bar on the first floor door. It didn't move. Frantic, she pushed again, harder. Same result. Then she rammed it with her shoulder. It still wouldn't budge.

She remembered that all the first floor auxiliary exit doors were locked so students couldn't bypass the security sensors at the main entrance and steal books and dvd's.

She felt trapped. She hurried back up the stairs, praying she wouldn't run into her attacker. She tried the second-floor door. It had locked behind her. The third-floor door also held fast. Heart pounding, lungs burning, shoulder throbbing, she made it to the fourth-floor, put both hands on the push-bar, said a silent prayer, and shoved. It opened.

Row upon row of six-foot high metal bookcases greeted her. Foreboding even during the day, the dark, cavernous space seemed even more ominous at night with most lights turned off after hours to save electricity. The only sounds she heard were her own labored breathing rhythmically echoing in her ears and the pat-pat-pat of her footsteps as she half-walked half-ran down one of the rows, heading for the stairwell that led to the main exit, the only one she was sure would be open.

The good news was that she probably knew the layout of the stacks better than anyone at the college. When she started working at the university, one of her first duties was taking students on library tours. In addition to knowing the locations of all the exits, the freight elevator and even the dumbwaiters that at one time were used to transport books from one floor to another, she knew that the walls were lined with sound-deadening material so that students could study in relative silence. It also meant crying for help would be useless.

The fourth-floor stacks extended the entire block-long length of the building, which felt like miles to Jordan. As she got closer to the exit door she broke into a run when suddenly it flew open and a large, shadowy figure started towards her with an awkward gait, a result of Jordan striking his shin with the shovel. It was too dark to make out any of her attacker's features.

She screamed, turned and ran, darting from one row to another, trying to use the labyrinthine layout of the stacks to her advantage. As she ran she heard the heavy arrhythmic footfalls of her pursuer. He was limping, she thought. Maybe that would give her a chance.

Arriving at one of the freight elevators, she hit the button, hoping luck would be with her, the door would open and the car would be waiting to carry her to safety. It wasn't. And she couldn't risk waiting around for it to arrive. She turned and ran again, with no real destination, just trying to put some distance between herself and whoever it was that was chasing her, probably the same homicidal maniac who murdered Dr. Berg and Josh.

She reached another exit door, this one had an alarm on it. Hopefully, when she pushed it open, the alarm would blare, scaring off her attacker and bringing the police. She inhaled deeply, shoved the door open and...nothing. The police must have disabled the alarm system to process the crime scene. Exhausted and terrified, she ran down to the third floor. It was laid out differently than the fourth, with the Circulation desk and several book bins in the center. There was a large wire mesh security cage next to the circulation area where recently returned books were stored prior to reshelving. This meant that there were only five rows of stacks on either side.

Without thinking, she ran to her right. She could hear the heavy, uneven footfalls thumping down the stairs. The energy burst she had from the rush of fear and adrenalin had dissipated. Her head was spinning, her legs jelly. She leaned against the wall, gulping air. She willed herself to keep going but her body wouldn't cooperate. She couldn't see her attacker, but she could hear him coming ever closer. She moved some empty book trucks looking for someplace to hide when she saw the old dumbwaiter. It looked like an oversized medicine cabinet, about four feet wide, two feet high and another two feet deep, a perfect size for transporting books from floor to floor, but not so good for humans. Desperate, Jordan flung open door and squeezed herself in, folding her legs under her torso, her head tucked into her chest. She said a silent thank you to her yoga instructor and for the classes she'd been taking for the past year.

She could see the shadowy figure lumbering towards her as she reached for the rope that that served as the inside handle to pull the door closed. It broke in her hand. He was almost upon her. She desperately dug her fingers into it and managed to get it shut. She hit the first-floor button and prayed that after all these years the dumbwaiter still worked.

Nothing happened. She kept pressing it in panic and frustration. She steeled herself for the attack that was sure to come. Then suddenly she felt movement as the rusty gears screeched and rattled, then slowly it began to make its way down to the first floor. She could hear her pursuer banging on the dumbwaiter door. After what was surely the longest thirty seconds of her life, it jolted to a halt. She prised the door open. Ignoring her fatigue and pain, she unfolded herself from the small compartment and squeezed out, scraping her legs and arms on the sidewalls. She was just twenty feet from the main entrance. She hobbled to it, pushed open the door and was out on the central mall.

Utterly spent, she collapsed on a bench under streetlamp in front of the library. She hoped the lamplight and the smattering of students would be enough to keep her safe. She dialed MacArthur's number.

"Chief, I've been attacked."

"Where are you."
"In front of the library."
"Don't go anywhere. I'll be right down."

Chapter 24

"Welcome to Braveheart's," said the giant of a man in a voice as husky as he was. About six-five and easily 300 pounds, his thick, red, curly hair and full beard were tinged with gray. What commanded Gabriel's attention was the blue tartan kilt and the knife with the intricately designed handle tucked into his knee-high white socks. His accent, though, had the echo of the New York City streets, not the Scottish highlands.

"Hello Tommy, how are you tonight?" Semansky said with a grin as he and Gabriel walked into the bar.

"Can't complain. Getting a little chilly, though." He glanced quickly down at his kilt.

"I told my friend Harry that this is the best bar for single malt on all of Long Island."

"A whisky man, huh." The big man smiled and thrust out a meaty paw. "Tom Buchanan, glad to know you."

"Harry Gabriel." He shook the proffered hand.

"The writer?"

"You've heard of him?" Semansky said.

"Oh yeah, I've read a few Mr. Gabriel's books."

"Tommy, I never saw you as the literary type."

"Literary nothing, they're a good read."

Harry smiled broadly. "Thank you, Tom, always a pleasure to meet a fan."

Buchanan led them inside. The room was dark and smoky from a wood burning fireplace. On one cinnamon hued wood paneled wall was a huge gleaming steel sword that looked like it could easily lop off a man's head in one swing. The other walls were decorated with daggers, shields, helmets and Braveheart movie memorabilia and posters, one signed by Mel Gibson.

A half-dozen tables were scattered around the semi-circular bar, which featured an array of beers on tap with names like Jarl, Wolf, Ola Dubh and Elvis Juice in addition to standard Bud, Bud Light, Corona and Guinness. Behind the bar were four tiers of mahogany shelves, but instead of stacks of well-worn spines of venerable volumes, there was a seemingly endless array of single malt scotch bottles. Several were familiar to Harry but many more, with names like Auchentoshan, Bruichladdich, Glenglasswugh and Bunnahabhain, seemed totally exotic, more like the tipple of Beowulf and his pals than anything he might drink.

After seating them at the table nearest the fireplace, Buchanan turned to Harry. "How about an 18-year-old Laphroig?"

"Wonderful."

"And the usual merlot for you, professor?" Buchanan said disdainfully.

Semansky sat straight up in his chair and puffed out his chest. "Forget that. I'll have the same as my friend."

"Are you sure? Laphroig isn't for the faint of heart."

"Bring it on," he said with bravura.

"We'll make a man outta you yet." Buchanan winked at Harry and headed back to the bar.

"So," Semansky said slyly. "How were you able to spy on Tash when she was in Berg's house?"

"You know that Berg modeled his house after Shakespeare's birthplace."

"Yeah, I've been there."

"But I'm talking exactly. He must have gotten hold of the original plans. He had a priest hole built, a secret chamber behind the fireplace, as I'm sure John Shakespeare did in the original. I bet Berg used it to spy on his guests."

"How the hell did you find that?"

Before Harry could answer, Buchanan returned to the table. "Laphroig 18," he said with a flourish, setting down two Glencairn glasses, each with a generous dram of honey colored whisky.

Gabriel lifted the glass to his nose, took a quick whiff, then a taste. A contented smile wafted across his face. "Very intense, but not as harsh as the ten-year-old."

Buchanan nodded. "The extra age takes a bit of the bite off, makes it a drop milder."

Semansky took a hefty taste, gasped and made throaty noises.

"What do you think?" Buchanan asked.

"If this is the mild version I can't imagine what the harsh version would be like. From now on I'll stick to merlot," he said hoarsely.

"Islay Scotch is peat fire in a glass," Gabriel said to his colleague. "Laphroig most of all. It's not for the novice drinker. It's a drink you work your way up to."

Buchanan nodded approvingly, then lumbered off.

"Speaking of novices," Semansky said, getting his voice back. "How's the amateur sleuthing coming along?"

"Interesting. It seems there are a lot of people around here who couldn't stand Berg."

Semansky nodded knowingly. "To know Spenser Berg is to loathe him. It'll be harder to find people on campus who wouldn't want to murder him."

"Who would be on top of your suspect list?"

"I already told you, Peter Foote."

Harry shook his head. "I'm not saying he's incapable of murder. But beheading? I just can't picture it."

"Don't kid yourself. There's a lot of suppressed rage beneath that swishy exterior. Violence is his specialty."

"What do you mean?"

"He's one of the world's leading scholars on Shakespeare's use of brutality. Bloodshed and gore are his claim to fame. His office is decorated with authentic Elizabethan weaponry, swords, daggers, spears, axes

— some of the nastiest looking things I've ever seen. He's probably fantasized about cutting Berg's balls off with every one of those rusty old knives he has hanging on his wall."

"Could Berg have been blackmailing him?"

"I'd be shocked if he wasn't. He had dirt on everyone on campus and used it all to his advantage."

"Even you?"

Semansky stared dolefully into his glass of Scotch, then looked up. "I'm sure you'll find out eventually. I was arrested when I was in college. Domestic terrorism. I managed to get off, but somehow Berg found out. Since then, I've been his literary whore, writing most of his journal pieces, even the bullshit ones about authorship."

"I know."

"What! How?"

"Peter Foote told me."

"When?"

"He asked me to meet him in the campus deli. He couldn't wait to toss you and Natasha under the bus."

"Of course he did. That's University Career Advancement 101, 'Never miss an opportunity to promote yourself at your colleague's expense.' "

"You two weren't the only ones on Foote's hit list."

"I can imagine."

"I'm not sure you can."

"All right, I'll bite. Who?"

"Angie DellaRosa."

"Angie? That's insane. She loved Berg."

"According to Foote, she loved him too much. He said Berg got an offer from Tufts and was planning to leave. Angie took it very personally."

Semansky shook his head. "I'm not buying it."

"What about this?" Harry put a handkerchief on the table, the 'A.M.D.' monogram facing up. "I found it in Berg's house. If I'm not mistaken, her full name is Angelina Mariana DellaRosa"

"So it's a hankie with Angie's initials. She was Berg's friend. She could have left it there anytime. Besides, it might not even be hers."

"Do you know anyone else with the initials A.M.D. that could have been there?"

Semansky thought for a moment. "Arnie Dobbins is an assistant basketball coach and I think his middle name might be Marc. But I don't think he and Berg hung out together." He paused for a beat. "I wouldn't put much stock in your suspicious snot rag. Remember what happened to Othello when he jumped to conclusions about a handkerchief."

"Forget the goddamn hankie, who do you think did it?"

"My money's still on Peter. If you weren't so homophobic, you'd agree with me."

"What are you talking about. I have no problem with gay people."

"Your thinking that a gay person can't perform a vicious, violent crime, that his homosexuality prevents him from being an vicious axe-murderer, is soft bigotry. It's like assuming that if someone is black, he's a good dancer or a great basketball player. It's meant as praise but actually indicates an underlying prejudice."

"So now you're moonlighting as a sociology professor?"

"Stealth discrimination is one of my pet peeves. It's why I have a problem with affirmative action, but that's another discussion for another time."

"All right. So besides Foote, who else do you think could have murdered Berg?"

Semansky shrugged. "A lot of people despised him. He's been the most hated man on campus since he got here. Why kill him now?"

"I'm thinking it had something to do with the table."

"Table? What table?

"I thought you knew."

"Knew what?"

"When MacArthur was grilling me, he mentioned that Berg donated a table to the library that belonged to Shakespeare."

"You're sure he said 'table?'

"Positive."

"Has anyone seen it?"

"No. Nobody knows where it is."

"They'll never find it."

"How do you know?"

Semansky shook his head disdainfully. "Because it doesn't exist. Besides, he'd never donate anything to the library or anywhere else. He was as cheap and selfish as he was pompous and arrogant."

"So why claim he found it?"

"Good question. He's been talking about this so-called evidence he found for years and it's all bullshit. I know, I've been writing the journal pieces."

"Okay, so why the table?"

Semansky shrugged. "I bet he found one in an Elizabethan antique shop on his last trip to England and figured he could pass it off as Shakespeare's."

"So I guess I wasted my time looking for it in his house."

"I thought you were looking for clues to his murder."

"I was. But I was also looking for the table."

Semansky began to giggle.

"What's funny?"

"I just thought of something."

"Enlighten me."

"So you, MacArthur and Peltz, and half the campus Keystone Kops are running around looking for a really old piece of furniture that may or may not have belonged to William Shakespeare."

"What's so funny about that."

"Because the table isn't a table."

Harry looked at him as if he were somewhere between psychotic and demented.

"What the hell are you talking about?"

"I just thought of it. In Shakespeare's day, a table was what they called a notebook or a diary. Remember the term 'Tabula Rasa'.

"Clean slate."

"Very good. You didn't forget all your academic training. They wrote on slate, tabula, before there was paper. So tabula became table in English, signifying something you write on. We still use it today when we talk about a writing tablet. There's even a line in Hamlet, it goes something like 'I'll write it down in my tables.' "

Semansky took another quick sip of scotch to collect his thoughts. It went down a little easier this time.

"One of Shakespeare's handwritten notebooks would be the most important scholarly discovery of all time. It would be worth tens of millions, maybe more. If someone thought Berg had that in his possession, that's really something worth killing for."

Buchanan returned with the second round of drinks.

The burly Scotsman gave a quick salute and said, "Sláinte."

Harry lifted the glass, then his phone rang.

"Harry," said the young voice on the other end. "It's Tristan."

He could hear the panic in the boy's tone, even through the scratchy cell connection. "Are you all right? What's the matter?"

"Josh is dead...murdered. We found him in the library."

"Oh my God!"

"The campus police were there. They think you killed him. They think you murdered Spenser Berg too."

There was a pause. Then, more urgently, "Don't go back to wherever you're staying, they might be waiting for you there right now to arrest you."

"Where are you?"

"I'm at the railroad station."

"What are you doing there?"

"It's where I go to think."

"Stay there, I'll come get you." He ended the call and turned to Semansky. "I've got to go. I'll explain later." Harry headed for the door.

Semansky yelled after him. "What is it? What happened?"

No answer. He was gone.

Chapter 25

Two minutes after she called him, MacArthur was standing in front of Jordan, notebook in hand. She was still slumped on the bench, panting and quivering.

"If there was anyone besides you in the stacks, he's not there now," MacArthur said.

"What do you mean 'if'?" Jordan bristled. "I'm telling you I was attacked in Josh's office and he chased me up to the fourth floor and all through the stacks. Why won't you believe me?"

"It's not that I don't believe you, but I'm a firm believer in President Reagan's motto, 'trust but verify.' Right now the only thing we can verify is that your office was totally ransacked and any evidence that we might have found there is compromised."

"You think I did that? That I destroyed my own office?"

"Right now, you're the only one we can place at the scene."

"I told you. There was someone in Josh's closet. When I went in to get the shovel, he grabbed me. He tried to strangle me. How do you think I got this?"

She lifted her head and pulled down her collar to reveal a red pinstriped scar circling her throat.

"Can you see that? Do you think I did it to myself too? He did that," she screamed. "He ripped my necklace off trying to grab me. Trying to kill me, like he killed Josh and Dr. Berg."

"Please try to calm down, Ms. Day." He checked his notebook. "Yes, you mentioned that. A small emerald, diamond and ruby on a thin gold chain." He held up the notebook. "It's all in here. If we find it we'll give it to you after we're done with it."

"Of course I'd like the necklace back. It was a gift from my mother. The last thing she ever gave me. But that's not what this is about. Someone tried to kill me and you don't seem to care."

"Of course I care, Ms. Day."

"So why aren't your men out looking for this monster?"

"Who would you like them to look for?" MacArthur said sharply. "You haven't been able to describe anything about your alleged assailant. We don't even know if it's a man or a woman. What I do know is that I specifically asked you not to touch anything in your office and the next thing I know it looks like a bomb hit it."

"I'm not sure I appreciate your tone, Chief MacArthur," Jordan barked back.

"I'm not interested in what you appreciate, Ms. Day. Two people have been murdered on campus in the past 24 hours. If I have to ruffle a few feathers to find the killer, that's just too damn bad."

"I think Tristan might be correct. You're not following any evidence except if you think it implicates Harry Gabriel. Maybe it's no coincidence that he's the only person of color involved."

MacArthur's face turned crimson. "You think I'm a racist? Fifteen years on the New York City police force and eight more here, no one's ever accused me of that. And besides, I'm not sure Gabriel really is black. I think he's using it to sell books."

"What you believe about Harry Gabriel's race doesn't matter. I just want to know why you won't believe me."

"Because nothing you've said pans out. You told us about a table, there's no table. Now you're saying you were attacked but there's no attacker. We go to retrieve the head outside your office window. It's gone. Your credibility is wearing pretty thin. If you didn't mess up your office yourself, why didn't you call as soon as you saw it was ransacked?"

"I was in shock. I panicked. I wasn't thinking. I'm not trained to react to that kind of situation. I'm a librarian, not a policeman."

"Maybe you have an answer for that. What's your answer to why people around you keep winding up dead. First Berg's severed head is outside your window, then Campanella in your vault with a noose around his neck. There's something going on with you and I'm going to find out what it is."

"With me!" she screamed. "This has been the most horrible day of my life. And you're making it worse!"

"It was a lot worse for Berg and Campanella," he said harshly. Then softening, "Why don't you go home and have a drink or something. Try to calm yourself down."

"How can I be calm? My brother's still out there and there's a killer roaming the campus. He could already have Tristan."

"I'm sure he's fine."

"Well I'm not! "

"I'll alert my men to be on the lookout for him."

"Somehow, that's not very comforting." She headed for her car.

Chapter 26

Lizzie Peltz walked soundlessly to the open vault. "How's it going, Sherlock?"

MacArthur jumped, nearly dropping his phone. He had been taking pictures of Josh Campanella's body from several angles. "Can't you knock or something."

"Sorry." She walked back into the reading room and sat down. MacArthur followed.

"Where the hell have you been all this time? I figured you went home."

"I wish," she said wistfully. "I've been comforting a hysterical old lady."

"DeVere?"

"Well it wasn't Grandma Moses. She and Spenser Berg were a lot closer than we thought. When I told her that he was the other murder victim she went nuts. For a moment I thought she was going to stroke out right on the spot."

MacArthur put his camera on one of the long tables. "You're kidding."

"Do I look like I'm kidding?"

He scrutinized Lizzie. Her hair was disheveled, her clothes mussed, her skin ruddy.

"I'm surprised you didn't hear the scream. She shrieked like a banshee, started shaking violently, ripping at her clothes, talking gibberish and finally, she swooned and fell into my arms. I swear to God I thought she bought the farm, or the mansion, or whatever crazy, rich old ladies buy when they croak."

"So what did you do?"

"We were outside the Rotunda, I sat down with her at one of those picnic tables until she came to. She apologized and told me that Berg was the great love of her life."

MacArthur's face contorted as if he just bit into a lemon, rind and all. "What!"

"It seems she's a direct descendent of Edward de Vere, the Earl of Oxford. According to her, a lot of people, including Berg, think he's the guy who really wrote all the works we think were written by Shakespeare."

"Yeah, so?"

"When he was doing his Shakespeare research, he interviewed every known descendant of Oxford. That's when he met Lady DeVere and her brother, Anthony. He used to be the director of the Melville Institute for Mathematical Sciences, a real wiz."

"I thought he was some hotshot billionaire."

"He was. About twenty years ago he figured out a formula for picking stocks and started a hedge fund. Pretty soon, he was raking in billions."

"So the old lady must be doing all right."

"She is now. She was very close with her brother until he married a woman about half his age. She was a teacher here, Annie Macaluso, did you know her?

MacArthur shook his head. "Uh-uh."

"The old lady went ballistic. She called Annie a golddigger, a whore and some other names you can't say on TV. Her brother didn't like it. They didn't talk for a year. It looked like the old lady was going to be left out in the cold until Anthony and his new wife got killed in a car crash a couple of months ago."

"Interesting, but what does it have to do with Spenser Berg?"

"Lady DeVere has been bankrolling Berg's research. He lost most of his funding when he started all that authorship crap. She's the one who paid for his trips to England and I think she even covers some of his salary. I guess you could say Berg was the world's oldest and ugliest gigolo."

"She told you all that stuff just now?"

"Of course not. I'm in charge of university public relations, so I knew a lot of it already, especially about her brother. When someone with a connection to the university becomes a billionaire, I'm all over it like psoriasis on the old lady's ass."

MacArthur winced. "Ugh! Did you have to go there?"

"No. I do it just to see you squirm."

"Where's DeVere now?"

"Home. After I drove her to her house, she asked me to stay for a cup of tea. I couldn't say no, she looked like she was on the verge of a nervous breakdown. She talked about Berg, her brother, Annie, the Earl of Oxford...all kinds of things. I just sat there and listened."

Wheeler yelled from the doorway, "Chief, you called?"

"Wheeler, is that you?"

"Yes, sir." He walked into the room.

"There's been another murder."

"Jesus! Who?"

"Josh Campanella." He pointed over towards the vault. "Over there."

"Do you want me to process, sir?"

"Negative, I took care of it. I need you to take care of the body."

"I don't understand. What do you want me to do with it."

"Put it somewhere where no one'll find it until after the weekend."

"Where?"

MacArthur shrugged, then gazed questioningly over at Lizzie.

"Don't look at me," she said, shaking her head. "I helped you stash the first stiff. You're on your own with this one."

"Do you think we can put it in the gross lab too?"

"I think Donnie would get a little suspicious if we just keep showing up with fresh corpses every couple of hours, don't you?"

"We don't have to tell Donnie." MacArthur looked at his watch. "It's after eight, he's been home for hours."

"With no Donnie, how are we going to get in?"

"I'm the chief of police. I have keypad combinations to every room, lab and lecture hall on this campus."

"Well, in that case, why not? All the bodies are in bags. I doubt Danny takes inventory. I bet he'll never notice one extra carcass."

"Let's hope so."

"Does Angie know?"

"No, of course not. This just happened. We better call her."

"You know what," Lizzie said thoughtfully. "She's not going to want to hear about another murder over the phone. Maybe I should go over and tell her in person while you and Wheeler here take the body to the gross lab."

MacArthur winced at the mention of the gross lab. "I'll go with you. Angie will want to know about proper police procedure in a situation like this." He turned to Wheeler. "Can you get the body over to the gross lab without me?"

"Uh, yeah, I guess so," he said halfheartedly.

"If you think you need help, call Suarez. No one else is to know about this, got it."

"Yes, sir. But how are we supposed to get the body there without arousing suspicion?"

"You're the police. You're investigating a disturbance."

"With a corpse?"

"Figure it out, Wheeler. I'm not here to do all your thinking for you."

"Sure Chief, no problem." He tried to sound confident but his eyes looked bewildered.

"Good. I know you can handle it," MacArthur said, not knowing any such thing. "I'll text you the keycode. Now I gotta go meet with the President. Text me when you're finished."

"Will do." Wheeler snapped a tepid salute.

A few minutes later, MacArthur and Peltz were in the President's Suite. Usually the offices close at six but with Whale-A-Palooza coming up tomorrow, Lizzie was sure she'd be there..

"Come on, Edie, all we need is a couple of minutes," Lizzie begged. "This is very important."

"I told you when you called that she had back-to-back meetings all evening, and she hasn't even had dinner yet."

"I don't care if she hasn't eaten in days," MacArthur yelled. "This is, literally, a matter of life and death. Now tell her we're here or I'm going inside unannounced."

Edie, exasperated, picked up the phone. "Excuse me, ma'am, Chief MacArthur and Ms. Peltz are here. They have urgent news and need to see you immediately." She paused to listen. "Yes ma'am," and hung up. "She'll see you in a few minutes."

A few seconds later, a man, about forty, stocky with curly brown hair and thick arms, wearing a white polo shirt, khaki slacks and tennis shoes, walked out of the President's office carrying what looked like a folding lounge chair of some sort.

"See you next week, Nick," Edie said as he walked past her.

"Yes, next week, same time," he said with a slight eastern European accent as he left the office.

"That's a portable massage table, isn't?" Lizzie demanded.

"That's right."

Both Lizzie and MacArthur glowered at Edie.

"You can go in now." Edie said, ignoring their icy stares.

Dr. DellaRosa gestured for them to sit by the small round table opposite her desk. Lizzie sprawled on the couch and MacArthur sat stiffly on a wing chair.

The President paced in front of them and asked, "Did you find out who murdered Dr. Berg?"

"Yes and no, ma'am," MacArthur said somberly.

"Don't talk in riddles!" she shouted. "Do you know who the killer is or not?"

"We think so, but that's not why we came." MacArthur averted his eyes. "There's been another murder."

"Oh my God, no! It can't be." She looked nervously from Peltz to MacArthur then back to Peltz. "Who?"

Lizzie said, "Josh Campanella, from the library."

DellaRosa's eyes furrowed. "Isn't that one of the names who was on your suspect list?"

"Yes it was," MacArthur replied, slightly abashed. "If you remember, he wasn't very high on the list."

"That's good news. I'd hate to have one of your top suspects eliminated," she said, her voice dripping with scorn.

MacArthur didn't reply. He just stood there sheepishly.

DellaRosa said, "All right, Chief. Tell me what you know about this latest incident."

"They found his body in the Special Collections vault around 7 pm. It looks like he was strangled."

DellaRosa winced. "How absolutely horrible. Who's they? Who discovered the body?"

"Jordan Day, her young brother, Tristan and Millicent DeVere."

The president shook her head slowly. "There's 50 million dollars down the drain," she said forlornly, then glared at MacArthur. "And are you any closer to knowing who did these terrible things?"

"All the evidence points to Gabriel. He was seen having a heated argument with Campanella just before he was found dead."

"People on this campus argue all the time. It doesn't usually lead to murder," DellaRosa snapped.

"Gabriel was also threatened by Berg the night before his body was found."

She turned to Lizzie. "How sure are you?"

"Ninety percent."

"I see." DellaRosa closed her eyes in concentration. Ten seconds later, when she opened them, her jaw was set and her eyes defiant. "That's not enough." She turned her gaze to MacArthur. "Harry Gabriel is a celebrity. And he's African American. Two murders on campus is bad enough. A misguided rush to judgment against one of the leading black literary voices in America would do irrevocable damage to this university."

"But suppose he did it?"

"I don't want suppositions," she screamed. "I want proof."

"Yes, ma'am," he replied obsequiously.

"If you find him you may question him but by no means are you to arrest him. Is that understood?"

"Yes, ma'am."

"Whale-a-Palooza is the most important event in the University's history. I'm holding you personally responsible to make sure nothing happens to ruin it." She pointed to the door. "Now go. And don't come back until you have something positive to tell me."

Chapter 27

The train station was eerily still as Harry pulled the Karmann Ghia into the dimly lit parking lot. The dozen or so remaining cars seemed tucked in for the night. He walked towards the end of the empty platform to the small cabin that housed the station's ticket office and waiting room. He tried the door but it didn't budge.

He thought back to Tristan's call twenty minutes earlier. He was positive the boy said he was at the railroad station, so where the hell was he? Could he have meant a different station? No, this was the only station close enough for him to walk to. He sounded so upset, panic stricken. Could the killer have him? Two people were already dead, could the murderer think that Tristan was a threat? Was he using the kid to set a trap? Harry didn't even want to think about it. His heart began to race.

He sat down on the bench outside the ticket office when a high-pitched voice broke the stillness. "Hey!"

Harry jumped up, fists clenched. "What? Who's there?"

"It's me." Tristan emerged from the shadows.

"Jesus, you scared the sh... the life out of me." Harry sat back down, his heart pounding.

Tristan paced back and forth in front of the bench. "Sorry. When I saw you pull up I hid behind the ticket machine." He pointed to a large vending machine next to the ticket office.

"Why?"

"I wanted to make sure you weren't followed."

"Followed?" Harry looked genuinely puzzled. "Who would be following me?"

Tristan stopped pacing and stood in front of Harry, arms folded, an exasperated expression on his face. "The police." He paused for effect. "Or the real killer." Another slight hesitation. "Especially if he's trying to frame you."

"You really think the killer wants to frame me?"

"Isn't it obvious? You didn't kill Professor Berg or Josh, did you?"

"No, of course not."

"Well, somebody did," Tristan said emphatically. "And whoever it was is trying to make it look like it was you."

Harry shook his head skeptically. "The only people who knew that Josh and I had words were you and Jordan. I'm pretty sure you're not trying to frame me. Do you think your sister is?"

"Of course not."

"Well then?"

"Josh knew." Tristan smiled, like he had just figured out a trick question on a tough exam. "He could have told whoever killed him."

Before Harry could answer, a sudden flashing of lights and clanging of bells shattered the stillness. He jumped off the bench, arms flailing in front of him. "What the hell..."

Tristan tried to stop himself from laughing. "The gate's coming down," he said with a giggle. "The train should be here soon."

Harry smiled self-deprecatingly. "Oh. I guess I'm a little jumpy."

Two minutes later, the eight-forty-six out of Penn Station screeched into the station, discharging about a dozen passengers. They shlumped, tired and rumpled, out of the train, after the two-hour trip from Manhattan. Most headed for the parking lot.

Out of nowhere, like so many nocturnal sprites, half-a-dozen scruffy men ran onto the platform shouting, "Taxi! Taxi cab here!"

Harry instinctively put his arm around Tristan so as not to lose him in the sudden burst of activity. From behind him he heard nasally, high-pitched, New Jersey twang. "Harry! Harry Gabriel. Is that really you?"

He turned to see a short, slender woman carrying a Louis Vuitton overnight bag striding resolutely towards him in black high heels. She wore a black, perfectly tailored business suit. Her thick, wavy brown hair was cut short and blunt. The upturned nose, the product of a modestly priced plastic surgeon from Teaneck, seemed too small for her face.

Harry forced a smile. "Hello Bethany."

He had met Bethany Bierstein, a former assistant district attorney from Passaic County, at several writers conferences. She made the front pages of the Bergen Record, the Daily News and the New York Post by prosecuting several members of organized crime as well as busting a counterfeit pharmaceutical ring. She cashed in on her fame by writing two moderately successful true-crime books detailing her cases. Then moved on to lurid romantic thrillers.

"Harry, I didn't know you were a White Whale" She favored him with a saccharine smile. "I thought you went to Kansas or Nebraska or some other God-forsaken farm belt college."

"I went to Columbia."

"Really? I was sure it was somewhere in the Midwest."

"After I graduated I attended the Iowa Writers Workshop. Maybe that's what you're thinking of."

"Oh." She shrugged. "So what are you doing here?"

"I came here to give a talk about Shakespeare."

"The playwright?"

"Yes, that Shakespeare." His derisive tone was lost on her.

"And who's this handsome young man? I can see a slight resemblance. Don't tell me it's Harry Jr."

"This is Tristan, he's a friend of mine." He put a hand on the boy's shoulder.

"I'm Bethany Bierstein, Melville University, Class of '86. I'm a writer, like Harry. Maybe you've heard of me?"

Tristan thought for a second, then shook his head. "I don't think so."

"How about my book, Guido Hunting?"

"Yes, I have heard of it. Weren't you sued by the Italian-American Anti-Defamation League?"

She smiled. "That's me. That lawsuit earned me an additional $150,000."

"You won?"

"No, I settled," she said smugly. "It cost me $10,000 to make fifteen times that in extra sales, at least according to my agent." She scanned him from head to toe. "Aren't you a little young to be in college?"

"I'm twelve," Tristan said defiantly. "I'm not a college student but I have taken several courses at the University."

"That's nice," she said, losing interest. She looked around. Frowned. "Crap, all the cabs are gone." She gazed pleadingly at Harry. "You don't by any chance have your car here, do you?"

He swallowed, sighed and said, "That's my Karmann Ghia over there." He pointed to the far end of the lot.

"Oh Harry," she cooed. "Do you think you could be so kind to give me a lift? It's not far and it would really save my life."

"Uh, I'm not sure you'd be comfortable," Harry said hesitantly. "The back seat is practically non-existent."

"Don't worry, I'm very flexible. I take two pilates classes every week." She smiled seductively. "You'd be amazed at how I can bend my body."

He glanced quickly at Tristan, then turned back to Bethany. "Where do you need to go?"

"The White Whale Inn. I always stay there when I come to the campus. I'm practically a regular."

"So you've been coming here fairly often?" Harry asked, as they walked toward the parking lot.

"I've been here several times this year, doing research."

"For another book?"

"We'll see," she said elusively. "I'm not sure if anything will come of it."

When they arrived at Harry's car, Bethany peered through the window and scowled.

"That back seat really is small." She glanced over at Tristan. "You know I honestly wouldn't have minded sitting back there but my sciatica is absolutely paralyzing me after two hours on that cramped train." She rubbed her back and grimaced for effect. "You'd be doing me a huge, huge favor if you let me sit up front for the few minutes I'll be in the car."

"Sure, whatever," Tristan mumbled and crawled into the rear, sitting sideways, with his back against the window.

Harry held the front door for Bethany, then settled into the driver's seat.

They drove in silence for a minute, then she said, "So Harry, are you working on anything right now?"

"As a matter of fact, I'm working on a murder mystery. It takes place on a college campus a lot like this one."

"Really?" Her face lit up. "How far along are you?"

"Oh, about halfway. I still have some plot details to work out."

"Could you tell me about it?"

"I usually don't talk about works in progress, but for you I'll make an exception." He paused to gather his thoughts. "An arrogant old professor who had been blackmailing several faculty members is murdered. All the preliminary evidence points to a young visiting lecturer. The prime suspect is black and almost everyone else on the faculty is white. I'm exploring the subtle sexism, racism and prejudice that still exists under the surface in many supposedly progressive colleges and the hypocrisy of academic integrity and collegiality."

"Sounds serious."

"It'll still have plenty of blood and gore."

"What about sex?"

"Not much. That's your ballpark."

"You should try it. It spices things up. When do you think it'll be ready?"

"I'm not sure. I'm still trying to decide who the murderer is."

"I can't wait to read it."

"I'll send you an advance copy," he said as they pulled into the Inn's parking lot.

"Oh Harry, thank you so much." She leaned over and pecked him on the cheek. "And thank you, too, ahh..."

"His name's Tristan."

"Oh yes, Tristan," she said as she left the car. "Harry, you really are a lifesaver. I have no idea what I'd have done without you."

Tristan had already scrambled into the front seat. As they drove off he said, "That stuff about racism and hypocrisy at the university. Do you really believe that?"

"There's racism and hypocrisy everywhere. Melville U. is no exception."

"Do you think that's why they think you killed Dr. Berg?"

"I don't think Lizzie Peltz has a racist bone in her body. The jury's still out on MacArthur." He looked at his watch. "It's pretty late. I better take you home. Where do you live?"

"What are you going to do after you drop me off?"

"I need to get some sleep. It's been a pretty rough day"

"Where?"

"I've been staying at the president's guest house."

"You can't go back there. MacArthur's men might be waiting for you."

"You're right." He paused and scanned the inside of the Ghia. "It's been a long time since I spent the night in my car."

Tristan's eyes brightened. "You can stay at my house. Nobody'll look for you there. We have plenty of room."

"I'm the last person your sister wants to see."

"That's not true, Harry. But even if it is, it's my house too."

"Thanks Tris, but no."

"You'll never get any sleep in this car. I can hardy fit. And you'll need your rest if we're gonna find the killer." He gazed at Harry with pleading eyes. "You have to stay at our place. It's the only way."

Harry shook his head slowly. "I still think it's a bad idea."

"Please! It'll make me feel safer."

Harry emitted something between a yawn and a sigh. "Only if it's okay with Jordan."

Chapter 28

Bethany Bierstein walked into Schooner or Later, the lounge of the White Whale Inn and sat down next to the only woman seated at the teak bar.

Natasha Ferette sneered at her as she sipped a martini. "It's about fucking time."

"I'm twenty minutes late. That's considered on-time for the Long Island Rail Road."

"In that time I've been hit on by a horny grad student, a drunk sociology professor and a Bulgarian physicist who smelled of stuffed cabbage and slivovitz."

"When they stop hitting on you, then it's time to worry."

The bartender walked over. "Ma'am?"

"Courvoisier. Neat."

"Coming right up."

"When you were an Assistant D.A., you drank beer."

"When I was an Assistant D.A., that's all I could afford. Now I'm a famous author...or should I say we are." The bartender set the cognac down in front of her.

"I didn't notice my name on the cover of any of those books."

"Most ghostwriters never see their names on the books they write.

But a lot of the royalties that resulted from those books found their way into your bank account."

"Good point." Ferette raised her glass.

Bethany did likewise. They clinked. As she lowered her glass, Bethany's face tightened in concentration. "From what I'm hearing, all hell's breaking loose on campus."

Ferette gave her a quick synopsis.

"Spenser Berg beheaded — I can't believe it."

"It's true."

"What the hell is going on at this university? First Annie gets killed, along with her billionaire hubby, now Spenser Berg. Something's rotten in the state of Melville."

"You think they're related?"

"I was never convinced that Annie's death was accidental."

"Who would want to kill Annie? Everybody loved her."

Bethany smirked. "Not everyone."

"But why?"

"I can think of a hundred million reasons."

"You mean DeVere's money? I don't think so. There was a prenup. Annie insisted on it. That goofy sister of his was getting all the money either way."

"Has she been acting any differently since the accident?"

"Naaa. She's still obsessed with who wrote Shakespeare, insisting that her great, great, great, great granddaddy was the true author."

"Don't you think that's a little too much of a coincidence: her coming into all that money, Berg murdered and both obsessed with Shakespeare authorship?"

Ferette shook her head. "DeVere was Berg's main benefactor. She thought he was going to prove her right. The last thing she'd want to do was kill him."

"So who do they suspect?"

"Looks like Harry Gabriel."

"No way. He's an egotistical jerk but he's no murderer."

"Is that your deductive or your seductive brain talking?"

"That little fling we had years ago has nothing to do with it. I was a

D.A. for fifteen years. I've seen my share of murderers. Harry Gabriel's not one of them. I'd stake my reputation on it."

Ferette smirked. "At least you're not risking anything of value."

"Talk about the pot calling the kettle heliotrope."

"All kidding aside, you really think that Annie's death and Berg's are connected?"

"I've been wanting to investigate what happened to Annie for awhile and I thought Whale-A-Palooza was a perfect opportunity to come out here and do some digging without drawing too much attention. Now with Berg being killed, I'll bet they're related."

Natasha raised her perfectly sculpted eyebrows. "Sounds like a future best-seller to me."

"If what I think is true, absolutely!"

"Maybe this time I'll get an author's credit."

"You've got a deal."

They high-fived.

Chapter 29

Harry followed Tristan up the front steps of the sage green two-story cottage. The house was dark. Tristan flicked on the living room light. The wide-screen TV looked out of place in the cozy room that might otherwise have been plucked from the set of Father Knows Best, with two small well-worn sofas and a fat, cozy club chair.

"Tristan, is that you?" came a voice from upstairs.

"Yeah, Jor, it's me. I'm here with..."

"It's about time" Jordan came bounding down the stairs, wearing a light blue terrycloth robe and pink ballerina slippers.

"I was just about to text you again." She stopped abruptly, almost comically, like in a Roadrunner cartoon, and glared at Gabriel. "What is HE doing here?"

"He drove me home."

"Oh," she said softly. Then severely, "Thank you, Mr. Gabriel, and good night."

"I told Harry he could stay here tonight."

A look of horror contorted her face. "Absolutely not! That's impossible."

"You don't understand. The campus police think Harry killed Josh and Dr. Berg." He looked pleadingly at his sister. "He's innocent, Jor, and he can't go back to where he was staying. The police are probably there now waiting to arrest him for murder."

She turned to Harry. "There must be someplace else where you can go."

"I'll figure something out." He started walking towards the door.

"Where are you gonna go?" Tristan asked, his eyes tinged with concern. "They'll be looking all over for you."

Harry smiled reassuringly at his young friend. "Don't worry, Tristan. I'll be fine."

His hand was on the doorknob when he heard, "Stay." Jordan's voice was suddenly calm. "Tristan's right, we can't let them arrest an innocent man."

Harry froze. "You believe I'm innocent? The last time I spoke to you I had the feeling that you thought otherwise." He turned and walked slowly back into the room. "What convinced you?"

She glanced over at her brother, then back at Harry. "Tonight, while you were with Tristan, I was in the library being chased by the real murderer."

Harry's jaw dropped. He stood motionless, silent.

Tristan ran to his sister and threw his arms around her. "Oh my God, Jor, are you okay?"

"Yes, I'm all right now."

Harry took a step toward her, then stopped. "What happened?"

"Let's sit down. It's a fairly long story."

She recounted the entire incident, stopping once or twice to berate herself for foolishly putting herself in such a perilous situation.

"You were awesome, Jor," Tristan added. "I can't believe you belted that guy with the shovel."

Jordan stood and walked towards the kitchen. "I was about to have a cup of tea when you walked in. Anyone else?"

"That sounds good." Harry followed her.

"What about you, Tris?"

"No thanks. I'm really tired." He stood and headed for the staircase. At the foot of the stairs he looked back. "Good night, Harry, Jor." Then he darted up the stairs to his room.

On the wall separating the kitchen and the living room were

several framed photos, most were of Tristan, with his Little League team, in a chess tournament, in the regional finals of the National Spelling Bee. Harry zoomed in on one, a vacation picture. Jordan, Tristan and an attractive woman in her forties on a beach, Harry guessed Hawaii or the Caribbean because of the translucent turquoise surf and palm trees in the background. A shorter and younger Tristan in floral print bathing trunks stood smiling behind a red boogie board, giving a thumbs-up to the camera. Jordan was ethereal in a long strapless white gauze dress. The older woman wore a large, floppy straw hat out of which flowed strawberry blonde ringlets. Her oversized sunglasses were perched on an upturned nose. The vivid red and green Hawaiian shirt draped over her swimsuit couldn't hide her shapely figure. Her wide smile showcased perfect teeth and full red lips. The glass in her hand held pink liquid and a purple paper umbrella.

Harry stared at the picture for several seconds before sitting down at the kitchen table. After a long couple of minutes, the tea was ready.

"That woman in the photo with you and Tristan on the beach, that's Diana Callahan, isn't it?"

"Yes, she's our mother. I thought you knew."

Taken aback, he shook his head. "I had no idea."

"You do know that she died, don't you? She passed away last June of an aortic aneurism."

"Tristan mentioned that his mother had recently passed away, but I had no idea it was Diana," he said sadly. "I'm so sorry. I knew her, you know."

"Yes, I know." Her eyes flashed anger.

Harry either ignored or didn't notice her venomous glare. "It must have hit him hard."

"It hit us both hard. But yes, Tristan was devastated."

"He doesn't seem that bad now."

She fiddled with her teacup but didn't drink. "He's better than he was. After Diana died he went into a deep funk. He's finally starting to return to normal."

Harry took a sip of tea. "Now it makes sense," he said more to himself than to Jordan.

She glared at him. "What, exactly, is that supposed to mean? What makes sense?"

"Never mind...nothing. Forget I said anything."

She took a deep breath and stood up, facing him. "Spenser Berg's severed head on a spike outside my office window, does that make sense? Or Josh being killed? Or a homicidal maniac chasing me around the library?" She glared at Harry. "If any of this makes sense to you, I'd love to know how."

"I didn't mean that. It's the way you've reacted to me today. Cold, aloof, standoffish. I was wondering why."

"Standoffish!" She shook her head disdainfully. "People are dying all around us and all you can think about is why one female on this campus didn't throw herself at your feet." She glared at him angrily. "You are the most self-centered, egotistical human being I've ever met."

He flinched, stung by her words. "I don't understand. We were friends once. I had hoped that we'd become more than friends. In fact, you were the one person I was looking forward to seeing when I came back here. What did I do to make you hate me so much?"

She stared down at him. "How do you think I should feel, after I found out that you were sleeping with my mother?"

"I, uh..." Harry stammered. "H...how do you know about that?"

"Diana told me, of course. She gloated over it."

"But why?"

Jordan sat back down. "Because that's who she was. She needed to be the center of everyone's attention. She couldn't share the spotlight with anyone, especially me. She couldn't stand the thought that someone she was interested in might be interested in me. It made her furious." She took a sip of tea. "Diana was seventeen when I was born. The studio kept her pregnancy out of the press, bad for the image of a wholesome teen sitcom star. She was never around. I was raised by governesses. She was more like my big sister than my mother. A big sister with a fragile ego. I confided in her that you and I went for coffee several times and I was hoping you'd ask me out on a real date."

She inhaled deeply, then grabbed the edge of the table with both hands. "I'll never forget what she said to me. 'He's out of your league, dear. A man like that wants a woman, not a child.' " Jordan's lip quivered for a few seconds. "I think she slept with you just to spite me." She took another sip, then said, "It wasn't until years later, when I was in therapy, that I realized that she was jealous of me and that was her way of protecting herself."

"But she was beautiful, successful, smart — what did she have to be jealous of?"

"She'd been a sitcom star since she was thirteen. Her whole career was built on her cute, bubbly personality. Then one day the producers told her that the audience had tired of her character. That was their way of saying she was too old. She was devastated."

Harry stiffened. "So Diana seduced me to do what...to get even with you for being young and beautiful?"

"She needed to prove to herself that she was still desirable, so she started collecting men."

"Collecting?"

"You weren't the only one."

Harry winced, bringing a small, satisfied smile to Jordan's face.

"There were three or four that year." She paused to let her words sink in. "Then she got pregnant."

"With Tristan?"

She nodded. "Once my brother was born Diana became a different person. She devoted herself to raising him. We both did, even though she never let me forget who the mother was." She took some more tea. "We left the city and came here. Diana became an Associate Dean in the theater department and head of the Film and TV Division. I transferred from NYU and changed my major from dance to English."

"Why?"

"Several reasons. Our apartment in Manhattan was barely big enough for the two of us and my mother couldn't afford a bigger one. After the sitcom let her go Diana had difficulty getting work. Money got tighter and tighter. A few guest shots and some commercial work but it wasn't enough. But Diana refused to change her lifestyle. She said maintaining her image was the only way she would be able to get back to the top.

"Angie DellaRosa had approached her several times about coming to the University. She wanted to start a Film and Television department and she believed a well-known name would propel the program into prominence. At first, Diana scoffed at the idea. She thought it was beneath her. She called Melville a farm school and its students a bunch of hayseeds. A year later, with very little work and a mountain of unpaid bills, Angie called again. She increased the salary and added free tuition for me. Diana jumped at the offer."

"I understand all that. But why'd you switch your major? As I recall, you loved to dance. You told me it was your life."

"My life changed. Tristan was an infant and Diana was very busy starting a department from scratch. All of my free time was consumed with taking care of him. A dancer, even a student dancer, has to go to rehearsals, recitals, off-campus performances and competitions in addition to regular classes. I couldn't spend that much time away."

"You gave up your dream to help raise your brother?"

"I have no regrets."

"You shouldn't. You did a great job with him. If I ever have a son, Tristan's exactly the kind of young man I hope he'll be."

She glared at him and shouted, "You still don't understand, do you? Tristan IS your son."

Chapter 30

Harry turned pale. His mouth dropped open but no words came out. He started shaking, sweating, feeling lightheaded, slightly nauseous. "I... I don't believe it."

"That's exactly how I thought you'd react," she said derisively.

Harry sat down, trying to collect his thoughts. It was about thirteen years ago that he was at the college as a summer sessions lecturer. He'd been introduced to Diana Callahan at a faculty cocktail get-together. Nothing happened that night, but a week later he ran into her at a campus bar and she was all over him. They had a couple of fun nights and that was that.

He stared deeply into her eyes. "What makes you so sure I'm Tristan's father?"

"Diana told me."

"You said your mother was with a lot of different men."

"Don't worry, we don't want anything from you. You won't have to take a DNA test." She spit the words at him.

"That never even crossed my mind. I just want to be sure."

"Diana hand-picked you to be the father. You were brilliant, handsome, athletic. She wanted her child to have your DNA, no one else's."

"She told me she was on the pill."

"She lied. She used you." Jordan leaned forward. "Just like you used me."

"That's not fair. I cared about you. You're the one who broke it off. You cut me out completely."

"What did you expect me to do after I found out about you and my mother!"

"I didn't know Diana was your mother. How could I?" he yelled. "Neither of you ever told me. Just like you never told me about Tristan. I guess that's one way you and Diana are alike."

"What would you have done if we did tell you? Your first book had just gotten rave reviews. You were the toast of the New York literary scene, the new voice of millennial African Americans, isn't that what the Times Book Review called you?" She sneered. "Don't tell me you would have dropped all that fame, money and adulation to come out here in the middle of nowhere to be the doting daddy."

"I don't know what I would have done," he said, his voice rising. "That was a decision for me to make. You and your mother never gave me the chance."

"Listen, right now I'm not concerned about you, all I'm worried about is Tristan."

"What's there to worry about? He's a great kid."

"For some strange reason he seems to have connected with you, but that was when all he knew about you was that you were a famous author who drove a cool car. If he finds our you're his father, who knows how he'll react."

"He'll be shocked and angry that you and your mother never told him, just like I am."

"We thought it was for the best."

"Whose best?" Harry yelled. "Not mine. Not Tristan's. A boy needs a father and you denied him that. And denied me the joy of raising a son and watching him grow up."

Jordan was quiet for a moment. "You're right. We were being unfair. We probably should have told you. But let's not argue about that right now."

"When is a good time to argue about it?" Harry yelled. "Tomorrow? The day after? If I really am Tristan's father I want him to know."

"Of course he needs to know," Jordan said, in a loud whisper, trying to tamp down the volume. "It's just a matter of finding the right time."

"How about right now?"

Now Jordan started yelling. "Right now you're the prime suspect in a murder investigation. You might be arrested at any minute. Finding out he suddenly has a father will be enough of a shock. Having his new father carted off to jail would be devastating."

Harry nodded. "You're right."

"We'll tell him as soon as things calm down and they find the real killer. That is, if you're really ready take on all the responsibilities of being the father of a teenage boy?"

"I'm absolutely ready."

"Are you sure? Being a parent, a good parent, is a major commitment. It'll put a big crimp in your Manhattan literati lifestyle."

"Tristan'll fit into my lifestyle just fine. It's you that I'm concerned about."

"Me?"

"Tristan and I get along great. But you're part of the package. So far we're not doing so well with each other."

"A lot of divorced parents who can't stand each other share custody."

"But we're not divorced. And you're not his parent."

"You wouldn't dare take him away from me!" she screamed.

"Of course not. What kind of person do you think I am?"

"You don't want to know."

"You're right. I don't." He yawned deeply. "Being accused of murder and finding out I have a son I never knew existed is about as much as I can deal with in one day. If I'm still welcome, I'd like to try to see if I can somehow manage to get some sleep. I'll need to have all my wits about me tomorrow. I'll be no good to Tristan or anyone else if I'm locked up for murder. I guess that's at least one thing we both agree on."

She gestured towards the living room. "The sofa folds out. There's bedding inside the ottoman."

She stood, stretched, arched her back like a cat after a nap, said a perfunctory "Good night" and walked towards the stairs.

Neither of them noticed Tristan crouching at the top of the landing. He scrambled silently back to his room before anyone saw him.

Chapter 31

Tristan sat on the edge of his bed, trying to make sense of what he just heard.

Harry...my father? No way! If it's really true, Jordan and my mom have been lying to me my whole life. And if Harry's really my dad, does he even want to be? He's such a cool dude. He probably thinks I'm an annoying little dork? No, he likes me. I know he does! What if he gets arrested? I can't let that happen!

As soon as he was sure that Harry and Jordan were asleep, he crept down the stairs and out the back door. He hopped on his bike and pedaled aimlessly into the cold, moonless night. The old bike had no lights and on some dark streets the only illumination was from the orange jack-o-lanterns glowing in the windows. Having no actual destination, he rode aimlessly until he wound at the Melville University main entrance. He cycled around the deserted campus trying to figure out where to go. What to do.

He stopped at a bench outside the library. He was cold, tired and confused. Chilly tears ran down his cheeks. He needed to talk with someone about what he just heard. But who? He didn't have a best friend. Nobody he would even consider a close friend. The only person he could ever confide in was Jordan. But not this time.

Fifteen minutes later, he was at Drew Wolcott's door. "Drew I didn't know where else to go. I need your help. It's a matter of life and death."

"Hey calm down little dude," Wolcott said, slouching in the doorway. "It's all good." Ponytail gone, his greasy black hair hung at his shoulders.

Tristan stepped gingerly into the apartment, navigating a minefield of pizza boxes, beer and soda cans and dirty clothing. He was no neat freak, but this was a whole new level of disgusting.

Wolcott shuffled in after him. He plopped on his lumpy, threadbare Salvation Army couch, motioning at the two rickety beach chairs that served as the room's other furniture.

Tristan stayed on his feet, pacing back and forth as Wolcott lay sprawled on the sofa, sucking on a can of Bud Light.

"Sit down, you're making me nervous."

The boy eased himself onto one of the chairs, expecting it to collapse beneath him.

"So what drove you out of your cozy house in the dead of night and brought you to my dungeon?"

"They lied to me, both of them," Tristan said angrily. "They've been lying to me since I was born."

Wolcott sat up. "Whoa! Slow down. Who lied to you?"

"My mother and my sister."

He leaned in towards Tristan, peering intently. "Sounds serious. About what?"

"My father."

Wolcott looked puzzled. "I thought you said your father was dead."

"That's what they always told me."

"He's alive?" Wolcott's slitty eyes bulged with surprise.

Tristan nodded.

Wolcott looked genuinely pleased for him. "I don't know why you seem so down. That sounds like a good thing. Maybe you'll get to meet him someday. Where does he live? Did they tell you?"

"He's here. I've already met him." Tristan paused, breathed deeply. "It's Harry Gabriel."

Wolcott's body shook as if convulsed. "Harry Gabriel? He's your father? He told you that?"

Tristan shook his head. "No. He didn't know either. Not until just now. I overheard my sister tell him."

"That's crazy." Wolcott jumped up from the couch. "How could he not know?"

"My mother never told him. That's how!" Tristan shrieked. "She went out with him when he taught some summer sessions classes here. He never even knew she was pregnant." He took a long breath. "If the campus police weren't after him, he still wouldn't know. And neither would I."

"Hold on, hold on. This is too much for me to take in all at once." He held up his hands and said very slowly. "The cops are looking for Harry Gabriel? What the hell for?"

"They think he killed Spenser Berg."

"No way."

"They think he murdered Josh too."

"Josh? Josh who?"

"Josh Campanella. You met him this morning. He worked with my sister at the library."

"He's dead too? Holy crap! You sure about that?"

"I'm positive. I saw the body."

"So Spenser Berg and Josh what's-his-face are dead and the police think Harry Gabriel is the killer? That's un-fucking-believable."

"That's why I need your help. Harry's innocent. I know it! You have to help me prove it."

"Me? What can I do?"

"Berg trusted you. You were always at his house, putting his stuff away in those secret hidey-holes. I'm sure you overheard a lot of his phone calls. Is there anything you can think of that would lead us to the murderer?"

Wolcott sat up straight. "Jeeze. That's a pretty long list. A lot of people hated his guts."

"Really?"

"Oh yeah. He was a real son of a bitch. He crapped on everyone. A real equal opportunity asshole."

"Even you?"

"Me worst of all."

"So why did you stay?"

"I had to. I got into a little trouble with the police when I was younger. Berg sorta vouched for me. Got them to release me into his custody."

"Really? How did you know him?"

"I didn't. A distant relative of mine is a good friend of his. She talked him into taking me in."

"Dr. Berg didn't seem like the kinda guy that would take a stranger under his wing."

"More like under his armpit. He treated me like stink. Like I was his fuckin slave. This was his apartment and he let me stay here rent free. He paid me just enough to get by. If I leave, I got nothing — no money, nowhere to live, no job. And with a police record, not much chance of getting one. He had me by the balls."

"So you hated him?"

"Like poison."

"Enough to kill him?"

"And put myself out on the street?" He shook his head derisively. "What do you think?"

"I get your point. So who hated him enough to kill him?"

"Let me think."

"Is it okay if I get a drink of water?"

"Sure, grab a glass, there should be one over there." He pointed to a table near the sink.

Tristan walked over to it. It looked like somebody dumped a junk drawer on top of a pile of dirty dishes. In addition to food encrusted knives, forks, spoons, plates and glasses, there was a small screwdriver, a pair of sunglasses, some loose change, zip ties, rubber bands, matches and a key ring.

Then he noticed something glittering underneath key ring. Three small stones on a thin gold chain. He picked it up to take a closer look. The stones were white, green and red. He had seen that necklace many times before. It was one of his sister's most cherished possessions.

He gasped. His hand shook as he lifted the necklace out of the junk pile and put it in his pocket. The voice in his head shouted, He did it.

He's the one who tried to kill Jordan. He killed Josh and Dr. Berg. This is the proof. Now all he had to do was tell Harry and the police.

He peeked furtively over at Wolcott who was sprawled on the couch, eyes closed.

"Holy crap!" he cried, looking up at the clock over the refrigerator. "I didn't realize what time it is. If my sister wakes up and I'm not there, she'll freak. Thanks for your help." He walked tentatively towards the door. "Text me if you think of anything else, okay."

Wolcott stood lazily up and walked towards Tristan. His crooked smile was belied by his snakish eyes. "What's your hurry, kid. You just got here," he said smarmily. "Anyways, your sister's the one who's been lying to you all this time, the hell with her. And you know, I've been thinking…I'm pretty sure I know who did those murders."

"Really? Who?"

Wolcott giggled cruelly. He grabbed the front of Tristan's shirt and twisted it into a knot, choking him. "Me."

Tristan's legs turned to Jello. Tears ran down his cheeks. He shook uncontrollably. After several seconds he gasped out, "Why?"

"Cause I fuckin felt like it," Wolcott hissed. "Gimmee your phone." He twisted harder. "Now!"

As Tristan reached into his pocket, the tremor in his hand caused him to drop the phone.

"What are you, a fuckin wise guy? One more stunt like that and you're dead," Wolcott yelled. "Three or four, it won't make no difference."

"Three? There are only two."

"Shut the fuck up!" Wolcott pushed him to the floor. "Now, pick up the phone."

Tristan did as he was told.

Chapter 32

"Wake up! Wake up!" Jordan screamed as she ran down the stairs. "We've got to find him!"

"What...who?" Harry said groggily. He was sprawled diagonally across the sofa, his head under a pillow, still wearing his clothes from the previous day. He lifted his head slowly and peered over at the digital clock. It read 7:13. "What's going on?"

Jordan stood over him in her blue flannel robe. Her face was red. Her hair disheveled. She had no makeup on. "It's Tristan. He's gone. His bed wasn't slept in. His clothes weren't put away."

Harry sat up, his eyes out of focus, his mouth tasting of dry parchment. "What? Where? Where did he go?"

"I don't know!" she screamed. "He's never done anything like this before." She covered her eyes with her hands. "What are we going to do?"

"Calm down. We'll figure it out."

"Don't tell me to calm down," she cried shrilly. "There's a murderer out there and he could have Tristan. He's your son, goddammit. Do something!"

"So now you want me to be his father? Last night you were hoping I would just go away."

"I don't care about last night. We can argue about that later. Right now we have to find Tristan."

"You're right. Let's think this through." His face tightened in concentration. "Did you hear him leave?"

"No." She paced nervously back and forth. "Did you?"

Harry shook his head.

"Do you think he heard us talking about me being his father? That would have set him off, wouldn't it?"

Jordan didn't answer, just nodded her head slowly.

"Enough to make him run away?"

She stood silently for a few seconds. Then her face contorted and tears rolled down her cheeks.

"It's my fault! It never occurred to me that he would be listening. If anything happens to him I'll..."

"Nothing's going to happen." Harry spoke very deliberately. "Most likely, he just needs some time to come to grips what he heard. It was a lot for me to digest all at once. I can just imagine how a twelve-year- old would react."

"You don't understand, Harry. He means everything to me. Now he's gone and I don't know where he is. He could be scared, hurt or..." She covered her face with her hands and sobbed. "Oh God!"

Harry stood up, guided her to the couch and sat down next to her. "He's probably at a friend's house right now, trying to make sense of this whole thing."

"He doesn't have many friends. None he would go to with something like this."

"If not to a friend's house, where? Where would he go to collect his thoughts?"

Jordan closed her eyes in concentration. "There are a couple of places I can think of."

"Okay, so that's where we start. I'm assuming you tried his phone."

"That was the first thing I did."

"Well?"

"It went right to voicemail."

"Did you text him?"

After an exasperated nod, she said, "No response."

"Don't worry, we'll find him."

A few seconds later the opening notes of "Shaft" by Isaac Hayes pierced the silence.

Jordan jumped. "What's that?"

"It's my phone. I'm getting a text." He hurried to the table where left his phone, wallet and keys. "Hang on. It's from Tristan!"

"Are you sure it's from him? What does it say? Is he okay?"

"This is weird. All it says it 'PFOOTE." He handed her the phone.

"PFOOTE?" She glared at it for several seconds. "I don't understand. What does it mean?

"I have no idea. I thought maybe you would know."

Harry closed his eyes. His face taut with concentration. "Pfoote. Pfoote," he said aloud. "Maybe he was trying to spell 'foot'."

Jordan shook her head. "I don't think so. Tristan can type better on his phone than most people on a regular keyboard. Besides, the 'P' and the 'F' aren't anywhere near each other on the keypad. And why would he put an 'E' at the end?"

"I don't know. He's your brother. Think. What's he trying to tell us?"

"I wish I knew," she said, her voice rising in panic.

"Pfoote." He said it again, this time it was more of a whistle. "It's like the sound of air rushing out of a pressure sealed container, like when you open a can of coffee."

"Why would Tristan text us the sound of a coffee can?"

Harry shrugged. "I don't know. He wouldn't. I'm grasping at straws here."

"Maybe it's a name," Jordan said, hopefully. "Do you know anyone named Pfoote?"

Harry concentrated for a few seconds. Then he hit himself in the head with his palm. "Of course! Peter Foote. That's it, P. Foote. He's on the English faculty. He's the Vice Chair. I met him yesterday. Does Tristan know him?"

She shook her head. "No, I don't think so."

Harry's eyes widened. "Maybe it has something to do with the murders."

"How?"

"Peter Foote was next in line to be department chair. He was on my suspects list. Could be Tristan found something to implicate him in Berg's murder."

"In the middle of the night? What could he possibly find?"

"I know it sounds ridiculous, but at least we know he's all right."

"We don't know any such thing! We don't even know if it was Tristan who sent the message. I doubt he's ever heard of Peter Foote." Tears welled in her eyes. "Oh my God! Peter Foote sent that message. He's the murderer. And he has Tristan!"

Harry shook his head. "If he's the murderer, why would he implicate himself? And if he's not the murderer and he has Tristan, why would he send a message to me? No one knows that I'm his father but you."

"I don't care about any of that. I just want to find my brother."

"So do I. But we're not going to find him standing here."

Five minutes later they were in Jordan's Volvo. They hit all of the places she could think of where he might have gone. No one had seen him. After a fruitless hour, they wound up in the library parking lot.

"I give up," Jordan said forlornly. "I don't know where else to go."

"Then go where you're supposed to go."

"What are you talking about?"

"Didn't you tell me you're supposed be in the Scholar's Showcase tent to give a presentation this morning?"

"Ugh! That's the last thing I want to do," she said with an exasperated sigh.

"Does Tristan know you're scheduled to be there."

"Yes, of course."

"If Tristan is on his own there's a chance he'll go there to see you."

She nodded slowly, hesitantly. "Maybe...but it's a long shot."

"Right now, it's the best shot we have. While you're there, I'll go to Peter Foote's office and see if that text means anything."

"I should go with you."

"Bad idea. We'll have twice as good a chance to find Tristan if we split up. Besides, if we're together and the police find us, they'll detain us both. Then no one will be looking for him."

"Do you really think he's all right?"

"I do," he said with as much conviction as he could muster as he headed for the Humanities building, praying silently to a God he didn't believe in, that he didn't inadvertently cause the murder of the son he never knew he had.

Chapter 33

The multipurpose room at University Police headquarters was filled beyond its 50-seat capacity. Uniformed officers and members of the Student Emergency Response Team sat shoulder to shoulder on white molded plastic chairs rented especially for the occasion. Latecomers stood along the back wall.

The Dean of Students, Director of Development and President of the Alumni Association had each described, in explicitly excruciating detail, the events, exhibitions and festivities planned for the day. Whale-a-Palooza was scheduled to begin at 9:00 with the Melville Mardi Gras, a student parade complete with floats, costumes, dancers, bands and young performers of all description. The extravaganza would conclude twelve hours later with the Student Symphony's performance of Tchaikovsky's 1812 Overture, complete with fireworks and a still-functioning World War I cannon on loan from the Riverhead Armory. Sandwiched in between would be a football game, barbecue, carnival rides, speeches, lectures, class reunions, a petting zoo, wine and beer tastings and the crowning of the Whale-a-Palooza king and queen. One of the most highly anticipated events was to have been a groundbreaking talk by Spenser Berg, which could forever alter the landscape of literary scholarship, a line written by Lizzie Peltz that she was especially proud of.

Chief Gregg MacArthur, the final speaker, stood at the podium, an American flag pin on one lapel, a small ceramic White Whale pin on the other. He wore a crisp blue pinstripe suit, white shirt and red and white whale-print tie. His shoes were shiny, as was his hair. If you looked closely, you could see his left eye twitching slightly. His fingers — cuticles red and swollen, nails chewed to the nub — drummed the top of the lectern as he spoke. A quick glance at his watch told him that they were running uncomfortably late. He had a five-minute speech prepared but left it in his pocket as he bent the mike closer to his mouth and started to speak.

"They're expecting close to 20,000 visitors to the campus today, including the governor, at least one U.S. senator, several congressmen, state legislators and God knows how many other bigwigs of various shapes and sizes. And don't forget the 30,000 students, faculty and staff who are here every day. That's the most people who have ever been on the academic mall at one time." He paused for gravitas. "And if that's not enough to worry about, I just got a message that some left-wing student group intends to stage a demonstration in front of the Engineering Quad to protest government-supported military research." He shook his head in dismay.

"It's up to all of us in this room to keep them safe." He looked out over the room, Lizzie, a late arrival, was standing near the door. "Remember, this is a party, the biggest celebration in Melville U's history, so it's probably gonna be a little wild and a little rowdy. You can cut the revelers more slack than usual but not so much that it comes back to bite us. So smile, be friendly, keep your eyes open and be mindful out there."

As the members of the Melville University Police filed out of the room to head to their assigned posts, Lizzie walked over to MacArthur. "Nice speech. You forgot to mention that we have a mass murderer roaming around campus."

"It slipped my mind." He rolled his eyes. "C'mon, I'll give you a ride." His cruiser, a Ford Crown Victoria, was parked in front of Headquarters.

In a few minutes they were on the main campus road. Whale-a-Palooza was just getting underway. The academic mall, a wide walkway that was the main campus pedestrian thoroughfare, had been transformed into a fairground midway, with colorful tents, booths and tables scattered all across the grounds. Hundreds of exhibitors were busily putting the finishing touches on their displays. Carts from Starbucks, Peet's, Dunkin Donuts and the university's own Kampus Koffee were doing a brisk breakfast business. Portable grills and outdoor ovens were being fired up for burgers, pizza and tacos, as well as Thai, Tandoori and Asian Fusion dishes. Long Island's many wineries and brew pubs were also setting up shop, much to the chagrin of Chief MacArthur. "Just what I need," he said as they pulled into the VIP parking lot. "Fifty thousand drunks on the mall."

"You're not getting into the Whale-a-Palooza spirit," Lizzie said as she extricated herself from the car. "Take a look at the circus over there."

"This whole goddamn campus is a circus."

"Not like this." She pointed to the large expanse of grass, known as the Great Meadow, where students usually sat, studied, made out, played Frisbee or kicked around a soccer ball. There was now a huge inflatable bounce house in the shape of a whale as well as a stilt walker a unicyclist and a clown juggling coke bottles.

"Holy Christ!" MacArthur exclaimed. "If they bring in elephants and a flying trapeze I'm quitting."

The theme to "Hawaii Five-0" sounded. MacArthur pulled the phone from its holster on his belt. "Yeah, yeah, got it, thanks. I'm on my way." The Chief slammed his phone shut. "And so it begins," he said, shaking his head and gazing skyward.

Lizzie raised her eyebrows. "What's goin' on?"

"That was Dispatch. They got a call about some kind of disturbance in Humanities. Figures, it's all the way on the other side of campus." It gotta go check it out. Wanna come?"

"Why not."

Chapter 34

The Scholars' Showcase tent was the size of a small airplane hangar. It was where the leading lights of the Melville University faculty were put on a pedestal like so many trained seals, performing academic tricks for potential donors, state and local politicians, members of the New York State Higher Education Council and other selected dignitaries deemed important enough by President DellaRosa to receive VIP status.

The finishing touches were being added to the various exhibits, poster presentations and art installations featuring dinosaur fossils, lunar modules, sculptures, paintings, and an odd wedge-shaped vehicle produced by the Department of Mechanical Engineering capable of driving 50 miles per hour for more than 100 miles on a single gallon of ionized water. Dozens of tables held displays, inventions and books of all shapes and sizes.

One of the tables, though, was empty except for a gold enameled papier-mâché Venetian mask about the size of a child's balloon with the face of William Shakespeare and a hand-lettered sign next to it that read "The Bard. Unmasked." Behind it stood a scowling Natasha Ferette, clutching a 20-ounce Starbucks coffee container and nervously chewing on a red lacquered thumbnail. She wore a black leather blazer and charcoal gray slacks. She didn't notice Isaac Semansky calmly ambling over from the rear of the tent.

"Hi Tash, what's up?" he said, probably a little louder than he intended.

She jumped, spilling some coffee on the table. "Ike, what the hell are you doing. You scared the piss out of me!"

All the eyes in the room instantly darted in her direction, a few of the younger, priggish faculty shook their heads with disdain, then just as quickly looked away, as if she were a car wreck on the side of the highway.

"Good morning to you, too," Semansky said with a grin. "A little jumpy this morning, aren't we?"

"You're damn right I'm jumpy. Did you check your phone today?"

"Are you kidding?" he said with a grin. "You know I'm a technophobe. I don't have a smartphone. And I have trouble making a call on my stupid old flip phone, much less figuring out how to get a text message. I still type my papers on the Smith Corona I used when I was an undergraduate."

"I think you should take a look at this." She thrust her phone in his face.

"C'mon, Tash, I don't feel like fishing for my glasses. Can't you just tell me what it says?"

"It's from Peter. It says, and I quote, 'Just heard from Angie. I'm the English Chair in Spenser's absence. I can't help with the Showcase. Too much to do. Keep calm and carry on.'"

"What do you mean he can't help!" Semansky yelped, his voice cracking with alarm. "This is HIS goddamn presentation."

"That self-centered, self-important ass." Her decibel level was edging ever higher. "He was the one who insisted that we go on with this asinine dog and pony show, even though without Berg and his supposedly world-changing revelation, I don't know what the hell we're supposed to talk about."

"We'll have to have something or else we'll look like a couple of prize jackasses."

"Okay, like what?"

"We can talk about our books. Between your *Shakespeare's Bitches* and my *Regina Fascista*, we could do a reading and have a discussion. It might work."

Ferette shook her head skeptically. "Do your really think these people are ready to discuss Shakespeare's shotgun marriage and subsequent misogyny or that Elizabeth I was a female Mussolini?"

"You have a better idea?"

"Not really. But since we don't have any of our books here, I don't know how we could pull your plan off."

"What do you mean no books!" Now he was the one yelling. "Where the hell are our books?"

"Ask Peter," she said angrily. "He was in charge of getting them here, remember."

"So where the hell is he?"

"If I knew, I'd be there now, wringing his turkey neck."

Semansky looked at his watch. "We have about an hour to find Peter and get those books." He grinned nervously. "If we don't, I don't know, we could sing some Sonny and Cher songs. Do you know 'I Got You Babe?' "

"Don't be stupid."

"How about Peaches and Herb? I bet you could do a mean 'Shake Your Groove Thing.' "

"You may think this is funny but I'm not in the mood to be humiliated," she said sharply. "There are posters all over campus about our supposed groundbreaking lecture. And without those books the only ground being broken will be to bury us."

"Where do you think Peter has them stashed?"

She shrugged. "No clue."

Semansky bit his lower lip. "I say we go to his office. If the books aren't there, he can tell us where they are."

"Suppose he's not in his office?"

"We'll go to Plan B."

"You mean break in?"

"Exactly. What's the worst that could happen?"

"Oh, I don't know...we get fired, we get arrested, we get murdered."

"See? No worries."

Chapter 35

Harry entered the rear door of the Humanities building. He checked the directory and saw that Peter Foote's office was on the second floor. He walked up the spiral staircase, staring at PFOOTE on his phone and trying to think of why Tristan would text Foote's name to him. The more he thought about it, the more convinced he was that Foote was involved. That he arranged the meeting in the Jewish deli to throw him off the scent. He paused at the top of the landing, breathed deeply and prepared himself for the possibility that he might be about to confront a multiple murderer who, according to Semansky, had an array of ancient but still deadly weapons hanging on his wall and probably knew how to use them.

When Harry arrived at Foote's door it was not only unlocked, it was wide open. The first thing he saw was the back of a leather desk chair. There was a shock of light brown hair protruding over the top of it. He guessed that Foote was taking a nap before his big lecture. He marched in, ready to confront the dozing professor and demand to know Tristan's whereabouts. Beat the answer out of him if necessary. Harry steeled himself, grabbed the back of the chair and spun it around. "All right Foote, you sonuvabitch, you better tell me..." then he gasped.

The rusty hilt of an ancient knife protruded out of the space where Foote's right eye should have been. His face was contorted in a hideous death mask. Blood blotches of vibrant red covered the front of his white oxford shirt.

Harry lurched backward. His legs turned rubbery. He grabbed onto the back of the chair, trying to steady himself. He barely regained his equilibrium when he heard voices coming down the corridor. He scanned the room, looking for somewhere to hide...another way out...a window. There was nothing. He was trapped.

Isaac Semansky walked through the door with Natasha Ferette right behind him, one of her trademark Gitanes cigarettes dangling from her lips. "Harry, I didn't expect to see you here?" Semansky said. "Have you seen Peter?"

Harry stood paralyzed at the other end of the office, unable to move or speak.

Natasha sashayed over to him. "Well, I'm glad we found you. We could use your help with our presenta...." She glanced over at Foote's desk, saw the bloody spectacle and screamed.

Semansky cried, "Oh my God Harry, not Peter too!"

Gabriel recoiled as if he'd been struck, "You think I...Whoa...hold on. You think I killed him?"

Semansky turned pale as he averted his eyes. "It sure as hell looks like it."

Harry shook his head strenuously. "I just got here about a minute before you. I found him like this."

"Why the hell are you here at all?" Semansky demanded.

"I was looking for my son."

"Your son!" Ferette exclaimed. "Since when do you have a son?"

"Since last night."

Semansky shook his head in disbelief. "I was with you last night at Braveheart's, remember? You didn't say anything about having a son then. Even a stud like Harry Gabriel can't magically acquire a son overnight."

"I know it sounds unbelievable, but this is what happened," Harry told them about Josh Campanella's murder, Jordan being chased in the stacks, how he found out that Tristan was his son and finally about Tristan going missing and the text message that said PFOOTE.

Semansky stroked his beard pensively. "I actually believe you. That story's too ridiculous not to be true."

"So do I, God help me," Ferette said. "What the hell do we do now?"

Harry shrugged. "I wish I knew." He took a deep breath. "All I know is that whoever killed Foote is trying to set me up. And he did it with Tristan's phone, which means..."

Semansky cut him off. "Don't even think about that. Tristan's fine. Unless I'm totally off-base, these murders are all about Shakespeare's table. It's the only thing that connects Josh Campanella to Berg and Foote. If the killer thinks Jordan Day knows where it is, then hanging onto her brother gives the him leverage, but only if he's alive."

"I hope to God you're right. But we're still no closer to finding him."

"Maybe we are. We know the killer has Tristan's cell phone. We can use that to find him."

"How?" Harry and Ferette asked at the same time.

"I'm sure the phone has a GPS. It'll lead us right to him."

"Since when do you know about that stuff?" Ferette said. "You're a techno-moron."

"That's true," Semansky said. "But that's how they do it on NCIS."

"But we're not NCIS," Harry said.

"We're better. We have a whole department full of brilliant computer nerds and a couple of them are in the Scholars' Showcase right now."

"Jordan's there too. We have to warn her," Harry said urgently. "If you're right and it's all about Shakespeare's table, she's the next target."

Semansky shook his head. "Not we, it has to be Natasha and me. You can't go anywhere near that tent. The police want to arrest you for two murders — three, once they find poor Peter. They'll lock you up as soon as they see you. That is, if those trigger-happy Neanderthals don't shoot you first. You have to let us handle it."

"No way!" Harry exclaimed. "Tristan's my problem. I appreciate the help, but I have to take care of this myself."

Ferette scowled. "I usually like all that macho stuff, I find it sexy in a

Bogie kind of way. But this time it's just stupid. You won't do anybody any good if you're locked up in a jail cell. Or dead."

Semansky's face lit up. "I have an idea."

Ferette took another drag on her cigarette. "I've seen that look before. It's never good."

"This is better than good, it's brilliant," he said with a mischievous smile. "The marching band director's office is right across the hall. It's where he stores all of his band paraphernalia. I'm pretty sure there's a spare Moby costume in there and you're just the right height."

Harry's eyes widened in horror. "You want me to walk around campus dressed as a furry fish? I don't think so."

"A whale's a mammal, not a fish."

"I don't care if it's a king sized crustacean. I won't do it."

"Why not? Moby is a big part of this event. He's the whale in Whale-a-Palooza. I'm sure they're using two Mobys at a big shindig like this, one on the Mall and one at the game. As long as you stay clear of the other ones, no one will be the wiser."

"I hate to admit it, but the little shit has a point" Ferette said. "Wearing that stupid costume the only way you can keep looking for Tristan without the University Police goons grabbing you. And today the whole force is out there."

Harry shrugged. "I don't know. It sounds pretty ridiculous to me."

"That's why it'll work." Semansky handed him a key. "This should open up his office. It's 213, a couple of doors down."

"Why do you have his office key?"

"It's my key. It opens every office door in the building."

"Really. Why would they do that?"

"Budget constraints. It's a lot cheaper to put the same lock on all the office doors, buy one key and make copies for everyone."

"I still think this is crazy," Harry said, shaking his head. But he took the key and started walking towards the door.

"Moby has special whale fin boots," Ferette said. "You better leave your shoes here."

Harry slipped out of his loafers and handed them to Ferette, who put them on the table next to her bag. "I really appreciate your help. I don't know what I'd do without..."

"Yeah, yeah, whatever." Semansky said, brusquely. "Now go change so we can get back to the Showcase."

As Harry walked barefoot down the hall to the band director's room Ferette whispered nervously, "Are we helping a mass murderer?"

"You really think he might have done it?"

"Guns don't get much smokier than Gabriel standing over Peter's bloody body."

"I don't care if the gun's on fire," Semansky said emphatically. "Harry's no killer. I'd bet my life on it."

"You just did."

Sounds of heavy footfalls and muffled voices emanated from the central staircase.

"Christ!" Ferette cried. "Someone's coming."

"Just stay calm." Semansky said, trying to sound more self-assured than he was.

He stepped into the hall, straining his eyes trying to see who was walking down the corridor.

"Shit! It's MacArthur and Peltz."

Chapter 36

Jordan stood apprehensively on the stone threshold of the library, like Indiana Jones before the invisible bridge. She stared up at her office on the second floor, wondering how she could ever set foot in it again. Then she thought of Tristan out there somewhere and the infinitesimal chance that he might show up at the Scholar's Showcase. She had to take that chance. Phil Bergstrum would be there. And he would expect her to bring the archival material for the "Early American Masters" exhibit. She braced herself, opened the front door and stepped inside.

Standing at the Special Collections door, her hand shook as she unlocked it and walked quickly through the main reading room into her office.

Three large padded envelopes containing the first editions of Typee and Omoo and the other original Herman Melville documents were on the credenza, exactly where she left them. She dropped them into the oversized canvas tote bag with the Melville Library logo. The urge to bolt was strong, but the Walt Whitman material, which Bergstrum specifically asked for, was still in the vault. In addition to collecting the Whitman papers, she had a nagging feeling that MacArthur's men missed something, something that might lead to finding Tristan. The police had no idea what they were looking at, while she was in that vault every day and could tell immediately if anything was missing or out of place.

The thick metal door was open, with several strips of thick yellow police tape draped across it. Fighting anxiety, Jordan took a deep breath, ducked under the tape and walked inside the room-sized, climate-controlled chamber.

The boxes and file cases, though in their proper location, were slightly askew. She checked the shelves that were reserved for the rare and fragile items. These precious pieces included a first edition of Walt Whitman's Leaves of Grass. There were also some court documents from Southold, a town on Long Island's north fork where Whitman was employed as a teacher, accusing the poet of 'bloody bedding' with local schoolchildren, and other acts of moral turpitude.

Jordan put on a pair of white cotton gloves and carefully placed the Whitman documents into a protective envelope and put it in her bag next to the Melville items.

She then pulled two more boxes off the 'Rare and Fragile' shelves and began delicately sorting through the papers to see if there was anything else she could use. The first box contained nothing of particular interest, some colonial-era deeds and other innocuous legal documents.

The second box looked even less promising, all it held was a small leather bound volume. Surprisingly, she had never seen it before. Between cataloguing, reshelving and assisting researchers, she thought she had come across every piece in the collection. But on closer inspection, she saw that it wasn't a published book at all, more like some kind of ledger or diary. It was very old and in extremely poor condition. She was about to place it back in the box when she thought perhaps it could be one of Whitman's diaries.

She thought she could see the faint outline of hand-carved initials scratched near the bottom, it looked like 'NS' but in the dim light of the vault she couldn't be sure. What she saw on the yellowed title page drained the color from her face. It was a faded handwritten signature, scrawled in an uncouth hand. The name was 'Will Shaksper.'

Her mind raced as she stared at the decrepit old volume cradled in her quivering fingers. Could this really be one of William Shakespeare's notebooks? If it was, how did it get into the vault?

She reached into her back pocket and pulled out the Post-it she took from Josh's office. 'STRAREFRAG.' It wasn't a name from one of Josh's science fiction books, it was a reminder to himself. RAREFRAG was Rare and Fragile, and the ST must have been for Shakespeare's table. But this was a notebook, not a table. Then it struck her, in Shakespeare's time, notebooks were called tables.

She stared, awestruck, at the withered diary. Could William Shakespeare have actually held this in his hands? Did he write these words with his own quill? Then another thought intruded. Is this why Spenser Berg is dead? And Josh?

Now that she had Shakespeare's table, what should she do with it? If she put it back where she found it, the killer could just walk in the way she did and make off with it. But if she took it with her, she would probably be the murderer's next target. After a moment's thought, she carefully put the ancient tablet into a padded envelope, then placed it very carefully next to the other items in her bag. She took one last look around the vault, decided there was nothing else she needed, and hurried out through the central reading room, down the stairs and out of the library, constantly on the lookout for sinister assassins lurking in every shadow.

Chapter 37

As MacArthur and Lizzie walked down the corridor Semansky stood outside the band director's office and yelled, "Chief MacArthur, is that you?" hoping that Harry would hear him.

MacArthur jumped. "What is it? Who's calling me?"

"Thank God you're here. I think you'd better come inside," Semansky said, walking casually back to Foote's door. "There's something you need to see in here."

By this time, Ferette was standing next to him.

MacArthur eyed them suspiciously, staring down at Semansky's sandals. "Who the hell are you two and what are you doing here?"

Lizzie said, "They're all right. They work here."

"Sorry, Chief, I thought you'd remember me. I'm Isaac Semansky. This is my colleague, Natasha Ferette. We're on the English faculty."

"Yeah, I guess I've seen you around." MacArthur scowled at Ferette. "You know there's no smoking in here."

"Sorry, Chief," she said timidly, dropping the cigarette on the floor and crushing it into the carpet with her shoe.

MacArthur turned to Semansky. "If you dragged me here on a bullshit wild goose chase there'll be hell to pay."

"Take a look in there. Then you tell me if it's bullshit or not."

Semansky led them into Foote's office.

When MacArthur saw the chair with Foote's body he stiffened and hollered, "Holy Christ!"

Lizzie, who was right behind him, stopped and stared at the body like it was an exceptionally interesting museum exhibit, finally saying, "I've seen that knife before somewhere."

Semansky followed behind. "It's an authentic 16th century bollock dagger."

He gestured up at the wall. "Peter was a collector of medieval weaponry. It was part of his collection. Some of the pieces are missing. You can see the spaces where they used to be."

"Yes. We did a piece about Foote's collection a while ago. Fascinating. I was always curious about those orbs on the handle."

"They're the bollocks, made to resemble men's, uh…"

"All right, that's enough!" MacArthur growled. "We got another faculty member murdered and you two are discussing the finer points of male anatomy and ancient knife design." He turned to Semansky. "What were you two doing here?"

"Dr. Ferette and I are scheduled to give a reading at the Scholars' Showcase, along with Professor Foote." He pointed to a cardboard box in the corner of the room. "When he didn't show up, we came over here looking for him. That's when we found…"

"When did you get here?" MacArthur cut him off.

"Just a couple of minutes ago."

"Were you the one who called it in?"

"No. We were just about to."

"Was anyone else here when you got here?"

Semansky hesitated for a few seconds. "Uh…no."

"So who called it in?"

"I have no idea."

"We'll find out. Did you touch anything, move anything?"

"Absolutely not." Semansky gestured at the body. "When Natasha and I found Peter like that, we were shocked. Wouldn't you be? We were just regaining our composure when you two arrived."

"All right." The Chief glared sternly at Semansky, then at Ferette. "Don't leave the campus. I'll want to talk to you both later."

Semansky said, "You think we had something to do with this?"

"I don't think anything. I know that this guy didn't stick a knife in his own eye. And you two discovered the body. I know that this is the third murder here in the last two days it all has something to do with Berg and a goddamn table. And I know that Angie wants to keep it all hush-hush until this ridiculous Whale-a-Palooza is over."

He looked over Natasha's shoulder and spotted her handbag and Harry's shoes.

"Whose are those?"

"That's my bag," Natasha said. "I imagine the shoes are Peter's. I mean were Peter's."

MacArthur shook his head. "I don't think so. Those shoes look like size 11 or 12. Foote's foot is about the same size as mine. No bigger than an eight, nine tops."

Lizzie eyed him skeptically. "Since when did you become such a footwear expert?"

MacArthur picked up one of the loafers and, very gingerly, held it next to a shoe on the dead man's foot. The one in his hand was considerably larger. He looked at the others triumphantly. "You don't have to be Thom McAn to know that these shoes don't belong to the same person."

There was an awkward silence for a few seconds until MacArthur said, "I think the last time I saw Gabriel he was wearing shoes like these." He glared at Lizzie. "Let's see what DellaRosa has to say about that."

"Are we free to go?" Semansky asked.

"Yeah. Just don't go too far. I'll need to talk to you later. Right now, I've got to find the foot that belongs to these shoes."

MacArthur glared at Lizzie. "And I'm in no goddamn mood to hear a Cinderella crack from you."

Chapter 38

Semansky banged on the Band Director's door. "Okay Harry, the coast is clear."

"Are you sure?" Harry's muffled voice came from the other side.

"Very."

For about 15 seconds the doorknob shook and twisted from left to right and back again without actually turning. Then, finally, it made a complete revolution and the door opened. Out stumbled Gabriel, wearing the body of the Moby costume, holding the big plastic whale head.

"Hello Moby," Semansky said with a grin. "Looks like you lost your head?"

"I'm gonna lose my mind if I have to wear this ridiculous costume for too long."

"If you don't you'll lose your freedom. It's all hands on deck for the University Police. They're all out there. And every one of them has your picture. You'll be arrested in two minutes if you show your face out there."

"I don't know if I can do it. It's about 200 degrees in this thing. I can hardly walk. I can't see through the eye slits. And the head keeps falling off."

Semansky tried and failed to stifle a chuckle. "But besides that, it's not so bad, right?"

"This isn't funny! My son's life is at stake. I've got to find him and I can't do it wearing this thing."

"We have 18-year-old kids who do intricate dance routines in that costume. You should be able to figure out how to walk in it without falling down."

"I can do a better job of looking for him without it."

"Not if you're behind bars."

Harry brightened. "Hey, I just thought of something. I had no reason to kill Peter. I hardly knew him. Maybe I'm off the hook."

Semansky glanced uncomfortably at the uncharacteristically silent Ferette, who averted her eyes. Then he sighed and said, "Sorry, Harry. You're still number one on MacArthur's hit parade. With a bullet."

"That's crazy! There's absolutely no evidence that I had anything to do with any of those murders. Especially Peter's."

"Actually, there is," Semansky said, shaking his head sorrowfully. "Tell him, Tash."

Ferette reached into her handbag, pulled out a blue Gitanes box, extracted a cigarette and lit it as the two men looked on. She took a long drag then blew the gray smoke over their heads. Finally she spoke. "I left your shoes out by Foote's body. MacArthur found them." She put her hand on Harry's furry shoulder. "I'm so sorry."

Semansky clapped Harry on the shoulder. "Listen, now you really have to keep your head on straight, in every sense of the word. We'll do everything we can to help."

Harry tried, unsuccessfully, to force a smile. He lifted the cumbersome Moby headpiece and put it on. Ferette and Semansky straightened it out, tucked the extra fabric into the back of the costume and fastened it with Velcro strips.

"That's about as good as it's gonna be," Semansky said. "Good luck." He patted Harry on the back.

Chapter 39

Phil Bergstrum jumped up from behind the library's exhibit table. "Oh Jordan, Jordan, thank God you're here." He pointed at her tote bag. "I hope you have something wonderful in there. Because I'm just dying."

She handed him the bag and looked around the Scholars Showcase tent, hoping to see her brother.

Bergstrum put on a pair of white gloves. He opened the bag and placed each of the envelopes gently on the table, carefully removing the material and skimming through each piece as he laid them out. When he was finished, he uttered a contented sigh as a wide grin swept across his face."These are wonderful, just wonderful! Jordan, you have absolutely saved the day."

"Thank you. I was hoping they would be of some value. Would you mind if I went outside to get a little air? It was a little stuffy inside the vault."

"Of course not. You go ahead while I set this up," he said, happily arranging the items. "By the time you get back we'll have a fabulous display."

"Thank you." She slowly made her way out of the tent. As she left she could hear Bergstrum exclaim, "Bloody bedding? My goodness! Walter Whitman, you are a naughty, naughty man."

Jordan sat down at one of the brightly colored metal picnic tables that lined the academic mall. The campus was filling up with Whale-a-Palooza revelers. The food vendors were out in full force, as were the Frisbee players, jugglers, folksingers, hacky sackers and others enjoying a warmer-than-normal October day.

Hoping to spot Tristan in the crowd, she scanned the faces but to no avail. She tried calling him again but the phone went right to voicemail. "Tristan, if you're all right, please call me, I'm very worried about you," she pleaded after the beep.

She tried Harry but got no answer there either. She closed her eyes, trying to decide what to do next when she felt a light tap on her shoulder.

"Jordan dear, are you feeling all right? I looked for you in the Scholars tent and Mr. Bergstrum said you came out for some air." Millicent DeVere sat down next to her. She wore a gray Irish fisherman's sweater beneath a green tweed jacket and matching skirt. She had replaced her Hermes scarf with a white Whale-a-Palooza baseball cap that vendors on the mall had been hawking all morning.

"You seem upset. Have you been crying?" She took a white lace hankie out of her handbag and handed it to Jordan.

Tristan's missing," she said, her voice cracking. "I looked everywhere. I don't know what to do. I think he's been abducted."

Lady DeVere took Jordan's hand in hers and massaged it gently. "I'm sure he's all right. Boys that age get involved in all manner of mischief. Perhaps he spent the night at a friend's house."

"No. He was home last night. He came in with Harry." She patted her eyes a second time with the tissue. "Then this morning he was gone."

"Harry?" Lady DeVere cocked her eyebrows. "Harry Gabriel? Why was Tristan with him?"

"They met yesterday in the Rotunda and they seemed to have taken a liking to each other."

"Maybe they're still together."

"No. Harry was with me this morning when we discovered that Tristan was missing."

"I see." Lady DeVere smiled and nodded knowingly.

"I don't think you do," Jordan said, a little more forcefully than she intended. "There's nothing between Harry Gabriel and me. He needed a place to stay and Tristan invited him to the house so I let him sleep on the couch. I couldn't just throw him out into the street."

"Of course you couldn't, dear." She patted Jordan on the knee as if she was calming a fidgety cocker spaniel. "Now about your brother, why would anyone want to kidnap him?"

"The same reason why Professor Berg and Josh were killed." Jordan looked around furtively to make sure no one could hear what she was saying. "To get Shakespeare's table."

"Don't be silly," Lady DeVere said with a benign smile. "I've always thought that was one of Spenser's little ruses, something he told people to impress them. I doubt very much that it actually exists, let alone that someone would kill for it."

"But it does exist, Lady DeVere," Jordan said emphatically. "I saw it. I held it in my hands."

Eyebrows raised, the old woman clasped her hands together and said in a throaty whisper, "No. I can't believe it. Are you sure?"

"As sure as I can be."

"You didn't say anything about this last night."

"I didn't know about it last night. I found it this morning, by accident. I was in the vault looking for material for the library's Showcase exhibit. It was hidden among the Early American documents on the Rare and Fragile shelf."

"But how could it have gotten there? Aren't you the only one with access to the vault?"

"Josh also has access." Jordan put a hand up to her mouth. "I mean had."

"My goodness! Have you mentioned this to anyone?"

"No, no one."

"That's good. The fewer people who know, the safer you'll be." DeVere reached into her bag for another tissue and dabbed at her nose. "All this excitement has left me absolutely parched." She pointed to a nearby food cart. "Do you think they have mineral water?"

"I'm sure they do. I'm thirsty too. I'll get us both some."

"Thank you, dear."

As Jordan waited in line at the cart she stared intently at all the young faces walking past, hoping her brother's might be among them.

Lady DeVere was fumbling with her phone when Jordan arrived with their drinks. "I'll never get the hang of these things." She dropped it disdainfully into her bag.

"They do make them overly complicated." Jordan handed Lady DeVere a bottle of Poland Spring.

"Thank you, dear."

Jordan smiled, nodded and took a long sip when her phone rang.

"Jor, it's Tristan."

"Tristan!" she cried. "Where are you? Are you all right?"

"I...I'm okay. I'm on campus...by the Tail Fountain." His voice was hesitant, fearful.

"What's wrong?"

She heard a rustling noise on the other end of the line. Then another voice, deeper and harsher. "Listen Blondie, if you don't want your brother to get hurt, get that sweet little ass of yours down to the fountain. Come alone. And bring the Shakespeare book with you. No book. No brother. Got that?" The phone went dead.

"Jordan, what's the matter? You're pale as a ghost."

"They have Tristan!"

"Who?"

"I don't know," she said between gasps. "They want me to go to the fountain."

"Whale or Tail?"

"The Tail Fountain, down on the lower campus."

"Shouldn't you contact the Campus Police?"

"I can't take that chance. The voice on the phone said to come alone. If I don't, they might hurt him."

Lady DeVere grabbed her hand. "Then I'm coming with you."

"No. It's my fault that Tristan's in danger. I won't let you put yourself at risk for me."

"I'm sorry dear, but you have no choice."

Just then, they heard the sound of horns, drums and stomping feet. "Oh God!" Jordan shrieked. "It's the Homecoming Parade."

She looked around and saw hundreds of marchers highstepping

down the academic mall. The Melville White Wave, as the marching band was called, lived up to its name, from the white feather plumes atop their white brimmed helmets to the white brass-buttoned jackets and pants, down to the white rubber-soled shoes. They came in wave after cacophonous wave, first the flutes, then the clarinets, horns and drums, followed by a half dozen sousaphones, their huge round white bells like giant cannon barrels facing forward, poised for attack.

"It's hopeless," Jordan said despairingly. "We'll never get through that."

"Oh yes we will!" Lady DeVere grabbed Jordan's shirtsleeve at the elbow and pulled her into the fray.

Chapter 40

After several minutes of pushing, shoving, twisting and contorting their way through the thundering throng, Jordan and Lady DeVere, only slightly the worse for wear, found themselves looking down at the fountain from behind a retaining wall at the top of the terraced path leading to the lower campus. Jordan saw two shadowy silhouettes. Certain the smaller one was Tristan, she turned to the older woman. "There they are."

"Who?"

"Tristan and whoever is holding him hostage."

"Are you sure?"

"Positive." Jordan's face hardened. "I'm going down there."

"Please don't." Lady DeVere clutched her arm. "I'm an old woman and you're a lovely but very slender young lady. We're no match for the ruffian down there. If we act hastily, it may place your brother in jeopardy, as well as you and me. If you want Tristan to be safe, the wisest course is to inform the police"

Jordan was pensive for several seconds. "You're right." She stared down at the fountain then back at the bustling academic mall. "I'll go get a policeman."

"I think it would be better if I went. If I stay here and they leave, I'm not sure I could keep up with them. We don't want to lose sight of Tristan now that we've located him. I shan't be long."

"Okay, I'll stay here and keep watch. If they move I'll follow them and call you to let you know where they are."

"Good. And remember, under no circumstances are you to initiate a confrontation," DeVere said firmly. "I'm certainly in no position to attempt a rescue."

* * *

Harry could hear the marching band as he left the Humanities building in his Moby costume. He was shocked to see the academic mall flooded with people of all ages clapping, cheering and shouting the Melville fight song, "Fear the whale, Fear the whale, Melville U will never fail."

Squinting through the hazy eye slit, he saw what he was pretty sure was Jordan and an elderly woman making their way through the crowd toward the lower campus. He was about to follow them when a mob of children came running at him, screaming "Moby! Moby! We love you, Moby!"

Dozens of kids swarmed around him, waving what looked like small pamphlets. "Sign my book. Please sign my book." He squinted to see that they were thrusting their "Moby the Wondrous White Whale" coloring books at him.

One of the kids shoved a stubby Sharpie pen into his furry fin. Harry grabbed it tightly and slowly scratched out MOBY in big block letters across the front cover. Hanging onto the pen, he signed several more books in the same manner. Then, as suddenly as they appeared, the kids ran off. The Long Island Reptile Rescue exhibit had just opened and it seemed that they found an eight-foot boa constrictor more interesting than a six-foot furry white whale.

Harry waved regally to the onlookers as he lumbered toward the lower fountain walkway, hoping that Jordan would still be there.

* * *

In stark contrast to the hullabaloo above, the lower level of the campus was empty, save for two figures, one much larger than the other, sitting on a bench near the fountain, facing away from the stone steps leading up to Main Campus.

"You've been doing very good so far, kid," Wolcott mumbled at Tristan. "I like you. I don't want to hurt you. After this is all done, maybe we can hang out or something. Play some chess."

Tristan didn't answer. He sat motionless, scowling at the fountain.

"Don't worry. Pretty soon, your sister'll be here, she'll give me what I want and everything'll be fine."

"You promised you won't hurt her," Tristan blurted, his voice cracking with fear.

"I'm not gonna hurt her, you or anyone else. As long as no one does anything stupid."

* * *

As she watched Lady DeVere disappear into the Whale-a-Palooza crowd, Jordan was surprised to see the University's white whale mascot trudging clumsily in her direction. She glanced down at the lower fountain to make sure that Tristan and his captor were still there, then turned back to see the large white whale mascot lumbering right at her.

When he was about five feet from her, the whale began gesticulating wildly and yelling something. She thought she could hear the words "Jordan" and "Harry" but she couldn't be sure. His voice was muffled by the costume.

The whale was upon her.

"Go away, Moby!" she yelled.

"Jordan, it's me, Harry," came the muffled voice.

"Harry? What are you doing in that stupid whale suit?"

"Trying to look for Tristan without getting arrested."

"Tristan's down there." She pointed at the fountain.

"So let's go get him."

"He's being held hostage."

"By who? For what?"

"I don't know. But he wants to trade Tristan for Shakespeare's table."

"Did you tell him you don't have it?"

Jordan shook her head. "I do have it. At least I did."

"What are you talking about! You had Shakespeare's table the whole time and didn't say anything? But now you don't have it?" Harry thrust his furry fins in the air "You're not making any sense."

"Of course I didn't have it the whole time. I found it when I went to the vault this morning to get material for the exhibition. Josh must have hid it there."

"Josh? What the hell was Josh doing with it?"

"I have no idea. But it's probably why he was killed."

"So where is it now?"

"Phil Bergstrum has it."

"Bergstrum! This is getting more convoluted by the minute. Don't tell me Bergstrum's involved in all this too,"

She scowled. "No, of course not. He has nothing to do with it."

She took a deep breath to collect her thoughts. "When I found the Shakespeare notebook in the vault I didn't know what to do with it so I put it in with the other archival material. I must have given it to Phil by mistake."

"How could you make a mistake like that?"

"I don't know." Jordan's voice cracked. "I was panicked...stressed out. Finding my friend murdered and my brother held hostage by a crazed killer tends to unnerve me. I guess I just don't have your equanimity."

"This isn't about you and me. It's about Tristan," Harry yelled.. "He's in danger and I'm going to help him."

"Don't Harry," Jordan grabbed a fin. "You might make things worse."

"A murderer has my son. Things can't get much worse than that!"

Harry pulled away. Before Jordan could reply, he started lumbering down the steps.

She was about to follow when she saw Lady DeVere marching towards her with Chief MacArthur and Lizzie Peltz.

Chapter 41

Phil Bergstrum smiled contentedly as he carefully arranged the musty manuscripts on the oak presentation table, a few early editions of Poe on one side, the Walt Whitman documents and a first edition of Specimen Days on the other. The centerpiece of the presentation was the Herman Melville display, signed first editions of Omoo and Typee, along with several hand-written manuscript pages and three sheets of correspondence with Holden's Dollar Magazine, the first periodical to publish his stories.

Bergstrum didn't know what to make of the small, ancient, leather-bound notebook. It didn't seem to fit with the other pieces. Holding it gingerly, he leafed through some of the barely legible handwritten pages and realized that the language was some variation of Early Modern English.

Cradling it like a wounded bird, he walked three tables over to where Ike Semansky sat in front of two stacks of books.

"They left you here, all by your lonesome?"

"Tash is outside grabbing a smoke."

"Don't feel bad, Jordan deserted me too. I guess standing in front of a table trying to look intelligent is man's work."

"It's asinine work that you and I were too stupid to get out of."

Bergstrum smiled. "I thought they chose us for our dashing good looks." He handed the small leather notebook to Ike. "What do you make of this?"

Semansky examined it intently, turning it over and upside-down, bringing it very close to his face. "Where did you get it?"

"It was mixed in with the Early American manuscripts and papers Jordan gave me, but it looked ancient and British, more up your street."

"It's a very interesting piece."

Bergstrum turned and started walking back to his table. After a few steps he turned and said, "Do you know what it is?"

"At first glance it looks Elizabethan or Jacobean."

"I thought so." He grimaced slightly. "Not really our bailiwick at the library. It's the American masters we crave."

"Phil, would you mind if I hung on to this for a little while?"

"Not at all. I'll make sure to tell Jordan you have it."

"Thanks for bringing it over."

Bergstrum nodded and walked back to the library's table.

Ferette, who had reentered the tent a minute earlier, stood, arms folded, her face puckered into a scowl. "Did Bergstrum really want something or was he just here to gloat about our crappy exhibit?"

"He wanted to know about this." Ike handed the book to Ferette.

She stared at the cover for a short while then carefully checked out some of the inner pages. "Is this what I think it is?" she said excitedly.

"I'm not sure. But if it is…"

* * *

After trudging down the 50-odd steps to the lower campus, Harry lumbered towards Wolcott and Tristan doing his best imitation of the Moby strut — head bobbing, feet wide apart, fins thumping his chest with every stride. They both gaped at him in surprise and amazement. Harry threw off the Moby headpiece, charged at Wolcott and yelled, "Run, Tristan, run!"

For a moment the boy froze, then he realized what was happening, jumped up and sprinted for the steps. A stunned Wolcott made a desperate grab at him but missed. He then reached into his jacket, pulled out a small knife and jabbed it at Harry, who deflected the initial thrust, knocking it out of his hand. The blade pierced the costume and left a bloody gash in Harry's forearm. Fueled by pain, rage and adrenaline, he leaped at Wolcott, knocked him onto the ground and landed on top of him. He grabbed Wolcott's head and pounded it into the fountain floor again and again, yelling, "I'll kill you, you sonuvabitch! Don't you ever go near my son again."

* * *

Tristan reached the upper level and saw Jordan, Lady DeVere, Lizzie Peltz and Chief MacArthur huddled together.

As soon as Jordan saw her brother she ran to him, enveloping him in a hug for the ages. "Tristan, thank God! Are you all right?"

"I'm fine," he said and pointed to the fountain below. "Harry's down there."

MacArthur hurried over to them. "Harry Gabriel is down at the fountain?"

"Yes, sir."

The chief drew his gun and ran for the steps. "Don't worry son, I'll make sure he never hurts you again."

"But Harry didn't..." Tristan never finished his sentence. MacArthur was already halfway down and out of earshot.

Chapter 42

"Why'd you kill them?!" Harry roared. His velour covered knees dug into the other man's shoulders, pinning him to the ground. "Why'd you do it?"

Groggy, bloody and in pain, Wolcott struggled to push him off, but Harry's 195 pounds plus the extra 30 pounds of the costume were too much for him to budge. He finally groaned and said, "I don't know what the hell you're talking about."

"You know exactly what I'm talking about, you bastard! You killed Spenser Berg, Josh Campanella and Peter Foote. And you kidnapped Tristan"

"You're crazy!"

"I'll show you who's crazy!" Harry put his hands around Wolcott's neck and squeezed.

"Okay, okay," he said, gasping for breath. "I'll tell you everything. Just let me up."

Harry loosened his grip slightly when from behind he heard, "Freeze, Gabriel!"

He stopped, craned his neck around and found himself staring into the barrel of a large black pistol. Behind it stood Chief MacArthur, crouched in the shooters position, his hands shaking slightly.

"Stand up slowly," MacArthur continued. "Very slowly."

Harry eased himself off Wolcott and clumsily made it to his feet, the bulky whale suit making every move a chore. "You don't understand. He's the one who..."

"Shut up!" the police chief screamed. "Clasp your hands together behind your head."

"I can't."

"Don't get cute with me, Gabriel. I'll shoot you right now and save myself a lot of paperwork."

"I'm not trying to be cute." Harry held up the two white mitts that covered his hands. "I can't do it because there are no fingers in this costume."

"All right, just put your hands up and move over there by the fountain."

As Harry thrust his hands into the air, MacArthur turned to Wolcott, who was still lying on the ground, groaning dully.

"Are you all right?"

Wolcott sat up, wobbling from side to side. "I didn't do nothing."

"I know," MacArthur said benignly. "Just sit down on one those benches and try to pull yourself together. I'll want a statement from you in a few minutes."

Wolcott stood, walked slowly to the bench area and sat down to catch his breath. As soon as MacArthur turned his back, he stood back up, broke into a slow ungainly trot and ran up the steps, hoping to lose himself in the Whale-a-Palooza crowd.

"Chief, he's getting away!" Harry yelled and pointed at the escaping Wolcott.

"Don't move!" MacArthur leveled the gun at his head. "Get your hands back up."

"But he's the one. He killed Berg and the others."

MacArthur shook his head derisively. "I don't think so. Harry Gabriel, you're under arrest for the murders of Spenser Berg, Josh Campanella and Peter Foote." He unclipped the handcuffs from his belt. "Now put your hands behind your back and turn around."

Harry did as he was told.

Even using both hands, MacArthur couldn't secure a cuff around the bulky sleeve of the Moby suit. "All right," he said, his face turning red with agitation. "Take that stupid costume off."

"Hold on Mac." It was Lizzie. She, Jordan and Tristan walked purposefully towards him. "Before you arrest anybody, I think you better hear what the kid has to say."

Tristan ran to where MacArthur and Harry were standing. "Please Chief, you can't arrest Harry," he pleaded. "He didn't kill those people, Drew Wolcott did. He told me, himself."

"Drew Wolcott?" MacArthur furrowed his brow. "Who the hell is Drew Wolcott?"

"He's the guy that you just let get away," Harry said, turning to face MacArthur.

"Shut the hell up, Gabriel." MacArthur turned back towards Tristan. "All right son, tell me what you know about all this."

As Tristan hesitated, Lizzie said, "Tell the Chief what that Wolcott creep said to you."

Tristan shuffled his feet a few times, bit his lip, then said, "Drew texted Harry about Peter Foote from my phone. He said Harry would be arrested for the murders because the University Police are too stupid to figure out who the real killer is."

MacArthur shook his head. "That's a pretty good story to get your newly found papa off the hook."

Jordan yelled. "It's true." Then said more softly, "We did get a text of Professor Foote's name sent from Tristan's phone. That's why Harry went there."

MacArthur glared at Gabriel. "So you were in Foote's office."

"I never said I wasn't."

MacArthur reached inside his jacket, drew something out and waved it in Harry's face. "And this is yours, I suppose." It was Harry's shoe.

"Yes, that's mine."

There were several seconds of silence, four pairs of eyes were on MacArthur. The Chief stared back at Lizzie, Jordan, Tristan and, finally, Harry. He shook his head resignedly. "I just don't buy it."

"You're wrong, Mac," Lizzie said. "The kid's telling the truth. I'm sure of it."

"Sorry, I gotta go with my gut."

"And I gotta go with mine." She pushed Harry out of the way, ran at MacArthur and wrapped both arms around him in a bear hug. "Gabriel, get the hell out of here," she yelled as MacArthur struggled to free himself from her grasp.

Tristan grabbed the Moby head that was on the ground next to the fountain. "Here," he said, thrusting it at Harry. "You better take this."

Harry took the head and ran up the steps.

Still clutching the struggling chief, Lizzie said. "If I let you go, promise me you'll listen to what Jordan has to say."

MacArthur was silent.

"I can stay here all day."

"All right," he said petulantly.

She released the Chief and turned to Jordan. "Tell him what you told me."

"Yesterday you didn't believe me when I told you someone chased me through the library."

"I didn't say that. I said that there was no evidence of anyone but you being in the library at that time."

"Do you remember me telling you that he ripped my necklace off?"

"Vaguely."

"Check your notes." She shot him a withering glare. "An emerald, diamond and ruby on a gold chain."

"Yeah. It rings a bell."

Tristan thrust his hand into his pocket and held the necklace in front of MacArthur's face. "Here's the necklace that Wolcott took from my sister. I found it in his apartment. He saw me grab it. That's when he took me hostage."

"So you see, Chief, while I was being chased around the library by the murderer, Harry Gabriel was with my brother."

"That's a good story, but I'm still not buying it." He turned to Tristan. "You could've got that necklace from your sister's jewelry case. And anyway, why would the killer be in Josh's closet?"

Before Jordan could answer, Lizzie said, "He was looking for Shakespeare's Table, you dolt."

"We searched in there, no sign of a table. I'm starting to doubt that it even exists."

"It exists," Lizzie said.

"How do you know."

"I found it this morning," Jordan said, much more loudly than she intended.

"Where?"

"In the preservation vault."

"No way. I told you, we were all over that vault. It was full of all kinds of crap — books, papers, tools, even an old pair of shoes, but no table of any kind."

Lizzie looked over at Jordan. "Tell him."

"Shakespeare's Table isn't a table, it's a book. A notebook. A very old notebook."

MacArthur shook his head spasmodically, pummeling the air with his fists. "You people are all insane!" he screamed. "I don't care if it's a table, a book or a freaking ice cream sandwich. All I know is that people are being killed all over this campus because of it and I'm going to make it stop." He took a deep breath. "I'm going to find Harry Gabriel and lock him up. And if Angie doesn't like it she can fire my ass." He stomped away.

Chapter 43

"Whew, that was fun." Lizzie winked at Jordan and her brother and headed back to Main Campus. After a few steps she stopped, turned back and hollered, "You guys be careful."

No sooner was she gone when Jordan's phone rang.

"Hello beautiful." Jordan recognized Wolcott's voice. "You cleaned up your office real good, but I still can't find that Shakespeare book. I need you to get it for me."

"How dare you!" she yelled into the phone, her hand shaking. "I'm calling the police."

"I wouldn't do that," he sniggered. "I got this sweet little old lady here. If I see a cop I might get nervous and accidentally break her neck."

"You're lying!"

The phone made a rustling sound, after a few seconds a different voice came on. "Jordan..."

Jordan thought she recognized it but she wasn't sure. "Lady DeVere, is that you?"

"Please do what he says." Then silence.

"Believe me now?" Wolcott said a few seconds later.

Jordan's hand shook as she yelled into the phone. "You do anything to hurt her and I'll..."

"You'll do what I tell you, that's what you'll do," he said malevolently. "Or else whatever happens to the old bag is on you. Now tell me what you did with that fucking book."

"I can't tell you, I'll have to show you. It's hidden in the vault and you'd never find it by yourself."

"Then get your ass over here. Now!"

The phone went dead.

Jordan stood, transfixed.

"Jor, what's the matter?" Tristan asked nervously.

"That was Wolcott. He's in my office and he has Lady DeVere. He wants Shakespeare's table."

"Just give it to him. Who cares about a stupid book."

"I wish I could, but I don't have it."

"Then let's get it. Where is it?"

"It's in the Showcase display. I put it in with the other exhibition pieces. I can't just take it and leave. Phil Bergstrum will want to know where I'm going."

"So what are we gonna do, call the police?"

"He said he'd hurt her if he saw a policeman."

"We have to do something!"

"I'm going up there."

"What are you going to do? Wolcott's a moose"

"I don't know. But I can't let him hurt Lady DeVere. This is all my fault."

She headed resolutely towards the library.

"I'm coming too." Tristan sent a quick text to Harry, then ran after his sister.

Chapter 44

The Homecoming Parade was still going strong when Harry, in full Moby regalia, lumbered up the granite steps that led back to the academic mall. He fell in behind some of the student marchers and joined the parade.

"Hey Moby," came a voice from behind. "You're gonna lose your head."

"Too much partying last night, huh?" said another. "You forgot to put your head on straight. Mine feels the same way."

The headpiece of his Moby costume had gone off kilter. Harry peeled off the procession near the Rotunda restaurant to try to find an out-of-the-way spot where he could Velcro it back in place. He noticed Bethany Bierstein sitting alone at one of the outdoor tables. He walked over and sat down next to her. She stiffened and said, "Uh...hello there, Mr. Whale."

"Bethany," he whispered. "It's me, Harry."

"Harry? Why are you in that crazy costume?"

"It's a long story but right now I need your help."

"Of course. What's going on?"

"I'll tell you all about it later."

"It has something to do with Spenser Berg's murder, doesn't it?"

"What do you know about that?"

"More than you think. I can help if you tell me what's going on."

Harry exhaled deeply. "The campus police think I murdered Berg and two other people."

"What!" she screamed. "Two more murders! Who?"

"Peter Foote and Josh Campanella."

"Oh my God! I just saw Peter yesterday. Are you sure?"

"Very sure. I found his body this morning with a knife stuck in his eye."

Bethany grimaced. "That's horrible." She paused for a second and said, "And the campus police think you did it?"

"Gregg MacArthur is totally convinced of it. That's why I have to wear this." He gestured up at his costume. "I have a good idea who the actual murderer is and the only way I can clear my name is to find him. I can't do that if I'm locked up in a holding cell."

"Who do you think it is?"

"I don't want to say until I'm absolutely sure. I know what it's like to be falsely accused and I don't want to do that do anyone else."

She hesitated for a moment. "Okay, what can I do to help?"

He turned so that she was facing his neck. "You see those two Velcro strips?"

"Yeah."

"Just fasten them inside the back of the suit so the head doesn't fall off."

In less than a minute she said, "It's done. But I can do a lot more than that."

He sat up at attention. "What do you mean?"

"I haven't been completely forthright with you either, Harry. I'm not here for this idiotic Whale-a-Palooka or whatever they call it. I've been looking into some sinister goings-on at the University for the past few months."

"Seriously? Like what?"

"I'm fairly sure that Annie Macaluso was murdered, along with her husband Anthony. Annie was my favorite professor when I was a student here. A mentor really. After I graduated, we became friends. Really good friends. We talked all the time."

"Really?"

"When she met Anthony they fell head-over-heels in love. She was in her 50's and he was almost 70, but they were like a couple of school kids experiencing their first crush. About six months after their first date they went away to Las Vegas and came back married. A lot of people were very upset."

"About what?"

"Anthony's last name was DeVere.

"The Billionaire?"

Bethany nodded.

"So your friend went to Las Vegas and hit the biggest jackpot of them all."

"It wasn't like that. A lot of people thought she did it for the money, him being so wealthy. But it wasn't true. She signed a pre-nup. The money had nothing to do with it."

"So what's the problem?"

"There were people on campus who got screwed by their marriage, specifically Millicent DeVere and Spenser Berg. Before Anthony met Annie, he doted on his sister. If you ask me, it was a little creepy. She was obsessed with proving that their distant ancestor, Edward De Vere, the Earl of Oxford, was the real author of Shakespeare's works. That's all she thought about, night and day. Anthony didn't care one way or another, but he loved his sister. He gave her the money to finance her crusade to prove Oxford was Shakespeare. The old lady gave most of the money to Berg, who, supposedly, was of the same mindset. For the past several years he claimed to be hot on the trail of some important evidence that would prove them right. I think he fabricated the whole thing just to pry the cash out of her."

"Sounds like Berg."

"Once Annie and Anthony got married, things changed. He still gave his sister a very generous allowance, but not enough to fund Berg's so-called research indefinitely. The old bastard was furious.

"Then, four months later, Anthony and Annie got killed in a car crash, Millicent was the sole beneficiary and Berg's gravy train was back on track."

"Sure things worked out well for Berg but that's a long way from making him a double murderer."

"I'm sure the car was sabotaged."

"Do you have any proof?"

"Just a gut feeling."

"What did the police think?"

"They thought it was a run-of-the-mill one-car collision. An old man in a fast car loses control and hits a tree at 70 miles an hour."

"Sounds logical to me."

"That's because you didn't know Anthony DeVere. Driving was his passion. They were in his 1964 Jaguar XKE. He kept it in perfect condition. He was also a regular at the High Performance Driving Academy at Riverhead Raceway. I've driven with him a few times. He was the best driver I've ever seen. There's no way he crashes that car."

"How'd you find all this out?"

"The same way I did when I was a DA, do a lot of research, ask a lot of people a lot of questions."

"Like who?"

"Everyone who knew Annie, Anthony, his sister or Berg. I also talked to the police, the insurance investigator and the entire Melville English department. I even went over to England and spoke to some of the people that Berg worked with over there."

"And they all talked to you?"

"Are you kidding? Academics are bigger gossips than school girls. I thought it would be hard to get them to open up." She rolled her eyes. "The hard thing was to get them to shut the hell up."

"Let's say you're right and Berg murdered Anthony and Annie. How did he do it? Berg knew nothing about cars. I don't even think he knew how to drive."

"His flunky Wolcott used to work as a mechanic. It would be easy for him to do something to the brakes or the steering."

"So if you're right, how does that help me find Berg's killer?"

"I don't think it does. The only one who cared enough about Anthony to avenge his murder was his sister. But she needed Berg for her Oxford obsession."

"So who do you think killed him?"

"Peter Foote would have been first on my list but he's been eliminated."

Harry snickered. "In every way. But why would you suspect him? I thought he was the only one in the department who got along with Berg."

"That's because Berg had him by the short and curlies."

"What do you mean?"

"Foote was gay."

"So what? College campuses are probably the most gay-friendly environments in America."

"That's true, but Foote had a sexual relationship with one of his students, probably more than one. That's immediate expulsion whether you're straight or gay. Berg found out about it and he's been holding it over his head for years."

"All right. So Foote had a good reason to kill Berg. But who would want to kill Foote?"

"No one that I can think of."

"So let's concentrate on Berg. Who's next on your list?"

"How about your friend Semansky?"

"Yeah, I heard about that one. The Red Panthers incident. I'm not buying it. I don't care how much he hated Berg, Ike's no murderer."

She nodded approvingly. "I'm impressed. You have been doing your homework." Then, after a brief pause. "I bet I have someone you haven't heard about."

"Who?"

"Jordan Day, everyone's favorite librarian."

"Are you saying that she killed Berg because of that Shakespeare table that no one's ever seen? That's even more farfetched than Ike."

"I don't know anything about a table, Shakespearian or otherwise. Jordan hated Berg because she blamed him for her mother's death."

"How can that be? Diana Callahan died of an aneurism."

"That's what Jordan told everyone. But the rumor was that it was a drug overdose. It seems she was addicted to painkillers. She had some kind of accident setting up one of her productions in the theater. I think a light stand fell on her, or something like that, and she was on heavy doses of oxycodone. Berg found out about it and threatened to expose her."

"Why should he care about whether Diana Callahan had a drug problem or not?"

"He was a control freak and Diana couldn't be controlled. He wanted her out so he could get one of his cronies in."

"Still. That doesn't seem like a reason for her to kill herself."

"I didn't say she did. It was probably an accidental overdose. I'm thinking she overmedicated because of all the stress he was putting her through."

"And Jordan knew about all this?"

"They were very close. If Diana confided in anyone it would be her daughter."

"Do you think Tristan knows?

"I have no idea. All I know is that if Jordan blamed Berg for her mother's death, that's a much bigger motive for murder than disagreeing about who wrote Shakespeare."

Harry shook his head in disbelief. "Are you sure about all this?"

"I'm not sure about anything. But I heard about the Diana Callahan situation from a number of different sources while I was looking into the deaths of Annie and Anthony, so I think the information is pretty reliable."

"Jesus, what a bastard! It looks like the only person on campus who didn't despise Berg was Angie."

Bethany shook her head vehemently. "Not true. Angelina DellaRosa had plenty of reasons to hate him."

"I thought she was crazy about him."

"She was." Bethany grinned lasciviously. "She and Berg were an item."

"You mean she and Berg were...?"

"That's right. They were making the beast with two backs, until Berg dumped her. And the university."

"I don't understand."

"The word is that Berg had accepted a position at Tufts. He was gone at the end of the semester." A sinister grin crossed her face. "A woman scorned personally and professionally. How's that for a motive?"

"Not bad."

"I still have one more suspect."

"Who?"

Just then, Harry's phone, unreachable underneath the costume, signaled an incoming text.

"Sorry, Bethany. I gotta go," he said abruptly. "That text might be important."

"Where are you going?"

"The men's room in the Rotunda. The phone's in my pants pocket. I gotta get out of this stupid whale suit. I obviously can't do it here."

Once there, he wriggled out of the costume and grabbed his phone. The text was from Tristan. "Wolcott & DeVere in Jordan's office. We're on our way."

He left the remnants of Moby inside one of the stalls, ran out of the Rotunda and headed towards the library.

Chapter 45

MacArthur grabbed onto the rail at the top of the 52-step stairway he just ran up. Gulping for air, his chest and head throbbed simultaneously. He promised himself that he would get back into shape, then he scanned the dense crowd, looking for a man in a whale suit.

His eyes darted across the hundreds of faces enjoying the festivities. Then, in the distance, he saw what he was looking for.

He grabbed his phone and pressed the push-to-talk key. "Suspect Harry Gabriel outside the Chemistry building, dressed as Moby. I'm on route. Keep him in sight but stand down until I arrive on scene."

As he got closer, he could hear what sounded like polka music. It was an accordionist in lederhosen, seated on a stool in the middle of a great expanse of lawn, playing the "Chicken Dance." Surrounding him, Moby and about ten small children were dancing, flapping their elbows and shaking their behinds. A dozen parents were sitting on the grass, watching their kids, clapping their hands and singing along.

MacArthur could see Wheeler and Suarez at the periphery of the crowd watching the performance. He engaged the walkie-talkie. "Stand down. Stand down. Suspect is with multiple civilians. Possible hostage situation. Will assess. Await further instructions."

MacArthur walked over to the accordion player who had segued into the "Hokey Pokey." He ordered him to stop playing. When the music stopped, Moby did an exaggerated shrug and the children meandered back to their parents.

MacArthur barked into his phone, "Take the whale into custody. Now!"

"Excuse me, sir," Wheeler said, his voice betraying his puzzlement.

MacArthur yelled into the mouthpiece, "That dancing whale is our murder suspect. Get over there and arrest him, goddammit!"

They stared at their phones in disbelief, then at each other. They walked tentatively toward Moby, who was entertaining some kids on the lawn.

President DellaRosa appeared on the scene and asked the accordionist why he stopped playing. He pointed at MacArthur.

She marched over to the Chief. "I hope you have a good reason for upsetting all these children," she said with a fierce scowl.

"I have a very good reason," he answered smugly. "The man inside that whale suit is a killer."

"I think you have lost your mind," DellaRosa yelled.

When she saw people staring at them she forced a smile.

"Moby's not a killer whale you silly man," she said gaily, "He's a white whale." She waved benignly to the crowd.

Then in a whispered growl, "You say anything about murder or murderers again and I'll have your job."

She grabbed the Police Chief by the shirtsleeve and marched him out of earshot of the spectators. "Now tell your men to let him go."

"I'm sorry, Dr. DellaRosa, I can't do that. There have already been three murders on campus and I won't risk a fourth, even if you will." By this time, Wheeler and Suarez were standing behind Moby. "Take him!" MacArthur shouted.

They each grabbed a furry fin.

"Huh!" came the muffled cry from inside the whale head.

"Stop this!" she screamed. "Let go of that whale immediately."

The officers looked over at their boss, who shook his head. They shifted their gaze to DellaRosa, who did not make eye contact with them but continued glaring malevolently at MacArthur.

The Chief took a few steps toward Moby and the two campus cops.

"This is the man who murdered Spenser Berg, Josh Campanella and Peter Foote," he announced triumphantly.

There was a gasp from the few people within earshot. A very discombobulated accordionist, meanwhile, ducked down on his stool, trying to hide behind his instrument.

"Chief MacArthur, I demand that you order your men to release Moby this instant."

"I'm sorry ma'am, I can't. do that"

He glared icily at the president. "I let this psychopath slip through my hands once today because of a woman's interference, I won't let it happen again."

"How dare you! I'm no woman, I'm the president of this university and your boss," she roared. "Mr. MacArthur, I hereby relieve you of your duties for the Melville University Police Department." She turned toward Wheeler and Suarez. "Please release the pris..." She turned to the crowd and smiled benignly. "I mean let go of our wonderful mascot, Moby."

"You're making a monumental mistake, President DellaRosa."

"I think you're the one who made the mistake." She held out a hand. "Give me your badge, gun and phone. They are all property of the University."

MacArthur handed them to DellaRosa, who carefully put them in her oversized handbag. Deflated, he shuffled dejectedly towards Wheeler, Suarez and Moby. He was a few feet from the furry whale mascot when he jumped at him, grabbed the head and started frantically trying to separate it from the rest of the costume.

Shrieks, screams and wails of panic cascaded from the crowd.

DellaRosa, quaking with anger, yelled at the other cops, "You, officers, make him stop. Arrest him if you have to."

Wheeler and Suarez froze in bewilderment. They couldn't bring themselves to put a hand on their chief.

MacArthur, meanwhile, had succeeded in loosening the head, even with Moby trying desperately to keep it on. Mustering all his strength for a final heave, he yanked it up and off. Turning his gaze to DellaRosa, he said, "Here's your murderer, Harry Gab..."

But it wasn't Harry Gabriel in his grasp, it was Chris Conway, the

Melville University senior who had been playing Moby for the last three years.

"Who the hell are you?" MacArthur demanded.

Before the dazed mascot could answer, DellaRosa screamed, "He's the young man who plays Moby, you idiot. Now that you've made a complete fool of yourself and horrified these children," she pointed to a group of kids huddled nervously in a corner, "leave this campus at once or I will I have you arrested."

"I don't understand." MacArthur stared blankly ahead, ambling towards the south gate.

She turned toward the young mascot. "Are you all right?"

"Yes, ma'am."

"Can you still perform for these children?"

"Sure." He smiled. "But only for a few minutes. Then I gotta get to the game."

"Of course. We can't have you disappoint your fans."

She turned to Suarez and Wheeler. "Help him with his costume!" she ordered.

They jumped to his aid, fastening the head back onto the torso with Velcro strips.

The excitement over, DellaRosa turned to the accordionist, who hadn't budged. "Okay, Fritz, let's have some music."

As he started playing the Chicken Dance, Moby gave his signature 'fins-up' sign and began a frenetic two-step. Within seconds, the crowd was singing and dancing along with him, as if the MacArthur debacle never happened.

DellaRosa gave a final wave to the crowd and headed back towards the center of campus.

Chapter 46

Tristan stood anxiously behind Jordan as she cautiously opened the door to her office.

"I'm not so sure this is a good idea. Drew's a psycho. We should call the police or something."

"No police!" Jordan said, emphatically. "All they ever do is make things worse."

She slowly pushed the door open.

"All right Mr. Wolcott, we're here," she yelled into the empty room. "What do you want with us?"

No response.

"Nobody's here," Tristan said. "We should go. Maybe it was all a joke."

"That was no joke. Let's look in the back."

They walked trepidatiously across the main reading room, Jordan's head swerving from side to side expecting Wolcott to jump out at them at any moment. They made it to her office door without incident. There were still some broken remnants of police tape on it. She pushed it open, flicked on the light and walked uneasily inside. Steeling herself for an attack that never came, she relaxed and scanned the room to assess any damage.

Suddenly she screamed and collapsed on a chair.

Tristan ran over to her. "Jor, what is it?"

She pointed to a corner of the room. Wolcott was curled in a fetal ball, his head resting at an odd angle in a pool of blood that appeared to come from a small, dark hole in his temple. Tristan ran over to the body.

"Holy crap, it's Drew!" he cried. His eyes were riveted on Wolcott's perforated skull. "He's dead, isn't he?"

"I think so." Her voice was thready. Her skin pale, almost translucent. Her breathing, labored.

Tristan gaped at his big sister. "What do we do now?"

Jordan shrugged. She was sapped physically and emotionally.

"What about Lady DeVere? Do you think she's dead too?"

"I'd rather not think about it," she said softly. "Call Chief MacArthur. His card is in my bag."

Tristan rummaged through the bag. After a few seconds he found the card and dialed the number. It rang five times, then he heard a scratchy recorded female voice. "This is the Melville University Police Department. No one is here to assist you at the moment. Please leave your name, location and the reason why you are calling."

"Chief, this is Tristan Day." His voice was laced with panic. "I'm with my sister in her office in the library. Drew Wolcott is here. He's dead. We can't find Lady DeVere. Please come as soon as you can." He walked back to Wolcott's prostrate body and started taking pictures with his phone.

"Tristan, what are you doing? Get away from there."

"When the police come they're gonna ask a million questions. I want to show them exactly what we found so we don't get accused of anything."

Jordan nodded. "That makes sense, I guess."

He grabbed a chair, pulled it next to his sister and sat down. "Now what do we do?"

She took both his hands in hers. "I wish I knew." Her face showed the unrelenting strain of the past two days. "Nothing makes sense. I thought it was Wolcott doing all these terrible things. Now..." she shrugged. "I know it has something to do with the Shakespeare notebook but I don't know what."

"Let's go get it. Do you know where it is?"

She pursed her lips and gazed up at the ceiling, then shook her head.

"I can't remember if I left it in the vault or put it in with the Scholars' Showcase material."

"I'll go look in the vault and see if it's there."

"No, I'll go. You don't know what it looks like." She willed herself to stand and marched resolutely back across the main reading room.

The vault door was half open. Jordan felt a chill as she approached it. This was once her favorite place in the entire library, her personal time portal to literary immortality, where history reached across the ages to touch the here and now. Where precious volumes, once held by the greatest writers who ever put pen to paper, were now available for her gentle caress. The events of the past few days slammed shut that portal forever. What had been a temple was now a tomb.

Her hand trembled as she pushed the door open a little wider. She took a cautious step inside, felt for the light switch and flipped it, blinking at the sudden brightness. She saw what she thought was a body in the corner. Then it moved and emitted a throaty groan.

Jordan screamed. It was a scream that was two terror-filled days in the making, that lasted as long as she had breath, that depleted her lungs and what was left of her strength. When she finally stopped she had to hold on to one of the shelves to keep from falling.

Tristan ran to her, as did Lady DeVere, who had been huddled in the back of the vault.

"I'm so sorry, dear. I didn't mean to frighten you."

Tristan took his sister's arm and walked her over to one of the carrels just outside the vault, easing her into a chair.

DeVere followed them. "Is she all right? With all she's been through, I'm afraid this might have been one shock too many."

"I'm fine," Jordan said. "You just startled me. I didn't expect to see anyone inside the vault."

Tristan stared at the old woman with bulging eyes. "Lady DeVere, we thought you were, uh..."

Jordan cut him off. "What happened here?" she said, gaining strength.

DeVere took a deep breath. "That Wolcott brute took me captive in the library. He was determined to get his hands on the Shakespeare diary and for some reason he thought I knew where it was. When I told him I hadn't the slightest idea as to its whereabouts he became violently angry. He grabbed my hair and I thought he was about to strangle me on the spot. That's when I said that if anyone knew where it was, it would be you." She brought her palms together in a prayerful gesture. "I'm so sorry. Please forgive me. I would have never gotten you involved if I hadn't thought my life was in imminent danger."

"But who shot Wolcott?" Tristan asked.

"That's where it gets very strange," DeVere said. "After he spoke to Jordan on the mobile phone and she told him she was going to come up and show him where the book was, he became convinced that she was going to send the police and that they would arrest him for the murders. Then he began to rant, screaming that he'd rather die than go back to prison."

"I never knew he was in prison," Tristan blurted.

DeVere ignored him and continued. "He began waving his gun around, screaming incoherently. I've never been so frightened in my life. I was sure he was going to shoot me. In his paranoia he went over to the window to see if the police were coming. That's when I ran out of the office and hid in the vault. I thought he would come after me but he didn't. A few minutes later I heard what sounded like a firecracker going off. I assumed it was a gunshot but I wasn't sure so I remained hidden in the vault. I can only imagine that he took his own life."

Tristan, who was staring intently at his phone, looked up and said, "He couldn't have shot himself. There's no gun."

Lady DeVere reached over towards him. "May I see that?"

"Sure." He handed the phone to her. "Do you know how it works?"

"Of course." She glared at him. "I'm old, not stupid." She flipped through all of Tristan's pictures of the crime scene, pausing several times to stare intently at certain frames. "You're correct, young man. If he shot himself there would be a pistol somewhere near the body."

"That means somebody else killed Drew," Tristan said. "But who?"

"I'm afraid the most likely candidate is your friend Harry Gabriel," DeVere said solemnly. "He was in the process of beating him to death when Chief MacArthur intervened. It looks like he came back to finish the job."

Chapter 47

Natasha Ferette glanced down at her watch, then at Semansky, who was assiduously leafing through the ancient volume.

"We're supposed to give our brilliant presentation on that stage in four minutes and I've got bupkis," she growled.

She pointed to the raised platform at the rear of the tent. "I hope whatever it is you've been staring at in that decrepit little journal for the past half hour will keep us from looking like a couple of first class douchebags."

"We're fine." He winked at her and was rewarded with a skeptical snort in return.

"Maybe you're fine. I'm not feeling so honky-dory right now."

"You can just stand next to me and smile."

"Sure I'll be your Vana White. If you screw up, I'll sneak off the stage. If you're a hit, I'll walk up next to you at the end and glom some credit. Isn't that the way they do it here in the hallowed halls of academe?"

"It is. And you have my permission to carry on that ignoble tradition."

About half the seats in the five rows of ten white metal folding chairs were occupied. The audience was a mixture of students, faculty and guests of various ages. Many held a printed sheet that read, "The

Bard. Unmasked. Who really wrote Shakespeare?" presented by the faculty editors of Yorick's Brain, Melville University's acclaimed Shakespeare journal."

Semansky walked onto the stage. He stood, looked out into the crowd and said, "I love mysteries, don't you?"

A murmur of assent buzzed through the audience.

"Today we're going to explore one of the most enduring literary mysteries of all time." He paused, scanned the room, then continued. "William Shakespeare was a glover's son from the small country town of Stratford Upon Avon. He left school in our equivalent of the eighth grade. His parents were semi-literate and the only book in the house he grew up in was the bible."

He threw his hands in the air. "Could this be the clay out of which the greatest writer in the history of the English language was formed? Was this unschooled bumpkin the true author of the most enduring literary works of all time? Or could it have been someone else? Someone with the education, breeding, knowledge and experience to have conceived and executed these masterworks. Someone who could not openly acknowledge that he was the author because it was either socially unacceptable or physically dangerous. Many people...brilliant people, including Sigmund Freud, Albert Einstein, Mark Twain and the great Shakespearian actor, Sir John Gielgud think it's not only possible, but an absolute certainly.

"Through the years there have been many candidates for the title of 'Alias William Shakespeare.' One was the great playwright Christopher Marlowe. His official death was recorded in 1593, but suppose that was a scam. Marlowe had ample reason to fear for his life. He was an outspoken atheist and homosexual when both were capital offenses. He was also a government informant whose testimony sent a lot of men to prison or the gallows. By the time he was killed under very suspicious circumstances, he was a wanted man, both by the law and the lawless. It's not a huge stretch to imagine that he faked his own murder and went into hiding, probably across the English Channel to France. Once safe on the Continent, he could resume his writing and send his manuscripts back to an obscure actor of his acquaintance, one Will Shakespeare. Marlowe was England's preeminent playwright when he died.

And, coincidentally, almost all of Shakespeare's plays were written after Marlowe exited, stage left, supposedly to the big theater in the sky.

"Or it could have been Sir Francis Bacon. Think that's not kosher? Think again." He paused to allow people in the audience to laugh at his joke. None did. "Bacon was one of the major intellects of the era and had all the credentials needed to be the author of the plays. He was a poet, a lawyer, a philosopher and a statesman. He had an intimate knowledge of history and was a prolific writer. But because he was a member of both the aristocracy and Parliament, working in the theater was out of the question. It would be like the Secretary of State taking a second job as a DJ in a strip club. Bacon was the first Elizabethan aristocrat to be touted as the real Shakespeare but he wasn't the last.

"Today, the most popular authorship candidate is the Earl of Oxford, Edward de Vere. Known to have been a gifted writer and poet, de Vere's life paralleled many of Shakespeare's plots. In fact, several of his contemporaries assumed that Shakespeare based the character of Hamlet on him. Oxford traveled to many of the locations of the plays and was even the patron of an acting company, giving him easy access to the theater. There are several books, dozens of websites and even a Hollywood movie all proclaiming de Vere to be the true author.

"So did William Shakespeare write those timeless plays? Was it Marlowe, Bacon, Oxford or maybe a collaboration of all those guys and more? No one really knew for sure until Spenser Berg found this little notebook." He held Shakespeare's table aloft with one hand. "Written by the one person who knew all the secrets. William Shakespeare, himself."

He paused, waiting for the stunned reaction to his startling revelation. It got the same response as his joke. Two young people whom Semansky knew to be grad students in English Lit seemed engrossed, others nodded in mild interest, but most of the audience was unfazed. In fact, a few people stood and left to go to the football game. It always amazed and disappointed him that something he and his colleagues were so passionate about, something that they spent their lives exploring, was of so little interest to most of the world.

Swallowing his disappointment, he soldiered on. "This is one of the personal journals of William Shakespeare, what the Elizabethans called a commonplace book or table book. Many men of prominence carried these small diaries to jot down their plans, their thoughts, their experiences, anything that came into their heads. Hamlet mentions his in Act I, after seeing the ghost of his father, he says, 'My tables — meet it is I set it down.'

"Our esteemed colleague, Dr. Berg, discovered this table of Shakespeare's last summer, and like many important discoveries, it was a total accident. He was researching the life of Philip Henslowe, the theatrical entrepreneur and impresario who owned the Rose Theatre, the home of the Admiral's Men, Shakespeare's company's main rivals.

"As you all know, Dr. Berg has been acclaimed as the nation's premier Elizabethan scholar. His quest to discover the true author took him to Dulwich College on the outskirts of London. Founded during Shakespeare's lifetime by the renowned actor Edward Alleyn, the college became a central meeting place for Elizabethan London's theatrical and intellectual elite. Actors, poets, playwrights, philosophers, they all spent some time at Dulwich. Dr. Berg, who devoted the past ten years to discovering Shakespeare's true identity, hypothesized that if any proof existed at all, it would be found there among the papers and artifacts of Shakespeare's colleagues, competitors and patrons.

Imagine his surprise when he found, tucked away among Henslowe's ledgers, bills and contracts, this small diary. A book that he verified to be Shakespeare's personal journal for the year 1599."

Semansky could have spoken for another fifteen minutes but his audience was fading fast so he decided to wrap it up.

"So what does this 400-year-old notebook tell us? It seems to indicate that William Shakespeare of Stratford was, if anything, a minor collaborator in the creation of the plays and poems that bear his name. He writes that he resented the other writers of his day, who scorned and belittled him as a mediocre playwright and banal poet. But because he was a favorite of the Earls of Essex and Southampton — perhaps their lover, possibly their procurer, maybe both — he was selected to be the front man for Oxford, Bacon and several others including the Queen, herself, and was paid handsomely for his efforts."

Semansky closed the ancient notebook gently and placed it on the lectern. "I'm afraid that's all I can share with you right now. Thank you for coming."

As they made their way out of the tent, he heard a familiar voice above the din.

"That was a very interesting little talk."

It was Angelina DellaRosa making her way slowly down the aisle, navigating through clusters of audience members heading for the football game or another activity. By the time she reached the stage the crowd had dispersed. Ferette was standing off to the side of the small stage, nervously nibbling on her cuticles.

"I sincerely hope you know what you were talking about," DellaRosa continued. "The reputation of the Melville University English department will suffer greatly if Spenser Berg, our most illustrious faculty member and the nation's foremost authority on Shakespeare, is proven to be either a fraud or a fool."

"In my opinion, he was both," Semansky said defiantly.

Instead of being shocked, DellaRosa smiled smugly. "What would that make you, Isaac…his enabler, his accomplice, his stooge…considering you wrote all of his scholarly articles for the last year and a half?"

Semansky flinched. "You knew about that?"

"I suggested it. I noticed Spenser's decline about two years ago and confronted him about it. He was exhibiting all the early signs of Alzheimer's. My father was stricken with that horrendous affliction so I was all too familiar with the symptoms. The stubborn ass wouldn't even see a doctor until I threatened to let the world know about his condition. He was put on Aricept, a medication which slowed the progress of the disease for awhile, but over the last few months it's gotten much worse. Some days he'd be fine, then without warning he'd become hostile, delusional, paranoiac."

"We've noticed," Ferette said, joining them.

"Be that as it may, I will not have Spenser Berg's descent into dementia drag down this university." She walked to the lectern, picked up Shakespeare's table, held it out in front of her like it was Yorick's skull and said, "This is the cause of all the trouble. If it wasn't a priceless literary artifact I'd throw it in the fire."

"Go ahead," Semansky said. "It's worthless."

DellaRosa gasped. A horrified look came over her face. "But you said it was proof of the true author."

"No, I said Berg believed it was proof. And I think he did. In fact, that book is a fake — a very old, painstakingly rendered forgery but still a forgery."

"How can you be so sure?"

"I've been examining it for the past half hour and I found a couple of anomalies. I'm sure, given time, we'll find many more."

He handed it to her. "Look very carefully at the cover." She held the reddish brown, leather notebook close to her eyes. "See the gold filigree border, that's what's known as Morocco binding. It wasn't used in England until the middle of the seventeenth century, about thirty years after Shakespeare died. So you see, this couldn't possibly be his diary.

"And that's not the only proof." He held out his hand. "Would you mind giving that back to me." She handed him the book and he carefully leafed through it. After a moment he found the page he was looking for. He pointed to a line in the middle of it. "See this?" The line read, 'He was quytte upset.'

Semansky slipped into his professorial mode. "I've read more than my share of Elizabethan manuscripts and none of them spell 'quite' quite that way. But let's ignore that for now and concentrate on the word 'upset.' It was originally a nautical term used by sailors meaning 'to raise up' as in 'upset the mainsail.' It wasn't used the way we use it today, to mean 'distressed or perturbed,' until around the middle of the nineteenth century, about the same time when there was a brisk trade in Shakespeare forgeries."

"You're absolutely positive about this?"

"I'm 99 percent sure."

"Well I'd like to be 100% sure. Until your findings are verified, I don't want any of what we just discussed leaving this room. Is that clear, Isaac?"

He nodded.

"Natasha?"

"Crystal."

"Now may I please have the book back? Forgery or not, it's the property of the University."

He handed it to her. She placed it gently into her bag next to MacArthur's phone, badge and gun.

She turned back to Ferette and Semansky. "You two have done good work today. You salvaged what could have been a disastrous embarrassment. No go enjoy the remainder of the festival." She held a finger against her lips. "Just remember, not a word."

On their way out of the tent, Ferette looked quizzically at Semansky. "That sounded like a giant load of bullshit to me. Are you really positive that diary was a forgery?"

He grinned slyly, winked and continued walking.

* * *

DellaRosa sat down on a chair in the first row of the empty tent. MacArthur's phone had been vibrating constantly in her bag. She fished it out to check his voicemail. There were three messages. The first was about a parking problem in the Stadium lot. The second was from a hysterical parent reporting a lost child. The third voice she heard was Tristan's, saying that he and Jordan were in the Special Collections office, someone named Wolcott was dead and Lady DeVere was missing.

She dropped the phone back into her bag and hurried out of the tent. As she headed towards the library she saw Harry hustling across the academic mall. "Is that you, Mr. Gabriel?"

Harry froze.

She ran over to him. "Come with me," she said, tugging on his sleeve. "Jordan Day and her young brother are in her office in the library and they may be danger. We must act quickly."

"I know."

Taken aback, she said, "You know? How?"

"I got a text from Tristan."

"Well, all right then. Let's go."

"No." As she started to move he grabbed her arm and held fast. "I'll go and see what's going on. You stay here and call the police, the real police, not those campus clowns. Send them up to the library. Hopefully they'll get there before anyone else gets killed."

Chapter 48

Lady DeVere sat on the sofa in the main reading room. Jordan was on one of the two Queen Ann chairs opposite her. Tristan paced back and forth between them.

"You know, I'm to blame for all this," the old woman said.

Jordan sat up with a start. "I don't know how you can say that. You had nothing to do with any of this awful business."

"Oh, but I did. Spenser was never really all that concerned with the authorship question. He thought finding out whether the true author was the man from Stratford, the Earl of Oxford or someone else was an interesting mental exercise but of no real consequence. He was much more interested in the words themselves — their beauty, their meaning, their power, their passion — regardless of who wrote them."

This made no sense to Jordan. "But he spent the last several years looking for proof that Oxford was the true author."

"He did that for me. He knew how important it was to me. We were very close, you know. In love actually." She smiled dreamily.

Then she gestured to Tristan. "Come sit next to me, young man." She patted the sofa. "We don't want you wearing a hole in the carpet."

The boy did as he was told.

"Now what were we talking about?" DeVere closed her eyes in

concentration. "Oh yes, proving that Oxford was the true author. Now that Spenser is gone, I'm going to need your help."

"I'm not sure there's anything I can do but..."

"Well, as a matter of fact, there is."

"Really?"

"Why yes. Do you know that little book that Spenser gave to the library?

"Shakespeare's table?"

"That's right."

"You know, he actually meant for me to have it. He pretended to donate it to the university so that he could avoid paying taxes. Spenser absolutely loathed the Internal Revenue. If he were alive, I'm sure he would ask you to give it to me."

"I'm sorry, Lady DeVere, but I don't have the authority to do that," Jordan said solicitously. "If it proves to be authentic, it will be the most important piece in the entire collection. Perhaps the most valuable book in the world." She smiled sweetly at the old woman. "I can suggest that we put it with the DeVere collection. That way it will be your legacy as well as Dr. Berg's. And of course, you can come up here whenever you like and use it for your own research."

"That's very sweet, dear but I don't think you realize how much that little book means to me. Neither my brother nor I had any children. With him gone, I'm the last of the DeVere line. That diary will be my only issue, a lasting epitaph, proving beyond a doubt that my ancestor, Edward de Vere, the 17th Earl of Oxford, was the greatest literary artist who ever lived." She bowed her head and looked plaintively at Jordan. "Now do you understand why it's so important for me to possess it?"

"Yes, of course I do. Nothing would give me greater pleasure than to give it to you. But unfortunately, I can't."

"Of course you can. All you have to do is go to the vault and get it."

"I wish it were that easy."

DeVere's benign smile morphed into a grimace. "It is easy," she said sternly. "It's you that's being difficult."

"You don't understand. It's not in the vault..."

"You told Wolcott you had it. That it was in the library. I heard you." DeVere's tone betrayed a hint of anger. "Why would you lie?"

"Because I was trying to save your life," Jordan said defensively. "I thought that Wolcott was going to kill you if he didn't get his hands on that book. I was playing for time."

DeVere forced herself to smile. "Of course you were doing what you thought was best. Where is it now?"

"I think I might have mistakenly given it to Phil Bergstrum, along with some other volumes that he needed for the library's Scholars' Showcase exhibit."

DeVere's smile vanished as suddenly as it had returned. "Do you realize, young lady, how extraordinarily valuable that little book is?" Her tone became more hostile with each word. "The greatest literary artifact ever discovered and you cavalierly toss it into a pile of dusty old relics that no one cares about. I demand that you call this Bergstrum person immediately and see if he has it."

"I have no idea where he is at this moment," Jordan replied, a little indignantly. "But even if I did, as I told you before, Shakespeare's table isn't mine to give. It belongs to the university."

"And as I told you, Spenser never meant for the university to have it. He always intended to give it to me."

"I think you'll have to take that up with President DellaRosa."

"I'll take nothing up with that harpy." DeVere bristled. "She never appreciated Spenser's towering intellect. She seduced him with her Etruscan charm and used him like a trained monkey to garner prestige for this second rate farm school."

Jordan couldn't believe what she was hearing. "I thought you loved this university."

DeVere stood and glowered at Jordan. "I would love for you to stop prattling and bring me my book," she yelled.

Then she reached into her purse and pulled out a small pistol, not much bigger than a computer mouse. With its pearl handle and tiny barrel, it looked like a toy cap gun.

"Please, Lady DeVere, put that away," Jordan pleaded, unsure whether she should be afraid or amused. "If that thing is real, you may hurt someone with it."

"It's real, my dear. And I fully intend to hurt someone if I have to."

She patted the gun in her hand like it was a kitten. "This little beauty is called a Velo-dog. When my grandmother was a young woman in London, she used it to protect herself from stray dogs and rats while riding her velocipede around the Serpentine in Hyde Park. Like me, it's an antique. But I can assure you we're both fully functional. And deadly when necessary." She turned to Tristan, who had been huddled silently in a corner of the sofa, and leveled the gun at him.

"What are you doing!" Jordan cried.

"I wouldn't want to harm the boy, but if you don't retrieve my book right now I will."

"Lady DeVere, I can't believe you're acting this way? You're not a murderer."

She shook her head malevolently. "You're quite wrong, dear. I am. I've already killed five people. I'm actually becoming quite adept at it."

Jordan's mouth gaped open. "Y-you killed Dr. Berg and Josh and..."

"Yes. Some with the assistance the late Mr. Wolcott. But he was acting on my orders. So you see I won't hesitate."

Jordan glanced over at her brother.

"All right, I believe you. I'll do whatever you want. Just don't hurt my brother."

"All I want is my book — now go find your Mr. Bergman or Bergstrum, whatever, and fetch it. I'll wait here with your brother until you come back. And you better have it with you."

Jordan was now fighting the onslaught of a major panic attack. As she willed herself to stand, the door flung open and Harry charged in.

"Where's Wolcott?" he yelled, slightly out of breath.

"Harry, be careful — she has a gun!" Tristan screamed.

He turned to Jordan, who was standing, unsteadily, about a dozen feet from him. Her empty hands hung quivering at her side. "I don't see a gun."

"That's because you're looking at the wrong she," DeVere said, holding the small gun with both hands, now pointing it at Harry.

"What's going on?" he said to Tristan. "I thought you said Wolcott was here."

"Wolcott's dead." He pointed at DeVere. "She killed him."

"Is this a joke?" He walked toward the old lady.

"Please stop right there, Mr. Gabriel. I will most certainly shoot if you take another step."

Jordan yelled, "She's serious, Harry. She did it. She killed them all. Please don't give her a reason to hurt anyone else."

"But why? I don't understand."

"I do." Angelina DellaRosa walked into the room.

"You!" DeVere shrieked. "You're the cause of all this."

Harry turned and glared at the University president. "I thought I told you to stay downstairs and get the police."

"I'm not very good at following orders," she said smugly. "I'm much better giving them." She glared at DeVere. "Put that silly little pistol down before you actually hurt someone."

"I intend to hurt someone." She turned the tiny pistol toward Della-Rosa. "You!"

"You were always envious of me," DellaRosa said disdainfully. "Jealous that Spenser chose me over you."

"Spenser never loved you," DeVere said, her voice dripping with contempt. "He considered you an unlettered guttersnipe...a superannuated street urchin...a philistine of the lowest order. He tolerated you only because he needed your support to pursue his research."

"There was never any research," DellaRosa shot back. "Spenser was dying. He had Alzheimer's disease. But he stopped doing any research well before that. He used you. He's been swindling you for years."

"That's a lie!" DeVere screamed. "He found that Shakespeare diary, the one that beyond all doubt proves my patrimony, that Edward De Vere is the one true author."

"That diary's a fake, a fraud, just like Spenser's feelings for you."

"You unconscionable bitch! I should kill you now but I'll wait until Miss Day goes to your insipid showcase and retrieves the book. Then you'll die knowing that Spenser loved me."

"It's not there. She has no idea where the Shakespeare diary is."

"And I suppose you do."

"That's right," DellaRosa said with a smirk.

"Where?"

"Why should I tell you? You're just going to shoot me anyway."

"I'll spare her, Gabriel and the boy."

"Why should I believe you?"

"I give you my word."

"That's not good enough."

"It's all you're going to get and more than you deserve."

DellaRosa closed her eyes for a few seconds.

"All right," she said resignedly. "It's in my bag."

DeVere smiled contentedly. "That was a prudent decision." She turned to Jordan. "Young lady, bring me the book."

DellaRosa handed her handbag to Jordan. "Be careful, dear. This is my portable office. It's crammed with all kinds of things I find useful in my travels." Then she winked.

Jordan opened the bag and peered inside. The ancient diary was on top. It's what she saw next to it that made her gasp. MacArthur's service pistol, the one President DellaRosa confiscated earlier that day. It sent a shiver down her spine. She abhorred guns. She had never touched one. The thought of shooting a gun made her physically ill.

She quickly composed herself, carefully lifted the notebook out of the bag and handed it to DeVere.

The old woman took it in her gnarled left hand, still training her pistol on DellaRosa with her right. She smiled contentedly and cradled the small notebook to her heart. Without changing her expression she fired at DellaRosa, who crumpled, bleeding, to the ground.

Jordan screamed as she, Tristan and Harry ran to her.

Harry felt for a pulse. "She's still alive. We have to get her to the hospital."

"I'm afraid I can't let you do that," DeVere said with mock regret. "I refuse to spend my last years in prison and I highly doubt that I can convince any of you to keep this to yourselves, which means I have no choice other than to take drastic action."

She turned the gun on Tristan. "I really am sorry, young man. I had actually grown quite fond of you."

Harry jumped in front of him, shielding his newly discovered son's body with his own.

"Run!" he yelled as he walked straight toward the gun barrel. "She can't shoot you through me!"

She leveled her pistol at Harry's chest. "A noble gesture, Mr. Gabriel, but ultimately futile."

A loud blast shook the room. Lady DeVere fell to the floor amidst an explosion of blood spatter. Jordan stood a few feet behind her, holding MacArthur's Glock in her trembling hands, tears streaming down her face. Tears of joy and relief that her brother was safe and the nightmare that was plaguing the campus was over. Also tears of sorrow that she had just taken a human life, something that no matter what the justification, she found abhorrent.

Chapter 49

A huge banner hung over the stage of the Richard Rogers theater, proclaiming "Congratulations December Graduates!" The audience was a sea of white. Young men and women in white gowns and matching mortarboards were in the center seats, with proud parents, relatives and friends seated along the periphery.

Ike Semansky stood behind a lectern at center stage.

"I have a great surprise for you today," he said into the wireless microphone. "Gracing our campus for the first time since that horrendous day last October, it gives me great pleasure to present, our esteemed president, Angelina DellaRosa."

The hall erupted in thunderous applause as President DellaRosa, slightly stooped, walked slowly but resolutely toward center stage. When she arrived at the podium Semansky kissed her gently on both cheeks. She steadied herself, grabbing either side of the lectern for support as Semansky walked off the stage, taking a seat in the front row. That row was usually reserved for wealthy donors and local politicians. But seated there today along with Semansky were Jordan, Tristan, Natasha Ferette and Harry Gabriel.

"I can't tell you how wonderful it is to be here with you today. I have missed you all so much," DellaRosa said, her voice cracking with emotion.

Someone from the back of the theater shouted, "We miss you too, Angie. We love you." Which started another wave of applause.

She wiped away a tear. "Firstly, I would like to thank everyone for your kind thoughts while I was in the hospital. The cards, notes, flowers, emails and texts are what kept my spirits up. Without them I'm not sure I would be here today. Second, there are some lessons to be learned from those awful events of a few months ago. Namely, good always triumphs over evil. Perseverance is one of the most important qualities you can have. And no one is indispensable."

She smiled. "To that effect, Melville University seems to have gotten along pretty well without me these last couple of months."

A murmur of dissent passed through the crowd.

"I'm extremely proud of all you graduates today. You have persevered through the most difficult semester this university has ever experienced. I have no doubt that what you have been through — the loss of beloved professors and valued colleagues, the intrusion of the police and media for weeks on end, the continual disruptions and distractions — will prepare you to excel in all manner of circumstances in the future.

"My doctors have limited me to no more than five minutes so I must be brief. But before I leave, I would like to acknowledge some people, who quite literally, saved my life and probably saved this university as well. Please stand when I call your name. And I ask the audience to hold your applause until the end.

"Isaac Semansky, one of the nation's premier authorities on Elizabethan literature, recently named the Anthony DeVere Distinguished Professor of Humanities and Literature.

"Natasha Ferette, the new Chair of the Melville University Department of Women's Studies.

"Harry Gabriel, just back from a cross-country tour promoting his latest best-seller, 'Alas, Poor Shakespeare,' has accepted our invitation to be the visiting Presidential Professor of Arts and Culture for the spring semester.

"Jordan Day, who today I am announcing will be the Associate Dean of Libraries and will be this year's recipient of the Presidential Medal of Merit.

"And finally, Tristan Day." She stopped and gestured towards him.

"Tristan, I have no lofty title I can bestow upon you. All I can say is that you are the bravest young man I have ever known and if not for you and your sister, I wouldn't be here — or anywhere — today. I can never thank you enough."

Everyone in the theater rose to their feet, clapped and cheered as deafening roar swept over the theater. Two minutest later it finally subsided.

"Congratulations graduates," DellaRosa said as loudly as she could into the microphone, then turned to walk offstage. Two male nurses entered from backstage and helped her into a wheelchair that was waiting for her behind the curtain as the audience erupted one more time.

After a few more speeches and the presentation of diplomas, the ceremony was over. Harry, who had stopped to congratulate Ike and Natasha on their promotions, walked outside. The next thing he knew, he was being bear-hugged by Lizzie Peltz. Gregg MacArthur stood stone-faced next to her.

"It's great to see you, Harry." She planted a big, wet kiss on his cheek. "I can't believe you're going to be here for a whole semester. We're gonna have a great time!"

"It'll be fun."

MacArthur ambled over, offering his hand. "No hard feelings, Gabriel."

Harry shook it. "None. You were doing your job. If I were in your shoes, I'd think I was guilty too. Though I have to say, I would have never guessed it was Lady DeVere."

"Yeah, it turns out she was behind everything, even her brother's death."

"I can't believe it. I thought she was very close her brother."

"She didn't mean to kill her brother," Lizzie interrupted. "She was trying to kill Annie Macaluso. She got Wolcott to sabotage the brakes in their car and disable Annie's airbag. She figured Annie would be killed in the crash but her brother would survive. It would've worked too, except the car hit a tree and exploded."

Harry grimaced. "That's awful. But why kill Berg? I thought she was in love with him."

"She was. She told Berg what she did and that he now had all the funds he would ever need to pursue his research."

"So far it doesn't sound like a motive for murder."

"Seems that Berg had some scruples after all," MacArthur said. "He called her a homicidal maniac and demanded that she turn herself in. Said if she didn't, he would. A couple of days later she poisoned him with Strychnine."

"But how did she get his head on the library finial?"

"That's where Peter Foote came in," Lizzie said, cutting MacArthur off. "She told him that Berg poisoned himself and left the evidence of Peter's um...indiscretions, along with his will. DeVere told him not to worry. That she was named executor and destroyed the incriminating documents. Foote was incensed. He felt betrayed academically, professionally and personally. He leaped at the idea of using his ancient battle-axe to chop off Berg's head and place it on the library finial. It was also his idea to take the torso back to Berg's House and burn it. He said that the Elizabethans knew the proper way to treat traitors. He got poor Josh Campanella to help him. It looks like they were lovers."

Harry shook his head. "If I wasn't there, I wouldn't believe it."

"DeVere couldn't trust Foote and Campanella to keep their mouths shut so they had to go too," Lizzie said.

"But why did she kill Wolcott?"

"He tried to extort money from her." MacArthur shook his head. "Bad idea."

"So are you back as head of University Police?"

Lizzie stepped in front and gestured grandly at MacArthur. "Much better than that. Let me introduce you to the new Riverhead County Chief of Police."

The scowl that was permanently etched on MacArthur's face morphed into a sheepish grin.

"Well congratulations, Chief." Harry thrust out his hand. "I mean it. I'm glad everything turned out all right."

"Thanks." MacArthur took Harry's hand and shook it briskly.

"One thing though," Harry said. "How did you find out all these details?"

"It turns out DeVere kept a diary," MacArthur said. "It was all in there."

"So everybody made out but me," Lizzie said in mock disappointment. "Mac gets a big new job and a hefty raise, and the rest of you got promoted. And your friend, Bethany, she did best of all. Got a huge six-figure contract for her new book, Ivory Terror. Guess what it's about."

Harry leaned over and kissed her on the cheek. "Lizzie, somehow I think you'll do fine. But now there's someone I have to talk to."

He walked to the other side of the lobby where Jordan and Tristan were talking with Phil Bergstrum.

"Well, hello Harry," Bergstrum said. "Welcome to the fold."

"Good to be here, Phil."

"I was just leaving. See you around the water cooler." Bergstrum walked off.

Tristan held out his hand. "Hi Harry."

"What's this handshake stuff, give me a hug."

Harry threw his arms around his son. Tristan hugged him back fiercely.

After several intense seconds they let go of each other. Harry turned to Jordan, keeping a hand on Tristan's shoulder. "How've you been?"

"Fine," she said haltingly. "Really, I've been fine."

"I never really thanked you for saving my life."

Jordan shrugged. For an awkward moment they stood silently facing each other. Harry began to speak but stopped himself when Jordan said, "Tristan and I were on our way to have a hot chocolate. Would you like to join us?"

"That would be great."

Tristan smiled contentedly as he walked off with his sister and his dad.